The Elderen Wood

ALLY STAY

The Elderen Wood
©2023 Ally Stay

print ISBN: 978-1-66788-719-7
ebook ISBN: 978-1-66788-720-3

PROLOGUE

Drowning is quite possibly the worst death Amaya could imagine. In fact, lately, she'd been having nightmares about that very thing. It was as if she saw nothing but water engulfing her, penetrating her lungs. But that didn't stop her from spending her last summer on the Truckee River. It was a tradition her friends and she had held onto since they were kids. Amaya wasn't gonna let that go because of some silly dreams.

During their last night together, she sat in disbelief, realizing that this was it for them. By this time tomorrow, they'd be home packing for college, preparing for angsty, heartfelt goodbyes. Laughter and adventures that had seemed endless had now come to an end. Amaya's uneasiness was evident to Luna. "Hey," she whispered, slightly nudging her, "It's gonna be okay."

"*Or* we'll be lucky, and never speak to each other again!" Iris yelled from across the campfire.

"Ha, ha, very funny. We all know you wouldn't last five minutes without us." For that comment, Iris threw a bag of marshmallows at Elle. Unknowingly to Iris, the bag was open and the marshmallows scattered in the dirt, pooling at her feet. "Oh, good going, you idiot. Now how are we gonna make smores?"

The night continued as any other. Elle's relentless bickering with Iris and her sarcastic remarks. Amaya's constant anxiety and looming existential crisis. Luna pointing out the various constellations in the sky and babbling about the Cosmos while the other three hadn't a clue what she was talking about.

Although so different, they wove together like fabrics of a quilt, each girl incomplete without the other. To tear them apart would be to disrupt the balance of the universe, ultimately leading to the apocalypse and the end of humanity as they know it. Or at least, that's how it felt to Amaya, as they were really the only family she had.

AMAYA BROOKS

A maya awoke to the gushing sounds of the river and Luna's foot in her face. "Lou, do you mind?"

With a smirk on her face, Luna traced her sweaty sock along Amaya's cheek. "No, I do not mind at all, actually."

Trying not to gag, Amaya climbed out of her sleeping bag and tackled Luna to the ground. Iris moaned in pure agony as the girls tumbled over her. "Ugh, so much for sleeping in."

Just as Amaya expected, Elle was already awake, dressed, and making breakfast for everyone. They would likely forget to eat if it weren't for her. Amaya hated her for it.

Elle rolled her eyes in the distance, as the three of them went at each other's throats, practically bringing down the whole tent with them. But Elle knew exactly how to get their attention, "Come on guys, your huevos rancheros are getting cold!"

Within an instant, they were on their feet, stuffing their faces.

"Okay, the raft is all ready to go. Once you guys finish eating like the wild animals that you are, we'll head out. We got lucky; it looks like it's gonna be a nice day. The waters seem calm."

There was a stillness in the air that morning. Each leaf and branch could be heard rustling in the wind. It was as if the world was holding its breath, waiting for something.

Rafting down the Truckee River was something they'd been doing for years. Their final day together was meant to be memorable, so they saved this for last. There was nothing that could ruin this day for them, and Amaya was sure of that.

Elle threw four disgustingly orange life jackets into the raft, causing Iris to roll her eyes. "Do we *really* need to bring these? I mean, come on. We've done this a thousand times, Elle. If you fall in, I will personally rescue you."

"I mean, about 3,960 people drown in the United States each year," Luna noted.

"You're insane for knowing that exact number, Lou," Amaya said, fidgeting a paperclip in her hands. It was a weird habit she had. For some reason, it calmed her.

"Trust me, one day, you'll thank me," Elle said as she threw them in the raft.

"Doubt it," Iris mumbled under her breath.

As the girls had surpassed the age of eighteen, they were no longer as small as they once were. Fitting into the raft was almost comical. Limbs spilled over the sides, elbows crowded faces, and feet were constantly stepped on. It was a claustrophobic, jumbling mess, and yet, none of them could think of a place they'd rather be.

With a paddle in hand, Elle pushed them away from the shore.

For them, a typical trip down the river took about four hours. Despite having paddles at their disposal, they never had any intention of actually using them. They found it much better to sit back and let the water carry them. This particular stretch of river was free of all hard twists and turns. It was a peaceful river that flowed with no rapids or falls. All was calm. No worries. No hurry.

Normally, these were the moments when they would be discussing the start of a new school year and all the exciting adventures they were going to share. Instead, a stale silence filled the air. Everyone was afraid to say what they were all thinking. Especially Amaya.

Growing up, her friends were all she had. Her mother had become very distant over the years, and she never knew her father. Her friends were all she knew and that terrified her. For Amaya, change was like the rain. It's easy to ignore the forecast, unphased by its inevitable nature. You can leave the umbrella at home, believing everything will be fine. But in the end, you're left wet with a dripping nose.

She buried her nose in a book, avoiding the uncomfortable conversation she knew was coming.

Iris was the first to break the cold silence. "You guys are really bumming me out. Come on, let's have some fun!" She gently nudged Amaya, making her lose her balance.

"Iris, be careful! I could've fallen in."

"What, you mean like this?" she said, pushing Amaya into the moving water. Amaya gasped at the sudden sting of the icy water hitting her skin. She watched as Iris clutched her stomach, overflowing with laughter.

"So, it's gonna be like that, is it?" Her lips moved stealthily as she moved closer to the raft. In a single movement, she grasped Iris' shoulders and pulled her downward. Iris screamed as her back hit the water. She tackled Amaya, pulling her back under.

From beneath the rushing water, Amaya could hear the muffled laughs of Elle and Luna. When she surfaced, Iris and Amaya exchanged a sinister glance before swimming underneath the raft. With all their combined strength, they flipped the raft, sending the lifejackets and their friends flying.

Suddenly, the water became a warzone; water flew through the air as the girls tried to drown one another. Elle prided herself on being the strongest and wasn't afraid to hold back. She climbed onto the capsized raft with an animalistic stare in her eye. In a single jump, she tackled all three girls.

They were laughing so hard they failed to notice the danger heading straight towards them.

Luna was first to notice the loud rumbling that vibrated around them. "Guys, do you hear that?" They stopped and listened. A deep, violent sound tore through the air, eerily similar to thunder and haunted screams. It wasn't a pleasant sound, and it was getting louder.

As they turned to face the sound, they held their breath. The girls knew the Truckee River like their favorite song. Every turn, rock, and current was familiar. But what was approaching them was unlike anything they had ever seen before. Faced with the tumultuous, merciless rapids, their eyes widened in disbelief.

Large, jagged boulders penetrated the surface of the white waters, towering over the shores. Between the rocks, the waves screamed. Every inch of their bodies became overwhelmed with fear as the sound grew louder and louder. Once the shock began to wear off, the panic set in. "Guys, everyone to the raft! Hurry!"

A feeling of impending doom swept over them as they swam to the raft. They somehow managed to flip the raft in a fierce battle against the now fleeting current. Elle pulled herself up into the raft, scrambling to help the others. "Grab my hand!" she shouted, screaming over the rapids that were now inescapable. Iris reached her hand up, desperately grasping onto her friend.

Quickly, Elle yanked her into the raft. Running out of time, they each held out a hand for Luna. She held on as they pulled her to safety. The hulking waves now surrounded them, pushing and pulling the raft. Still stuck in the water, Amaya's heart sank.

As she gasped for air, she watched her friends drift further and further away. Crying and begging, they held out their hands for her, ""Amaya! SWIM!"

The strong current grabbed hold of her like a hand from Hell, pulling her down to the fire. Hearing nothing but the roar of the water and muffled yells from her friends, her mind began to spin.

Burning from the inside out, she felt the water begin to slip into her lungs. Amaya began to think this was the beginning of the end. She was ready to give in and just let go, when two hands slipped beneath her arms, pulling her against the current. As her vision blurred, she saw Elle, Luna, and Iris grasping onto her. They watched her closely, waiting for any indication that she was alright.

Through the coughing, she let a faint chuckle escape her lips. They all collapsed in relief. "I bet you're all wishing we were wearing those lifejackets, now, aren't you?" Elle teased.

"Elle, now is *not* the time!"

Despite the brief moment of solace, the danger was just beginning.

As the waters grew still, a new, unfamiliar noise could be heard. It was a different kind of rumble this time, one that was softer and lower in pitch. A strange tranquility hung in the air, weighing heavily on them. Something was coming.

Edging near, water tumbled down the mountain, pounding on the rocks below. The water foamed at the bottom, filling the air with a drizzling mist. The waterfall's roar echoed throughout Tahoe, imposing its dominance.

"SINCE WHEN WAS THERE A FREAKING WATERFALL RIGHT HERE?" Iris yelled, pulling her friends close.

Caught in the chaos, Amaya's mind turned to her dreams. Was this what they had all been about? Had they all been leading to this moment? Her death by waterfall? At this point, it didn't matter.

She closed her eyes as they huddled together.

AMAYA BROOKS

Amaya's eyes shot open, followed by a desperate gasp for air. As her head spun, she checked her surroundings. Elle, Iris, and Luna were sprawled unconscious amongst the shore. She grabbed Luna's shoulders and tried to shake her awake. "Luna! Hey, wake up." Slowly, Luna's eyelids opened, revealing her piercing blue eyes. They glistened with confusion as she glanced up at Amaya.

"What? What happened?" Luna put her hand to her head and winced in pain. A small cut spread across her forehead as a single drop of blood ran down her face. Using her sleeve, Amaya placed her hand on Luna's forehead and gently cleaned the wound.

"Are you okay?" she asked, wiping the blood away.

"I think so." She paused. "Are you?"

Honestly, Amaya wasn't sure. In her last memory, she was moments away from death. Now she was here, with barely a scratch. "I'm fine," she lied.

Next, Iris woke up groaning in the sand. She looked like she had just woken from a bad nap. Muffled gurgles escaped her mouth as she stretched her arms. She *sounded* like she had just woken from a bad nap. "What happened?"

"What do you remember?"

"Um, I remember water. Almost drowning. Feeling hopeless," she paused. "And those goddamn life jackets."

9

Suddenly, Amaya's attention was drawn to the empty spot on the beach where her friend had lain just moments ago. "Guys, where is Elle? She was just there a second ago!" Of course, Elle had to wander off in the unknown. Amaya felt a pinch of relief feeling the outline of her paperclip in her pocket. She pulled it out and twisted it between her fingers.

She got up and began searching desperately for their friend. As she found herself deeper in the trees, Amaya noticed something rather peculiar. Within the forest stood a white door. No building or house was connected to it. It stood alone, watching them. Amaya slowly approached it, wondering why on earth there was a door in the middle of the forest. "Do you guys see this?" she asked, turning Luna and Iris's attention to the door.

"That's odd." The three crowded around it. With its chipped paint and withered appearance, it had obviously been there for quite some time. "I wonder if it still works." Luna lifted her hand to the shiny, golden knob. With a turn of her wrist, the door opened. With their curiosity getting the best of them, the three pushed and shoved, causing them to fall right through.

"Great going you guys. If I wasn't all bruised up from the waterfall, I certainly am now," Iris groaned.

Ignoring her comment, Amaya picked herself up and began to look around.

It didn't take long for her to realize they were not in the same place they were only seconds ago. Something was different about this place. Although she did not recognize the world around her, it felt startlingly familiar. It was almost comforting, like a hug from an old friend. Amaya became entranced by the magical expression of the swirling mass of trees that filled the empty spaces. They hung over the atmosphere like they held a thousand memories. They were that kind of green you wish you could bottle up and take home with you to dress your walls in. The bark took kinship with the soft grass beneath her feet.

The sun poured through every crack and crevice, illuminating paths for even the smallest creature to follow. The sky was clear and full of life, while bird's songs echoed through the wood. Amaya's heart was calmed by the sound of a waterfall that had once terrified her. Serenity emanated from its gentle flow.

Almost forgetting her missing friend, Amaya turned quickly around a corner, running into Elle. "Elle? Where have you been? You scared us!"

"I was looking for a way back to camp. Where have *you* been?"

"So, you're telling me you thought the way back to camp was through a random door in the middle of the forest. Elle, you can't just go wandering off! We need to stick together, okay?"

"Okay, whatever. I was curious. But we're all together now, so no big deal. And besides, the best way out is through."

Amaya rolled her eyes and turned around to go back through the door. But to her surprise, it had been closed shut. She reached out to open it, but it would not budge. Her heartbeat soared as she realized they were trapped.

"Guys, the door won't open," she said in a panic. This didn't make any sense.

"What? What do you mean?" Luna asked.

"I mean it's sealed shut."

They exchanged worried glances. Unsure of what this meant for them, Amaya felt sick to her stomach.

"It's okay," Luna assured her. "We'll figure something out. Let's look around, maybe we'll find something familiar. Elle, you lead the way."

Elle nodded her head and the others followed. Amaya stayed close to Luna for comfort. She could see her friends too were in awe of this place. "This forest," Luna noted, "I've never seen anything quite like it. Everything is so full of life." She placed her hand on the trunk, running her finger along the raised ridges. "Do you guys think we died and went to Heaven?" she asked, still admiring the lined mess of the tree bark.

"No, you guys definitely wouldn't be in my Heaven," Iris joked.

"Iris Yuki, if you don't stop talking, I will leave you here in the middle of the forest for dead," Amaya teased.

"I'm kidding, I'm kidding. But are we really not going to address the fact that we definitely just walked through a magical door or have we all just accepted that?" Amaya hadn't even had time to process it all. Iris was right. This couldn't be real, no. She hit her head on that river and was tucked away in a dream.

Before she was able to collect her thoughts, a man on a large, black horse stopped in front of them. He was dressed in what appeared to be chainmail and metal armor. It surely was quite an elaborate costume. "Excuse me? Could you help us? Do you know which way the Truckee River is?" Elle asked, grabbing his attention.

He tilted his head in confusion.

"I've never heard of such a river." The man jumped off his horse and stepped closer to them. Over his eyes, his curly, blonde locks hung like an umbrella; it was miraculous that he could see at all. His face was matted with dirt and sweat, with smear marks along his sharp jawline. The metal armor sculpted his broad shoulders like it was made just for him. His odor was seemingly unpleasant, but he was fairly good looking.

"I'm Sir Henderson, and who might you all be?"

Sir Henderson? Amaya wondered if he were simply portraying a character.

"Um, I'm Luna. These are Amaya, Iris, and Eldora. We sort of took a wrong turn and aren't really sure where we are."

He almost laughed. "This is the Elderen Wood. Why surely you must know that?" But Amaya did not. The name meant nothing to her. How far from home had they traveled? It did not make any sense. In Sir Henderson's face, confusion turned into concern.

"It seems odd that someone would not recognize the most famous place in the Five Kingdoms," he muttered to himself. "Well, I am riding for Camelot and can escort you there if you wish." Now that's a name Amaya recognized.

Amaya and her mother never really got along. Her mother was distant and closed off, upsettingly as she was Amaya's only family. Blood related family, that is. However, the one thing they did have was books. They both had a love for reading and would often sit together in their home library. Most of the time, they would read their respected books and not speak, but these moments belonged to them. Their library was filled with all kinds of books about King Arthur and his great adventures, as they were her mother's favorite. Every so often, her mother would read them to her. It was one of the only memories of her that Amaya held close to her heart.

"Camelot? As in King Arthur?" Amaya realized she must've hit her head harder than she thought. Everyone knew King Arthur's legends, and that they were just that. Legends. Well, almost everyone.

"Is Camelot the one with the wizard Marlin? And the magic ring?" Iris asked, trying very hard to piece it all together.

"*Merlin*, and that's not the...never mind." Amaya turned her attention back to Sir Henderson. "You don't really mean that we're actually in *the* Camelot right? King Arthur isn't just running around these woods somewhere. Right?" Although, she'd have to admit that would be probably the coolest thing ever.

"Well, no. Arthur died many years ago. And yes technically, the Elderen Wood has been within the borders of Camelot since the Great War. Listen, you must be cold in those wet—very strange—clothes. Let me take you to King Kay, he can take care of you."

Amaya pulled Elle aside. "I don't trust this guy," she whispered. "This is weird. There's no way we're not actually in Camelot. Let's just go back."

"Amaya, come on. You don't need to be so overly cautious about everything. I'm sure he means no harm. Plus, look around. We don't exactly have that many options. The door is shut, remember?"

Amaya still felt uneasy. She crossed her arms and sulked in her shoulders. Elle was right. They did not have any other options.

"Don't worry, Amaya, I'll keep an eye on him," Elle reassured her. She turned to face Sir Henderson, "You hear me? Yeah, I've got my eye on you. Now, please take us to Camelot."

Amaya assumed leaving them in the woods would have been easier for him. His intentions seemed honest, but she kept her guard up. Elle grabbed her arm and dragged her along.

The Elderen Wood grew more impressive with each step. The trees stood like soldiers, bowing to them as they passed. With its broad, succulent leaves, its branches tickled the sky in the wind. Taking in the beauty of the wood, Amaya had a million questions running through her mind. "Sir Henderson, you said that King Arthur died fifteen years ago. What happened to him?"

"He died in the Great War," he paused. It seemed he had a personal connection to this war. Sadness draped around him like a blanket. "We lost some great men that day. Although I was only a boy, the memories stuck with me." In response, Amaya decided not to ask any more questions, feeling guilty she caused him to relive his painful memories.

As they continued, it was clear Sir Henderson did not know what to make of the four girls.

"So, *Tahoe*, you say? Does everyone in the land of Tahoe wear such bizarre clothing?" he lifted his eyebrows.

"In Tahoe, you would be considered the bizarre one, dude," Iris responded.

"Hmm, well I would suggest a change of clothes when we arrive," he cheekily smiled.

"Anything else we should know about? I'm not exactly sure what to expect," Luna admitted.

"All you need to know is the Elderen Wood is full of the unexpected. It's where all magic resides. Look!" Their eyes followed as he pointed up. Through the sky, a hundred little lights twinkled. They fluttered like dancing ballerinas in the breeze.

"Fireflies?" Elle questioned.

"No. Fairies," Amaya responded, unknowingly.

Their movements resembled a school of fish. All of them moved in unison, appearing as one huge body in the clouds. Dusk now painted the sky with bright and wonderful colors. Fairies sparkled against pink and orange, creating an image of beauty and power. It was the most beautiful thing Amaya had ever seen. Her fear was slowly being replaced with excitement.

Could they really be in *the* Camelot? No, how could they? Magic wasn't real. But there it was, staring her right in the face. God, she was going to get a migraine.

The further into the wood they went, the more the thoughts about going home drifted from her mind. She wondered what other beautifully impossible things this place held. She could not wait to find out.

Camelot was in sight as sundown was nearing. Through the clearing of the trees, the castle sat. It was made up of a thousand stones, each different in size. Dark and intimidating, it was built to protect its people and all within. Amid the mountain, it stood tall and proud over the rest of the kingdom. Amaya was swept away by the same feeling of familiarity she had felt earlier. It was unexplainable, and to be honest, a bit terrifying.

She was stunned that Camelot was right at her grasp. It felt like a dream she hoped would not turn into a nightmare.

A throng of people crowded the city as they entered the citadel. Amaya noticed there was a sense of fatigue and overwork among the people. Their clothes were tattered and unwashed. The people were noticeably thin, small bellies on man and child alike, a frown plastered on every pale face.

Throughout the crowd, heads turned as they followed Sir Henderson's horse. They exchanged awkward glances with the peasants who filled the city, unsure what to make of it all. The wood had been so vibrant and alive, but Camelot felt sucked dry of all its life and color. It was gray and filled with melancholy. The legends of Camelot told her it was such a wondrous place. Her mother's stories were nothing like this. What had happened?

"Stay behind me and do not speak a word," Sir Henderson ordered, as he pushed through the doors to the throne room. They shyly trailed behind him. Due to her upbringing in the United States in the twenty-first century, Amaya hadn't a clue how to behave before royalty. Judging by the nervous nature of her friends, neither did they. Amaya anxiously fidgeted with the paperclip behind her back.

A deep red rug ran from the throne to the doors. From the ceiling dangled matching red banners, with what Amaya knew to be the Pendragon crest. In front of them stood two thrones fashioned from jewels and precious metals. One lay empty, collecting dust. In the other sat who she assumed to be King Kay.

With steady eyes, he watched them. Other than his gold crown, he wore nothing but black. His face was prickly with gray stubble that trickled into his dark hair.

"Sir Henderson," his voice was hoarse when he spoke.

"Sire," he bowed. "I found these young women wandering in the Elderen Wood. I believe they are lost and in need of aid. They speak of a place called *Tahoe*. It is unknown to me and certainly not within the Five Kingdoms." The way he spoke to the king was different than when he spoke to the girls. His tone was now more serious and firmer.

The girls stepped forward as the king gestured to them. "What do you call yourselves?"

Amaya nudged Elle forward, being too afraid to speak.

"I'm Eldora, and these are Iris, Luna, and Amaya. Um, sire," she awkwardly stumbled over the unfamiliar term.

His eyes turned to Amaya, leering as if she had something to hide. His look felt like daggers in her eyes. She feared they had said something wrong, causing him to turn them away, leading them straight back to that door. She clenched her jaw as he opened his mouth to speak.

"You may stay in Camelot if you wish. My servant, Edmund, will show you to your chambers. That will be all." She was taken back by his few words, feeling relieved and terrified all at once.

"Thank you, Your Highness," Sir Henderson turned to face the girls. "That was strange," he said under his breath. "I will take you to Edmund. Follow me."

Amaya turned her head, placing her eyes on the king. This unsettling exchange left her feeling disoriented. His eyes were still fixed on her. Did he not want to know more about from where they came? Is he truly willing to let just any commoner with a sob story stay in the castle? Would King Arthur have done this for them? Unfortunately, that was an answer she'd never get.

Sir Henderson brought them to the servant's quarters, a small room adjacent to the palace. The wooden door was opened by a boy they believed to be the king's servant, Edmund. Pale and thin, his bone structure was prominent. His black hair, which clearly had not been washed in days, stuck to his forehead. He could not be much older than Amaya and her friends.

"Edmund, the king has entrusted these four girls to you. Please take them to the guest chambers and gather anything they might need."

Edmund shot him a confused look. Sir Henderson shrugged his shoulders.

"Okay?" he said, standing there awkwardly.

"Hi," Iris said, obviously not being able to take the uncomfortable silence anymore. "I'm Iris. This is Elle, Luna, and Amaya."

"I'm Edmund. Welcome to Camelot. Follow me." Despite being awkward, Amaya could not deny he was charming. He walked quickly with his head down and tripped over his own feet. How did he end up in a place like this?

"From what kingdom are you traveling?" he asked, his head still hanging low as he trailed in front of them.

"Um, we're not from around here exactly," Elle answered.

"Outside of the Five Kingdoms?"

"Very much so."

"That's strange. We don't typically get visitors from outside the Five Kingdoms. The king is letting you stay? Here?" The girls remained silent. "Well regardless, I hope you enjoy your stay."

He brought them to the end of a long corridor that stretched beyond sight. The walls were dark, covered in crumbling stone. High arches, dressed with candles, lit the way. There was a chill in the air, like years of memories were trying to share their stories with them. Amaya wondered what extraordinary things these walls had witnessed.

They arrived at four doors at the end of the hallway. "This is where you will be staying. If you need anything, you know where to find me." Leaving the four girls on their own, he left.

LUNA ANBRIS

Luna entered her room, overcome by the marvelous architecture surrounding her. The room itself was bigger than her entire house back home. The walls were a stunning soft blue, dusted with gold. Ballgowns and silk dresses draped from the wardrobe. A soft crackle could be heard coming from the corner fireplace. She leaped on the bed, sinking deep into the pillows. She could get used to this.

It was no secret that Luna did not come from money. She spent most of her childhood living on other people's couches, never having a room to call her own. She lived with Amaya on and off throughout her upbringing, who always made sure she was well taken care of.

She thought of Amaya, as she lay snuggled in the pillows, wondering if she was okay. She knew how overwhelmed Amaya could get, especially in unfamiliar situations. And this might have been the most unfamiliar situation they'd ever found themselves in. She decided to go check on her.

"Amaya," she whispered, entering her room, "Are you alright?"

Amaya was sitting on the edge of her bed, gazing out the window that overlooked the kingdom. She did not respond. Her right leg was bouncing up and down. Luna sat beside her, taking Amaya's hand in hers. "What's going through your mind?"

"Just a thousand thoughts and questions. You know my mind."

"I do. It never stays quiet."

Amaya softly smiled, "No, it doesn't."

"Well, at least you have an amazing view to watch while you think. I mean can you believe this? It's all so beautiful. I never want to go home."

"No, I can't believe it. That's the problem," Amaya spoke softly.

"I mean, I'd say it's highly probable we are just living in a simulation. What even is the definition of real?"

"Lou, I love you, but sometimes I have no idea what you're talking about."

Luna let out a small laugh. Leaving Amaya's side, she walked over to the balcony, wanting to see all the stars in the sky. The moon shone bright that night, filling the sky with its warm light. It waved over the city as its protector. "The stars are different here," she said. "There's hundreds, maybe thousands more. And dozens of new constellations," she smiled. "It's amazing."

Luna stepped into the stream of light that pooled into the room.

After a brief moment, she began to feel a slight tingle on her skin. It was almost like a tickle. A gasp escaped her mouth as she glanced down at her arm. Light appeared to be emanating from her skin.

Amaya noticed this too. "Um, Lou? You're glowing! Like literally glowing."

Luna's face was filled with shock as she turned to face Amaya. The blue light was now radiating off her pale skin like water on a hot summer day. It ran through her long, red hair, lighting it up like neon fire. Her eyes that held oceans were as bright as the sun. In a musical dance, blue rays of light surrounded her, lifting up into the sky. Amaya's jaw fell as the brilliant display of light encompassed her friend.

"The moonlight," Luna said under her breath as she stepped into the shadows. Once her skin was shielded from the light, it went dark. The fantastic, swirling rays of light quickly vanished, as if they had never existed. Luna watched as Amaya reached her hand into the moonlight, curious if her skin would have the same reaction. But to her surprise, nothing.

"That's strange," Luna mumbled, stepping back into the moonlight. Once again she felt that tingling sensation and began to glow. Why was she the only one affected by this?

Suddenly, Edmund burst through the doors. "I heard shouting," he panted, out of breath, "Is everything al..." he paused, mid-sentence as he noticed Luna. He took a moment and watched as Luna brightened the room. He did not seem fearful or concerned, but almost pleased. Like he had seen this before. "Luna, no need to worry. Please come with me. There's someone I'd like you to meet," he smiled.

Luna looked back at Amaya, almost asking for permission to go with him.

"Go," she nodded.

Luna was escorted to the far end of the castle by Edmund. They entered a large room that was filled to the ceiling with old books. It was dark and dusty and smelled like the ground after it rained. The books were all different colors and sizes, sitting on shelves with ladders scattered throughout to reach the ones in higher places. She had never seen so many books in one place before.

In the center of the room was a large, wooden table. A young woman sat at this table, her nose buried in a book. She was dressed in a long, blue cloak that laid gently against her dark skin. She kept her head down, not noticing Luna and Edmund. Edmund cleared his throat, causing her head to shoot up.

"Oh, hello Edmund," her eyes shifted to Luna, "Who have you brought here?"

Luna stepped forward.

"This is Luna. She just arrived in Camelot. Luna, this is Liana, the Court Mage. I feel you two have much to discuss."

Liana stood, removing the hood draped over her dark curls. She did not speak, but reached her hand out to Luna, guiding her towards the window near the back of the room. The moonlight poured through the window with meaning and power. Slowly, they stepped into the light. Both of them watched as the blue rays tingled off their skin.

Luna looked to Liana, her eyes longing for answers. "I don't understand."

Liana smiled, softly.

"Luna, you are a mage, such as myself, my dear. You have the gift of healing powers. Our gift comes from the moon," Liana said, pointing to the sky. "This is why we react with its light. The moon is a part of us. As are the stars. We were created to heal and protect."

"But how is this possible? I'm not from Camelot." Luna was struggling to grasp the impossible concept that she might have magical powers.

"Surely you must've noticed signs of your magic before? Mage magic is very powerful."

"I'm sorry, but I have not. I didn't even know magic existed until today." Although, this would explain her lifelong love and fascination with the moon and the stars. She always felt drawn to them, like if you collected them in the palm of your hand and put them together like a puzzle, it would create her. And now she was beginning to understand why.

"Oh? Very strange indeed. Well then. You shall study with me, my dear. Alongside me, you shall come to understand what it means to be a mage. Visit me here tomorrow."

Luna agreed, having no idea into what she was getting herself.

The next morning, Luna was afraid to open her eyes, fearing it had all been a dream. But, as her eyelids slowly lifted she saw she was nuzzled in the soft pillows, guarded by those beautiful blue walls. She smiled in relief. *So, I really am in Camelot,* she thought to herself. Magical memories of the previous night trickled into her brain. She knew her friends would not believe what happened. She could hardly believe it herself.

She opened her door to the grand hallway and shouted at the top of her lungs.

"MY ROOM, TEN MINUTES!"

In a pretty yellow dress with a ribbon tying back her curls, Elle stepped into the hallway.

"Good morning, Luna," she said with a smile on her face. "I went to the kitchen and got these from Edmund." She held up a plate of scones.

"How long have you been awake?"

"Long enough."

"Of course, you're already dressed," Iris groaned, drool running down her chin. She stepped into the hallway and rubbed her tired eyes.

"Guys, I was having this crazy dream that we were all in Camelot," Amaya said, exiting her room, "Then I nearly fell out of bed when I opened my eyes."

"I know. I am still having a hard time believing this is all real," Elle added.

"You have to hear what happened last night," Luna said, leading them into her room.

They sat on the floor, surrounding a plate of scones. Luna began to explain all the wonderfully crazy things she had witnessed the night before.

"Wait, wait, wait. So, you're telling me, your skin was glowing? Like goddamn Edward Cullen?" Iris asked, with a mouth full of scones.

"Okay, not exactly like that."

"No, it's true!" Amaya chimed in. "I know it sounds crazy, but I saw the whole thing. Even her hair was like one glowing, orange highlighter."

"Okay, so what did this Court Mage say?" Elle asked.

"She told me that I am a mage, just like her. Our powers come from the moon, so whenever my skin touches the light, I glow. I still don't quite understand it, but hopefully meeting Liana today will help open my eyes. It's weird," she paused, "I feel like I should be freaked out. But I'm not. I actually feel the calmest I've ever been. I can't explain it."

Luna was experiencing the same sense of comfort Amaya had the day before. Unlike Amaya, she didn't question it. It felt right.

Suddenly, two maids entered the room, quite surprised to see the four girls awake and already eating breakfast. Their eyes widened when they saw Elle was already dressed.

"Good morning. We came to wake you, but it seems you are already awake. And have food?"

"Oh, thank you! Yeah, I went down to the kitchen this morning and grabbed these from Edmund," Elle answered. The maids exchanged glances.

"Will you require our assistance getting dressed this morning?"

"Uh, I think we can handle that ourselves," Iris said.

Did people here really need help getting dressed every morning? It was almost laughable.

The maids seemed frazzled and disoriented. It was evident that they had never encountered anyone like them before, and they had no idea what to do. "Very well. Thank you," they said, slowly leaving the room.

"Alright guys," Elle began. "What's the plan here? I mean, we should be figuring out a way to get home, right?"

Iris shoved another scone down her throat. "I don't know about you guys, but I'm good right here," she leaned back, placing her hands behind her head.

"I don't say this often, but I've gotta agree with Iris. I mean, how often do we get to experience something like this? We all know what's waiting for us back home. After last night, it just feels like we're supposed to be here," Luna said.

"Are you guys hearing yourselves? We're in another world and you guys just wanna hang out? You're not even worried about how we will get home?" Amaya stressed. "For all I know I'm in a coma and this is my weird coma dream."

"No, cause not all of us spend every waking moment worrying about every goddamn thing," Iris teased.

"Not funny," Amaya glared.

"No, it's actually very funny," Iris laughed. "Besides, even if you're dreaming, what's the hurry to wake up?"

"Okay, okay," Elle interrupted. "Amaya is right. We need to come up with a plan."

Iris crossed her arm and rolled her eyes. She clearly had no intention in participating in this conversation.

"How about we stay for one week," Luna suggested. "Just seven days of doing whatever we want." Her eyes shifted to Amaya. "Then we'll start searching for a way home."

"I'm in," Elle agreed.

"Yea, whatever, me too," Iris said.

"You guys are crazy. Absolutely crazy," Amaya insisted. "But I'm not gonna let you guys hang out in Camelot without me."

"Oh, and don't forget. Do not tell anyone about where we are really from," Luna said.

"Why does it matter?" Iris asked.

"We don't want to disrupt the balance of the universe! We need to be careful. We don't know what could happen."

"Oh my God, you're insufferable," Iris rolled her eyes. "Fine, we won't say anything. Can we have some fun now?"

Just then, Edmund entered the room. "The king has instructed me to invite you to the Annual Victory Celebratory Ball this evening. The maids will come to take your measurements later today. I will escort you to the ball once you are ready."

Going to a ball was something they had all fantasized about since they were little girls. They would try on their mother's old dresses and prance around the house, pretending they were princesses. Never once did they imagine they were going to make this dream a reality. But why did the king want them there?

"Edmund, what is the Annual Victory Celebratory Ball?"

"It is the anniversary of the Great War. We celebrate its victory each year." Much like Sir Henderson, they could see the topic of the Great War upset him. Although they had many more questions, they decided to stay quiet.

"Thank you, Edmund. We will see you tonight, then."

About a hundred scones later, Luna found herself back in the library with Liana. They sat in front of the large window, facing each other. There were many thoughts running through Luna's head. She felt anxious, in a way where she was about to jump from a plane with a parachute strapped to her back. And she was ready for the jump.

Liana's hands held a large leather-bound book. She placed it at Luna's feet. On the cover read, "The History of Mage Magic." It was overflowing with information, wanting to share all it knew with the world. She began flipping through it, studying the many stories and illustrations.

"Many years ago," Liana began, "a young girl was traveling through the Elderen Wood with her mother. She was very ill and could no longer go on. The girl was desperate. She fell to her knees and looked to the sky, begging for help. All hope had been sucked dry, leaving her heart empty and withered. As she cried to the heavens, she noticed something rather peculiar in the sky. The glistening full moon rained down a single droplet of light. She watched it fall, down, down, until it hit her skin. The light seeped into her veins, sending chills down her spine. She held her mother in her arms and began to glow. In that moment, she saved her mother, becoming the first mage."

She took Luna's hands in hers.

"Mage magic is only for the pure of heart. This means it will only work unless you have the purest intentions. You must never forget that, my dear."

Luna nodded. Did this mean she was pure of heart?

Liana grabbed her hand and placed it on the wound she had received during the waterfall accident. "We'll start with something simple. This cut is small in comparison to the things you will be healing one day. It should come naturally. Now close your eyes, and free your mind of all other thoughts. Simply focus on the healing, my dear."

Luna did as told and took a deep breath. From her fingers to her shoulders, blue light began to flow through her veins. It ran through her like a river of warmth, getting stronger and stronger. Liana stepped back, smiling at her student. "That's it. Keep going. Don't think. Just feel."

A surge of power swept through her body, making her hair stand up. She gasped at the sudden wave of energy. She felt dizzy and her head began to drift back and forth. She had never felt anything like this before. As she slowly pulled her hand away, the light faded.

"Did it work?" she asked, looking at Liana.

Liana pointed to a mirror, hanging on the wall, "See for yourself."

She pulled back her red hair to reveal her perfect skin. It was clean of all blemishes, not even a single scratch. She had done it. She had healed herself.

IRIS YUKI

"**M**iss Iris?"

"Uh, come in," Iris answered. Multiple maids rushed into the room.

"Please stand here and we will take your measurements."

She stood in the center of the room while they held out her arms, tracing her body with a measuring cloth. She was overwhelmed with the countless hands that pushed and pulled on her limbs.

"Ow!" she yelled when something sharp poked her back.

"Miss Iris, please stay still," one of the maids insisted.

Once they finished gathering what they needed, they left the room to retrieve a few dresses they believed would be the perfect fit. Iris waited, twiddling her thumbs, terrified of what the maids were going to return with.

After a few minutes, five maids poured through the door with giant, poofy gowns spilling from their arms. Each maid held up her dress for Iris to see. Each one was bright and colorful, with sleeves so obnoxiously puffy it had to be a joke. Iris almost groaned in disgust, but decided that would be very rude. Instead, she put on a fake smile.

"Which dress is to your liking?"

"Um," she was unsure what to say. "Would you excuse me for a moment while I think it over?"

The maids nodded and exited the room.

Iris opened the wardrobe and sifted through the colorful mess of dresses. *Come on, there has to be something.* She was not the kind of person who wore bright or flashy things. Her position in this new world was not going to change that. She had always been very particular when it came to her look. Throughout her life, she never felt like she fit in anywhere. With a father living in Japan and a mother in America, her life had been split in two. Her clothes gave her a sense of identity for which she longed.

Dresses flew into the air as she tossed them onto the floor behind her. There *had* to be a black dress in there somewhere. She searched and scoured, causing one big, chaotic mess.

Then, her eyes widened

In the furthest corner of the wardrobe hung a long, silk, black dress. It was the only one of its color, standing alone collecting dust. She reached her hand far back and removed it from the wardrobe. She quickly began to remove her clothes and slipped into the dress. As if made just for her, the long lace sleeves wrapped tightly around her arms. It was snug around the waist and pooled at her feet.

There was no doubt this dress cost more than anything she had ever owned before. The fabric was soft and smooth, laying gently against her beige skin. She agreed this dress was meant for royalty.

She noticed a golden hairpiece resting on the dresser. *Perfect,* she thought. This was exactly what the dress was missing. Hairpiece in place, she tied back her long, black hair. She walked over to the mirror and gazed at her own reflection. She almost did not recognize herself. For the first time, she truly felt beautiful.

"Iris, that dress! It's beautiful!" Amaya exclaimed as she and the others entered the room. They too were dressed in ball gowns fit for queens, styled with jewels and shiny jewelry. It was no secret, however, that Iris looked the best.

"I have never seen a dress fit you better," said Luna.

"I know. We need to discover magical lands more often," she chuckled.

There was more to a ball than the girls could have imagined. The Great Hall was filled wall to wall with people dressed in the finest silks and gowns. The mixture of loud conversations, heavy heels pounding on the floor, and live music filled the air like a symphony of sound.

Girls, with corsets so tight their waists were reduced to the size of a toothpick, fought over the knights' attention. They laughed and spilled their drinks, seeing nothing but the men who stood before them. Rolling her eyes, Iris felt ashamed for them.

The girls noticed a familiar face in the crowd.

"Good evening, ladies," Sir Henderson bowed to them, "I will say, I almost did not recognize you. Last I saw you, you were soaking wet in those outlandish clothes. The king must find you very special to invite you to his ball."

"You'll soon come to realize, we are full of surprises Sir Henderson," said Iris.

"Oh, I don't doubt that." He flashed a smile at Elle and vanished into the roaring crowd.

"Elle! Did you see that? He totally likes you!"

"Oh, please. Trust me, I am not interested. I know his type. Thinks he's better than everyone. He just sees me as some pretty prize to be won."

Although Iris thought Elle was insane, she always admired how headstrong she was. She knew exactly who she was and no one could take that away from her.

The guests began to quiet down as King Kay clinked a spoon against his chalice.

"Welcome, my friends, to the Annual Victory Celebratory Ball! This day marks the anniversary of our triumph over the great evil that tried to harm so many. Also, it marks the anniversary of the passing of my beloved brother, Arthur. I know he would be proud of what we have done. Tonight, we feast in his honor."

The guests began swarming around the large table that lay in the middle of the room. The

girls followed and sat in front of a wondrous mass of food. Iris couldn't remember the last time she had a full meal. Her stomach began to rumble. She filled her plate with all sorts of food she had never even heard of.

"Do you think if we gave any of these fools a shot of vodka, they'd just fall over and die?" Iris joked.

"Iris," Amaya and Elle groaned in unison.

"Strictly speaking, we might fall over and die just being present in this room due to the unhygienic conditions that our bodies are not accustomed to," Luna added.

"Okay, I didn't want a gross science lesson, thanks," Iris said while reaching her arm over the table for a plate of what seemed to be potatoes. In doing so, she stretched her arm a little too far, knocking over her cup of wine. Amaya shut her eyes, no doubt fearing the wine was heading straight for her green dress. However, the cup hovered above her in midair.

"Um, Iris?"

The cup remained in front of Iris's hand as she sat there, staring. Her jaw hung heavy. "What the hell?"

Silence fell over the crowd as they turned their attention to her. As they began to realize what had happened, small murmurs could be heard amongst them. "A witch!" someone yelled.

This startled her, making Iris pull back her hand. The cup fell, spilling the wine all over Amaya. "Thanks," she glared.

"Sorry." Iris caved in on herself, feeling the many pairs of eyes staring at her.

"There is nothing to fear, girl," said a man from across the table, "In fact, that is what we are celebrating today. The freedom to practice magic. So, by all means, levitate as many cups as you desire."

"He is right," interrupted the king. "Everyone return to your celebrations, there is nothing to fear." The people did as told and once again, the hall was filled with buzzing noise as if nothing happened.

"Iris, how in the world did you do that?" Elle asked.

"I have no idea. It just happened. Like an instinct, I guess."

How *did* she do that? She had never done anything like that before at home, had she? This was hurting her brain. She needed more wine.

"Now is not the time for reason or understanding," she said, gulping down a large sip from her cup, "It is time to party!"

"Uh, Iris, I don't know. I think we should–"

Iris cut Amaya off, placing a finger on her lips, "Shhh! No thinking. Just dancing."

While the live music continued to play, she pulled her friends onto the open floor. They all loved to dance, feeling the music vibrate through their souls as they glided across the floor. In motion, Iris' black dress looked even more stunning. It swayed like the tide, as if it were doing a dance of its own. It reminded her of going to Matsuri back home with her dad.

"Hey, isn't that Edmund over there?" Iris pointed through the sea of people to a boy standing alone near the doors.

"I think it is. Come on," Amaya said, making her way over to Edmund. The girls followed.

"Edmund, why are you all alone? You should be celebrating like the rest of us."

He crossed his arms and firmly stated, "I do not dance."

"Like hell you don't," Iris said, grabbing him by the arm.

"No, no, no. I mean it!"

She ignored his pleas and with the assistance of the other girls, she pulled him to the dance floor.

They all joined hands and began skipping around in a circle. Edmund tried his best to not trip on his own two feet, clutching onto Amaya and Iris for balance. The girls laughed and smiled while he kept his stone-cold exterior, pretending he was not having a good time.

As they continued dancing, Iris noticed a faint smiling creeping across Edmund's face.

"Is that a smile I see?" she teased.

"No," he quickly denied.

The music soared and so did everyone's spirits. Iris felt like nothing else mattered at that moment. Her silly little worries floated into the air like magic. At this moment, nothing could hurt her.

When Iris returned to her room, the sounds of music rang in her ears. She twirled around her room, never wanting this night to end. She got so lost in herself that she did not see the large pile of books that lay on the floor. Her foot twisted and she started to fall. When she braced for impact, her hands hovered inches from the ground. She stopped. She, herself, was now hovering, like a cloud in the sky. She had done it again.

Picking herself up, she gazed at the stack of books in front of her. She slowly lifted her hand, facing them. She was not sure what to think or what to do, but she focused her attention on them. Slowly, one by one, the books peeled themselves off the floor and lifted in the air.

Pleased with herself, she kept going. As more books ascended, her heart rate increased. Her warm, powerful presence filled the room. Soon books and papers filled the air and danced around her. She twirled on her toes as the sounds of fabricated violins rippled through her mind. She smiled brightly, amazed at what she had just done. There was no way she was going home anytime soon.

ELDORA PEREZ

E lle woke with the sky. It was the way it had always been. In her youth, she was burdened with caring for her abuelita. Her mother and father were far too busy with work. Being the eldest sibling, this responsibility fell to her. By now, she was used to early mornings, preparing meals, and making sure her life, and everyone else's, were in order. This may or may not have spilled into her friendship with Iris, Luna, and Amaya.

She peered out the window and watched the sun claim its space over the kingdom. As the kingdom slept, the city stayed quiet. Elle could only hear the howling wind and the faint sounds of metal clinking in the distance. Knowing her friends would not be awake for hours, she decided to explore.

Unlike the city, the castle was awake. Servants could be found on every floor, going about their usual business. They moved like a machine. Everyone played their own part, all working together to make the wheels of the kingdom turn.

It was no surprise she ran into everyone's favorite servant, Edmund.

"I see you're walking around bright and early again," he said, carrying a basket full of clothing. The basket was clearly too heavy for him. Elle offered him a hand.

"You know," she said, "It almost looked like you were having fun last night. You may try to hide it, but you can't lie to me, Edmund."

"Okay, so what if I did? I never said I did not like to dance, I just can't. If you have not noticed, I'm not exactly light on my feet. I was not about to embarrass myself in front of the lot of you."

That was the most she had ever heard him speak.

"Aww, Edmund. I quite like you."

Just then, she heard that same clinking sound from earlier. It piqued her curiosity.

"What is that sound?" she asked him.

"Oh, those are the knights. They always start training at dawn."

This interested her indeed.

"I'm going to go have a look. Thanks, Edmund!"

She handed the basket back to him, and followed the sound out to the training yard. She pursed her lips when she found Sir Henderson, along with four other men dressed in chainmail, out in the training yard. She should've known *he* would be here.

"Ah, if it isn't Sir Henderson," she said with a displeased tone.

"Elle," he smiled. "What a pleasant surprise!" His excitement was genuine. This made Elle's blood boil.

"My name is Eldora," she corrected him. "Only my friends call me Elle."

"My apologies, Eldora." He bowed to her with a smirking smile. "Now what brings you to the training yard? Did you lose your way to the kitchen?" he teased. The other knights chuckled behind him.

Oh, he would pay for that.

"Oh, so you think since you're such a *manly* man that you're better than me? I could do just as much damage as you. If not, *more*."

He straightened up and walked towards her. He lifted his arm and placed a sword in her hands.

"Then by all means, be my guest."

The other knights gathered around, peering over his shoulder. Elle knew they were attempting to intimidate her, but she was not going to let that happen.

"No," she said, handing the sword back to him, "Not with that." Looking around the yard, she searched for something. *Surely there was one around here somewhere*, she thought.

"Ah-ha!" she exclaimed, as she pulled a large bow down from the rack. Carved from deep maple, it glistened in the light. It was the most beautiful bow she'd ever seen. The knights laughed and rolled their eyes when they saw her weapon of choice.

There was one vital thing the knights did not know about Elle. She was a very talented archer. She had been training for as long as she could remember. It was a random hobby she picked up when she was a kid. She always wanted to be just like Katniss Everdeen. When her abuelita was asleep, she practiced every night with her own target in her front yard. Finally, it was going to be put to good use.

"You," she pointed to Sir Henderson. "Up against the door."

He did as told, with a grin plastered on his face. It was clear he did not know what she was capable of. She was going to love this.

She tucked her curls behind her ear and gently nocked her arrow in place, keeping her eye on Sir Henderson. She took a deep breath and drew back the string. She felt every muscle tense in her body as she locked eyes with her target. Then, in one swift movement, she let go.

The arrow cut through the air like water, almost instantly making contact with the wooden door. Sir Henderson gasped at the sudden loud noise as the shaft hit the wood. His eyes shifted to the left, where the arrow was only one breath away from his face. He reached his hand up to his ear that had been nicked ever so slightly. He looked to Elle in disbelief as the blood ran onto his fingers. The knights were silent.

"Next time, I won't miss." She dropped the bow and returned to the castle.

Elle trailed through the grand corridors, hoping to find her friends wide awake when she returned. As she walked past the Throne Room, something caught her attention. Through the large doors, she heard muffled words. It was the voice of the king. She paused and pressed her ear to the door, once again letting her curiosity get the best of her.

Although it was faint, she could make out a few words: wood, magic, and war.

Elle felt uneasy. Only a few short days had passed since she arrived in Camelot, but she knew whatever this was, it didn't sound good. She leaned in closer and gnawed on her bottom lip.

"But we've come this far," mumbled an unrecognizable voice.

"I am your king! And you will not…"

Suddenly, a strong grip took hold of Elle's arm. Her heart jumped as she turned to face the source of strength. It was one of the knights she had seen earlier on the training yard. He glared at her with anger in his eyes. For the first time since she had arrived in Camelot, Elle felt intimidated. Where's a bow and arrow when you need one?

"What do you think you're doing?" he growled, dusting her face in saliva. He tightened his grip on her arm.

"I was just…" she trailed off, unsure what to say.

"Don't mess with things that don't concern you." He clenched his jaw. He released her arm and left before she could say a word.

She stood there for a moment, wavering in shock. Embarrassed and unable to speak up, she felt ashamed.

AMAYA BROOKS

Awakened from a restless night's sleep, Amaya slowly opened her eyes. Sleeping was a troublesome thing for her. She found her mind wandering in places she did not want it to go. Her dreams would often turn into nightmares, leaving her drenched in sweat with shaking hands. Her three-day absence from her anxiety medication did not help.

She yawned and stretched her arms as she climbed out of bed. She walked over to the balcony where only a few nights ago Luna had discovered a whole new part of herself. It seemed like so much had already changed since then.

Amaya didn't like change.

She sat on the balcony and watched the kingdom open its eyes to a new day. As she watched the people trickle down the streets and alleyways, she thought of her mother. *She would love this,* she thought. Seeing Camelot through her own eyes felt like one of her mother's story books leaped off the page. Although it was a rare feeling, Amaya missed her.

She also missed her books and her favorite leather chair that she'd curl up on with a warm cup of tea. She missed watching her mom get so caught up in her book that she would lightly giggle to herself. She missed the way things were before her friends decided they were all going to go their separate ways. What if this was all a dream and her friends had already left her?

Oh no, she thought, as the room started to spin. She felt her heart banging against her chest while an eerie feeling seeped into her stomach. She held onto herself and sank to the floor. *Is the room getting smaller?* She panicked. Her mouth tasted bad and her throat went dry. As the bile crawled up her throat, her nails dug into her arms. She wanted to scream, cry, and disappear.

She closed her eyes and tried to focus on something. Anything.

She thought of her friends.

Elle.

Iris.

Luna.

They weren't gone. They weren't going to leave her. They were right next door. Even so far from home, they were here. Like they always were. And always will be. She took in a deep breath, filling up her lungs to their fullest capacity. She paused for a moment, then let it release, trying to let all the fear out with it. She repeated this for a moment, until she was finally back on her feet. *You're okay,* she told herself. *You're okay.*

Her head shot up at the sound of the creaking door. In walked Luna, still clothed in her night dress. She seemed to know Amaya needed her. Somehow she always did.

"Hey," she spoke softly, sitting by Amaya's side. "Are you alright?"

Amaya tried to disguise the fact that she'd been crying, despite there still being tears on her cheeks. She didn't have to say anything. Luna knew.

Amaya took a deep breath and looked at her friend. "I'm okay, Lou."

Luna smiled and placed a comforting hand on her shoulder. Amaya leaned into the touch, returning the grin.

"Listen, we were talking about having a picnic in the Elderen Wood this morning. It was Elle's idea. Are you up for it?"

That's exactly what Amaya needed. Time with her friends. Time with her family.

"Course. Couldn't think of anything I'd rather do."

The girls met in the hallway, all dressed in beautiful dresses that ran down to their feet. Amaya let out a faint laugh to herself as she looked at her friends.

"What the hell are you laughing at?" bugged Iris.

"Nothing, it's just, you all look so pretty," she smiled, "Like princess from my books. I wish we could dress this way back home. Although I will admit, corsets are a lot less comfortable than I thought they'd be."

They laughed as their eyes lit up with endearment.

"Come on, bud," Elle said, ruffling Amaya's hair. "Can't have you getting all sentimental on us before our picnic! I don't want you crying on the scones. I ran into Edmund this morning after a little stroll around the castle," Elle continued. "I convinced him to put together a picnic basket for us!" She held up a basket that was overflowing with treats and goodies.

"Wait, Elle. You already walked around this castle this morning? What the hell were you doing at the asscrack of dawn?" Iris asked.

"Oh, nothing."

Amaya knew that was code for "getting myself into trouble by letting my curiosity get the best of me." *Who's gonna look after us when this girl gets herself killed?* she wondered.

"Are you sure we can go out there on our own? We don't exactly know our way around here," Amaya noted.

"Yea, we'll be fine, as long as we don't go too far."

After chaotically running rampant through the castle with their picnic supplies in hand, the girls found themselves back in the heart of the kingdom amongst the peasants who were barely scraping by. Amaya wondered how King Kay could sit behind the castle walls, feasting with nobles and lavishing himself with precious jewels when his people were clearly suffering. It didn't make sense.

They came across a small boy curled up alongside the road. He watched them as they passed. His sad, tired eyes weighed heavy on Amaya's heart. It was clear he was hungry and all alone. His face was smeared with dirt and his clothes were severely tattered. Amaya noticed his eyes fell on the basket Elle was holding. She reached into it to take out a small piece of bread.

The boy carefully watched her as she placed the bread in his hands.

"It's okay. Take it" she said softly.

He did not say thank you with words, but with his eyes. He took the bread and began eating it like it was the last piece of food on Earth. She looked back at the basket in Elle's hands. Without asking her friends for permission, she retrieved four scones and handed them to Elle.

She took the basket and carefully handed it to the boy. They could have a picnic without it. Amaya smiled as he accepted the gift, but only wished she could do more.

The further into the city they went, the more the truth of Camelot came to light. That boy was only a small part of the reality of the kingdom. Every corner was filled with a starving mother or child. It was almost too much to bear. Were the legends of Camelot even true? Was it ever really the greatest kingdom the world had ever known like the stories say? Or was it all just one big lie?

IRIS YUKI

I ris had missed being amongst the trees in the Elderen Wood. It was almost as if the wood missed her, too. The trees leaned in as she stepped onto the grass, like a warm embrace. The slight breeze felt warm and inviting. The outdoors were much more appealing to Iris than being cooped up inside a dusty, old castle all day.

In a hidden grove of trees, they came to a beautiful spot. "Let's go here. It's freaking gorgeous," Iris said, laying down the soft blankets.

As they munched on their scones, they observed their surroundings in silence. They were the kind of friends who did not need to talk to enjoy each other's company. Simply being there with each other was enough. It felt safe. It felt like home.

Iris drifted onto her back and watched as the wind moved swiftly through the leaves and branches. It reminded her of a place she used to go to with her father when she was young. Her favorite part of visiting him every spring break was watching the cherry blossoms bloom. They would lay there together, just like this, and watch the beautiful pink flowers sway in the breeze.

"Do you guys know what I miss? Elle asked, breaking the silence.

"What?" Luna sat up and turned her attention to Elle. Amaya and Iris did the same.

"Two words. Indoor plumbing," Elle was laying on her back, arms crossed behind her head.

"Ha! I second that!" Iris agreed. She wondered what else her friends missed. Were they thinking about home like her? She was too afraid to ask.

"Not to mention sunscreen," Luna added. "My pasty white skin is probably burning to a crisp as we speak."

"So, Elle? When are you gonna get with that knight, huh?" Iris teased, trying to get her mind off home.

"Oh, shut up! I told you I don't like him," she rolled her eyes.

"Yeah, but he likes you." Amaya lifted her eyebrows.

"And your point?" she crossed her arms.

"Why are you always like this with guys? Oh my god, remember that one time Harry asked you to prom and you straight up rejected him in front of the entire school," Luna laughed.

"Stop, yeah! Elle, what was up with that? You know, sometimes you're just gonna have to give a guy a chance," Iris jumped in.

"Listen, I didn't like him, okay? I'm not gonna settle. Unlike the rest of you, *I* know my worth. This Henderson guy is definitely *not* worth my time. And that's that," Elle glared.

"Okay, fair enough." Iris left it at that. But deep down she knew there was more to it. Elle had always struggled with emotional intimacy. She knew she feared being vulnerable. Hell, after thirteen years of friendship, they'd never seen her shed a single tear. Iris wasn't even sure if she was capable.

She crashed back down on the blanket and watched the trees once more. As she gazed into the atmosphere, something peripherally caught her attention. She turned her head to face it and squinted her eyes. "What?" she softly spoke to herself as she watched a trail of light form in the grass. She sat up, getting a closer look. *What the hell?*

The light was bright with rays that shot in all directions. It glittered on each blade of grass with a sense of purpose. She felt like it was calling to her, yet the other girls did not even seem to notice.

"Hey, guys? Please tell me you're seeing this, right?" she asked, still watching as the light stretched deep into the forest.

"See what?" Luna asked, sitting up.

Iris pointed to the trail. "That!"

The three stared at her in utter confusion. How could they not see the light? It was right there.

"You're telling me you don't see that trail of light? How is that even possible?" She turned to it and then back to her friends. Then without a moment of hesitation, she got up and started running along the path. So, what if they could not see it? Clearly she could for a reason. She could feel it, and she did not have time to explain that to them now.

"Iris, wait!" they called out to her.

But she did not stop. She kept running and running, following the illuminated path deeper into the wood. She weaved in and out of trees like a rat scampering through a maze. She was light on her feet, feeling the soft grass beneath her toes.

"Iris!" her friends yelled, attempting to catch up with her.

She was much faster than them. Well, maybe not Elle. But she was too far ahead for them to catch her now.

She was starting to lose her breath when the light trickled out of existence. She was so focused on the path, she failed to notice what was right in front of her. She searched the ground, looking for the light, but it was gone. It was once again just grass.

Feeling defeated, Iris turned back to find her friends. She was surprised to see them standing right behind her. "When did you guys catch up with me?" she asked.

No one answered. They stood there with eyes wide and their jaws to the floor. "Oh my God," Elle whispered.

"What the hell are you guys looking at?" Iris turned.

Just then, her eyes were filled with the sight of an entire city hidden in the trees. There were beautiful wooden staircases that wrapped the trunks tightly, guiding lost souls to the world up above. The rest of the forest was devoid of trees like this. They stretched to the sky and stood with a purpose.

Tall, golden pillars stood in support of the beautifully crafted structures that sat in the atmosphere. They held windows of all shapes and sizes, framed with shining gold fixtures. There were draping bridges that connected one to the next. They did not sit awkwardly amongst the trees, but were a part of them. The two weaved in and out of each other, not knowing where one began and the other ended.

From up above, it seemed like fireflies were painting the sky with their light. As Iris looked closer, she could see that they were not fireflies at all, but small fiery balls of light. Like magic. It must be. She could feel it, just like she had the night before.

"Iris."

She gasped as the unfamiliar voice spoke her name. They watched as a woman slowly approached them. She wore a long dress that trailed behind her, collecting leaves. Her hair was large in volume, fitted by a black crown that seemed to be composed of leaves and twigs.

"So glad you found us. I assume you saw the trail I left for you?" she spoke. She looked at Iris like she knew her.

"That was you? Who are you? How do you know my name?"

"I am Marjorie, the protector of the Elderen Wood. I've been wanting to speak with you since the moment you arrived. I could feel your presence. Your *magic*. You possess great power, Iris."

Iris did not know what to say. It had hardly been twenty-four hours since she discovered this part of herself. And now some stranger in the woods was telling her she could sense her magic? It was all too much.

Yet, it excited her.

"Where are we? What is this place?" Luna asked, while Iris was still dwelling in her thoughts.

"You are in Castemaga, home of the witches. Here, we are able to practice magic freely, and protect the wood from within. It is a sacred place."

"I thought that magic was now legal after the Great War. Why can't you practice your magic in Camelot? Or any other kingdom?" implored curious Elle.

"Young girl, just because something is *legal*, does not mean it is welcomed by all. There are many people who wish for the return of the old ways. They view us as a threat—something to be feared. We do not always feel safe within the city walls. It is best we stay here, where we are assured our safety and the safety of the wood."

Marjorie spoke with a great deal of clarity to Iris. She remembered how she felt the night before when everyone's eyes were on her. Some had judgment, even *fear*, painted across their faces as they watched her levitate that cup. It didn't feel right.

"Iris." Marjorie stepped closer to her, reaching for her hand. "I need you to stay here in Castemaga with me for a short while. There are some things we need to discuss and it's best we do it here amongst our people."

Our people. Those words hung in the air like a thick fog. Her friends were her people. She couldn't possibly stay here without them. Could she? She didn't even know this woman.

"Stay here? For how long?" she asked.

"Just a few short days. Then you may return to Camelot, if that is what you wish. Please Iris. It is very important you do so."

She looked back at her friends, who very clearly did not want her to stay. Amaya grabbed her wrist. "Iris, you're not actually considering this, are you? We don't even know this person. And you're gonna stay here alone? Iris, no. I won't allow it."

But Iris wanted answers. She wanted to know who she was and of what she was capable. Maybe this would finally be a chance for her to fill that empty void inside her that had been troubling her for so long.

She looked into Marjorie's eyes. They were honest and held the truth. Maybe it would be okay. Just for a little while.

"But she knows who I am. I can't explain it, but I know I can trust her. Guys, they have magic like me. Come on, I just want some goddamn answers. If I don't show up after a few days, hell, just send Sir Henderson after me. I'll be fine."

"But Iris…"

"Amaya, stop," she spoke with dominance.

Amaya grew silent. Iris knew her friends would not understand. Especially Amaya. She could see the worry spread across her face like a bad rash. She had to do this for herself. Arguing with them was going to get her nowhere. *Amaya will just have to grow up and deal with it,* she told herself. Some things were bigger than their friendship. Sometimes she had to put herself first. Besides, it would only be a few days, right?

"Okay," she turned to Marjorie, "I will stay."

LUNA AMBRIS

The journey back to Camelot was weighed with heavy emotions. Their inseparable group had now been separated. Luna did not want to leave Iris, but she knew her decision had already been made. Due to Iris's innate stubbornness, attempting to change her mind would be pointless.

Luna watched her friends drag their feet through the blades of grass, traveling further and further away from Iris. With time passing, it crossed Luna's mind that they did not know their way back to the kingdom. Without the illuminated path to follow, they were hopelessly lost.

"I swear I've seen that tree before." Elle stopped in her tracks.

"Elle, they're trees. They all look the same," Amaya responded, in a monotone voice.

"No, I know we've passed this one. Look," she pointed, "It's got a large gash through it."

"Wait, you're right," Luna agreed, recognizing the marking. "We've been going in circles."

Amaya dropped to the ground and buried her face in her hands in defeat. "Great, first Iris now this? This day just keeps getting better. What are we gonna do? We should've never gone out here alone. What were we thinking?"

Amaya was right. The Elderen Wood was large and filled with mystery. It was impossible to predict what dangers awaited them. Nothing was impossible in this world. They were far from home and vulnerable.

"If only it were dark, we could use the stars as a compass," Luna said.

"Too bad cell phones don't exist here, cause that would be super helpful right now. We could just Google Map it or something," Elle noted.

"Quiet," Luna said, ignoring Elle. "Did you hear that?"

They paused and listened. A firm sound, pounding against the earth, echoed through the trees. At first it was faint, but the longer they listened the louder it grew. It was coming for them. And they had nowhere to go.

Luna and Amaya looked to Elle, hoping she would quickly form a plan. She usually did. "Elle, what do we do?"

Elle sat there, concern filling her eyes like tears.

"Come on, Elle! Think of something!"

Elle said nothing, gnawing on her lip. Luna's heart panicked as Elle's face filled with uncertainty. It was never a good sign when Elle was nervous.

"Guys, I don't know what to do. I'm sorry," she said with defeat.

Just then, approaching in the distance, were a dozen men on horseback. They were not Camelot knights. They were something else. As if on a mission, they rode with a strong presence. With swords in hand, they tore through the wood like burning flames.

It was too late to hide. The men had already seen them and they could not outrun the horses. The girls stood shoulder to shoulder, assuming the worst of these mysterious riders. Luna was afraid they'd hear her heart that pounded against her chest, as they drew near. She took a deep breath, not wanting to show her true fear.

Within seconds, the men surrounded them like they were animals being hunted. As if the men weren't intimidating enough, the black horses towered over them, making Luna feel small. A man covered in heavy, dark armor stopped in front of them. He jumped off his horse and walked towards them. He had crooked teeth and reeked of ale.

"Now, what are you pretty ladies doing out here all alone?" he asked, getting a little too close for Luna's liking.

"I think that's none of your damn business." Elle always had to open her mouth. Luna shook her head, knowing she was going to get them in trouble.

"Elle, no." She grabbed her arm and held her back.

"Oh, this one's got a mouth on her." He stepped towards Elle. "I like it." He reached out his hand, covered in thick leather, and wrapped it around her throat. She held her head high, remaining stone faced.

"Leave her alone!" Amaya blurted out. Luna was shocked at Amaya's uncharacteristic outburst. Amaya sighed and shut her eyes. Luna could tell she immediately regretted it.

The man drew his sword and pressed it against Amaya's neck. She winced as the blade slightly pierced her skin. Luna held back tears as she watched Amaya fear for her life. She looked at the remaining men who still surrounded them, wishing there were something she could do.

"I thought I asked you what you pretty ladies were doing out here in the middle of the Elderen Wood."

Elle reached for his arm, attempting to pull the blade away from Amaya's neck. The man ripped his arm from her grip, shoving Elle to the ground. She had pushed too far. He was angry. Luna knew Elle was going to get them into trouble.

In the distance, Luna heard what seemed to be a single horse, galloping through the wood. She turned her head and saw a flash of Pendragon red. The man also seemed to notice this, as he turned his attention away from Elle who was still cowering on the ground.

Upon recognizing his face as he drew closer, Luna exhaled in relief.

Sir Henderson drew his sword, aiming it towards the man.

"King Caradoc, you are trespassing on the lands of Camelot. Leave at once. This is your only warning," he demanded firmly.

"As the brave and noble knight commands," he mocked, re-sheathing his sword. Getting back on his horse, he glared menacingly at the girls. Just like that, he and his men were gone.

"Are you ladies alright?" he asked. "I've been scouring the wood looking for you. It was a mistake to let you travel here alone." He reached his hand out to Elle, but naturally, she rejected it.

"I don't need your help," she said, picking herself up.

"Right. Because you certainly had it all under control before I arrived," he smirked, causing Elle to scrunch her nose with anger.

"Yes, I think we're alright," Luna interrupted them. "Just a little shaken up, is all."

"Where's Iris?" he asked, noticing there were only three.

"She stayed with someone called Marjorie, I believe it was. She wanted to stay and learn about her magic."

"Ah, Castemaga. It's natural that she would find her way there. No need to worry. Marjorie will take great care of her. Now, let's get you back to Camelot."

Luna's gaze shifted to Amaya, who had stayed awfully quiet throughout this entire exchange. The red gash, where the man's blade had lain moments ago, sat prominently against her skin.

"Amaya," Luna gently placed a hand on her arm. "You're bleeding."

Amaya lifted a shaking hand to her throat and felt the oozing red liquid run onto her fingers. Just then, a brilliant idea crossed Luna's mind.

"Sir Henderson, can you give us a moment? I want to try something." Luna sat Amaya down in front of her.

"I don't know if this will work, but it's worth a try," she said.

"What are you going to do?" Amaya asked.

"I'm gonna try to heal you. Now just stay still." Luna gently placed her hand across the wound and closed her eyes. She focused on what Liana had told her, about having pure intentions.

This moment reminded her of when they were children. One particular day, Luna was pushing Amaya on the swing on the playground. "Higher, Lou! I want to go to the moon!" Amaya had said. Luna pushed her as hard as she could. Amaya soared through the sky, her cheeks aching from the permanent grin on her face.

Luna watched Amaya's limbs flail in the air as she leapt off the swing. Her smile quickly faded as Amaya tumbled down, slamming against the ground. Luna rushed to her side to comfort her. Amaya wailed as blood dripped from her elbow. Luna reassured her that everything was going to be okay. She cleaned her wound and placed a fresh bandage over it, allowing it to heal.

Now, thirteen years later, nothing had truly changed. Although they were in another world, Luna was still here, trying to heal Amaya.

She closed her eyes and focused on the healing. While she had previously healed herself, this felt entirely different. A surge of energy flowed from one to the other, tingling like a carbonated drink flowing through their veins. The intimacy Luna felt was difficult to ignore. She felt a warmth pressing against her hand. After taking a deep breath, she opened her eyes.

"Lou?"

Luna smiled. "It worked."

AMAYA BROOKS

Amaya felt the smoothness of her skin as she ran her fingers along her neck. It was like nothing had happened. She felt a bit uneasy, knowing that Luna had this great power at her fingertips. But she trusted her, probably more than anyone.

She looked to Sir Henderson, who was seemingly in disbelief. His jaw hung low and his eyes were wide. "Luna," he said, "I did not realize you were a Mage."

"Oh, right," she laughed. "I found out the night we arrived here. I know it's only been a few days, but so much has changed."

So much has changed. There was that word again, *change,* cutting through Amaya like an edged sword. This was a painful reminder of Iris' absence. She already missed her. Inhaling deeply, she tried to divert her attention elsewhere.

"Shouldn't we be getting back?" she asked with a shaky breath, gripping the back of her neck.

"You're right. Follow me." Sir Henderson climbed back on his horse and began leading the way, with the girls trailing alongside his horse. Amaya lingered extra close out of caution.

"You knew that man," Amaya said to him. "Who was he?"

"Someone very dangerous and not your concern right now," he said, eyes fixed ahead.

All the uncertainty weighed heavily on Amaya. It was becoming increasingly clear to her that something bigger was going on. Something no one wanted to talk about.

"So, Iris is a witch, Luna is a Mage, and Elle has archery skills the likes of which I've never seen. Iris was right. You girls are certainly full of surprises," Sir Henderson noted, changing the subject.

"Hey, how does he know about your archery skills?" Amaya asked Elle.

A red hue spread across her face. "Uh, no reason."

Oh, what did she do now?

"Now you are the real mystery, Amaya. What kind of secrets are you hiding? Are you a changeling? An elf? Maybe a troll, perhaps?" Sir Henderson teased.

Amaya laughed. "Not to my knowledge. I'm just me."

All joking aside, she realized he was right. There was something special about each of her friends in Camelot. Something useful. She was simply there, filling up space, making everyone's life a little harder, no doubt.

The sun still had a few hours to set when they returned to Camelot. Luna visited Liana, and Elle was out on the training yard, getting into more trouble no doubt. Amaya could surely find something to amuse herself for a few hours. *Now would be the perfect time for some reading,* she thought. There had to be a library around here somewhere. She was in a massive castle, after all.

She remembered Luna had told her about a library Edmund had brought her to that night she discovered her powers. Amaya figured it would not be too hard to find. She had been living here for three days now, and had seen very little of the castle.

As she walked down the hall, rough windows scattered the wall in an asymmetrical pattern. Hefty wooden doors hid rooms full of secrets. It was clear this castle had stood the test of time. The rocks of the walls were aged and vines and plants grew inside the cracks. In some ways, it looked exactly like she had imagined. But there was a dark energy that existed between these walls. It sent shivers down her spine like a cold breeze.

She reached the far end of the west wing, where the air grew silent. Unlike the rest of the castle, there were no servants, knights, or nobles. All she could hear was the sound of her own two feet vibrating through the corridor. She carefully placed each foot in front of her as she walked towards an open door she noticed near the far end of the wing. The towering gold encrusted door was opened ever so slightly, as if someone left it open just for her. Amaya placed her hand on the door and slowly peered her head into the room. She smiled when her eyes were met with a room full of books. She quickly looked around, making sure the room was empty before entering. The room seemed dark and lifeless. She quietly pushed open the door and stepped inside. As she entered, she was hit by the strong smell of books and aged wine. A long, maroon curtain draped over the window, shielding the room from the sun's light.

This did not seem like the library Luna had described to her. This one was smaller and felt much more personal. A rug matching the curtain covered the floor, collecting dust. Near the window sat a velvet, forest green chair. It looked lumpy, like someone had just been sitting in it, but comfortable. Next to it was a small wooden table overrun with papers and documents. On the wall hung a large painting, fitted in a golden frame. The painting portrayed a man who sat proudly with honor. His blonde hair rested gently against his forehead, while his clean-shaven face complimented his pronounced jaw. His fairly long sleeved, cloth jacket covered him, completely buttoned up at the right side. The sleeves of his jacket were narrow and reached down to just above his wrists. They were colorfully decorated with several thread linings from top to bottom. He radiated warmth like the sun.

On his head sat a crown, adding one more dominant detail to the painting.

"Arthur," she whispered to herself. This was King Arthur.

Amaya felt drawn to him, almost like she knew him. In a way, she did. Through her mother's stories, she had grown quite close to him. He was like an old friend. It filled her with great sorrow knowing he was gone.

"My baby brother," a voice behind her spoke. Amaya's heart nearly leapt out of her throat. She turned around to see King Kay standing over her shoulder watching the painting. It did not take her long to realize she must be standing in his library. His private library. *Oh, no,* she thought. She had broken into the king's private library. She felt sick. But he did not seem angry or disturbed. In fact, he barely batted an eye.

"The people loved my brother," he continued, his eyes fixated on the painting as he stepped towards it. "And rightfully so. He was a great man. They do not respect me the way they respected him. No matter how hard I try, I just cannot seem to win their affection." He reached his hand out as if Arthur were actually standing right in front of him. "It does not matter. I will never be Arthur Pendragon. If they will not love me," he paused, "then they must fear me."

Amaya was silent, practically holding her breath. Why was he telling her this? She knew she was not supposed to be here and feared what the king would do next. Probably throw her in the dungeon, or worse. His head turned to her, his menacing gray eyes meeting hers.

"I'm sorry, I shouldn't be here. It was an accident," she panicked, making her way to the door. His strong hand met her wrist before she could get any further. She watched his eyes study her face like a book. What did he want from her? As she attempted to avoid eye contact, she noticed a brass key dangling around his neck.

Amaya winced as he leaned in closer. "There is no such thing as accidents," he whispered.

She gasped as he released his grip, tearing straight for the door. Although she did not look back, she could still feel his eyes watching her.

Amaya did not know her feet could move so quickly. The adrenaline shot through her like electricity as she fled from King Kay. Servants turned their heads as she flew by them. She held the hem of her dress tightly in her hands, pulling it out of the way of her feet. Unfortunately, one of the many layers of fabric that built the dress unnoticeably slipped from her grasp. The long dress got caught beneath her feet, immediately halting her quick escape. Instead of feeling the cold, crushing concrete beneath her, she was met with two arms and a plate of food. The silver platter went flying through the air, making a loud banging sound as it hit the ground.

"That's funny. I'm usually the one falling into people," said a familiar voice.

"Edmund! Oh, I'm so sorry. I don't know what happened," she sighed.

"That is quite alright," he smiled. "You would laugh at how many times I have fallen in these halls. It is a miracle the king has not thrown me in the stocks all these years." He dusted himself off and helped

Amaya to her feet. He picked up the remaining scraps of food that lay scattered on the floor.

Amaya looked down at her dress that now fashioned a dark purple stain. She bit her lip.

"You're in luck, milady. I just so happened to be, well, *decently competent* at laundry," Edmund grinned.

Amaya was happy to see Edmund had warmed up to the girls since they first arrived in Camelot. Although first impressions were seemingly awkward, he was actually quite charming and charismatic. And it was humorous watching him carry out his duties in such a chaotic manner.

"Thank you, Edmund. You're a lifesaver. But what about the…" she gestured to the now uneatable food that he held in his hands.

"Oh, it's alright. It was just for the king. I will check in with him later. He usually does not eat it anyway," he said.

Amaya gulped at the sudden mention of the king. How was Edmund not afraid of him? She could only imagine what he would say if he knew Amaya was responsible for his soiled dinner.

"Edmund, wait. Are you sure? I wouldn't want to upset the king. I can go clean this up myself," she offered.

"It is no trouble, honestly. Come on," he grabbed her hand.

After stopping by Amaya's room to grab a fresh, clean dress, they found themselves in what appeared to be a designated room for laundry. The room was filled with servants, mostly maids, washing clothing in large wooden buckets. The air was humid and filled with sweat.

Amaya sat by Edmund and handed him the stained dress. He carefully rolled up his sleeves and dunked the dress in a bucket of water. She felt bad just sitting and watching. She wanted to help.

She reached her hand out, but he quickly stopped her.

"Amaya," he spoke softly. "You are a guest of Camelot. Guests do not do servant's work."

She wanted to argue back, but decided against it. He seemed too honest and sure. She watched his boney, calloused hands scrub back and forth.

"Edmund, I have a confession to make," she paused, fidgeting with her hands. "Earlier today I sort of broke into King Kay's private library by mistake."

"YOU WHAT?" he shouted, causing all the maids in the room to turn their heads. He leaned in and quieted his voice. "I'm sorry, I think I heard you wrong. You did not just say you went into the king's very secretive and very *private* library."

"It was an accident!" her eyes widened.

"I am the king's bloody servant and I've never even set foot near that place. No one has," he paused. "At least he did not catch you."

"Actually...he did," she scrunched her nose.

Edmund nearly fell out of his chair. "How is your head not on a spike? Surely, he must have been furious. How did you even get in? The door always remains locked and only he holds the key."

Amaya remembered the key she saw dangling from the king's neck.

"The door was open, I swear! I was only in there a few minutes before he saw me. At first, he did not seem upset. He barely acknowledged I was there. When I tried to run he made it very clear he was not happy." "You were very lucky, Amaya," his eyes were tinged with sadness, "The king can be a very cruel man," he whispered. "Promise me you will be more careful?" In a way, this felt like a threat. For once, he was strong and firm in his words.

"I will. I'm sorry. Camelot is all still so new to me," she admitted.

"Do not apologize. I should not have shouted like that." He returned his attention back to the laundry.

"Edmund, did you know King Arthur? Before he died?" she wondered, thinking of the painting in the library.

"Not as well as I would have liked. I was hardly two when he was killed. But I have heard a great deal about him. I feel like I know him in that way. Through words and stories."

Amaya smiled, knowing exactly what he meant.

"I can understand that. God, I wish I could've met him," she sighed.

"Maybe one day you will."

"But he's dead?

Before Edmund could answer, another servant came bursting through the door looking for him. "Edmund, the king is requiring your services at once."

"I'm sorry, Amaya. I should probably go. He might be wondering where his meal is. Not that you would know anything about that," Edmund teased. He placed the dress in her hand and quickly hurried out the door.

ELDORA PEREZ

The encounter with King Caradoc kept replaying through Elle's mind like a bad dream. This was now the second time she had let someone intimidate her in Camelot. How could she let herself be so helpless? Why didn't she get back up and fight? She almost felt embarrassed knowing she allowed her friends to see her so vulnerable like that. That wouldn't happen again. It couldn't. She just needed to get out of her head, that's all. Next time, she would be more prepared.

Some archery practice should help, she thought. *I'll just go to the training field and clear my head. You got this.*

"And you followed me to the training yard because?" Sir Henderson ran his fingers through his curly hair as Elle stepped onto the patchy grass.

"I did not *follow* you here. I came here to practice my archery. Please understand, it had absolutely *nothing* to do with you. Maybe you're the one following me," she said, taking the bow in hand. Although she did not care for him, she could not deny she enjoyed getting under his skin.

"Eldora, I do not mean to step on your toes, but this training yard is for Camelot Knights only. It is no place for a young girl, such as yourself. You're lucky I didn't have your head for your little archery display yesterday." Although he said this in a jesting manner, she knew it was not a lie.

She stepped closer to him and lifted her chin to meet his eyes. He was much taller than she was, but this did not intimidate her. Her deep brown eyes stared at him with purpose.

"Then make me a knight," she declared.

"You can't be serious," he laughed.

"I am. Make me a knight. I'm sure I'm far more than capable," she stood with confidence.

"But you're a woman." H raised his eyebrows.

"Wow, you're very observant! They must've knighted you for your intelligence."

"Women cannot be knighted. It's against the law," he said firmly.

"Just when I thought I couldn't think any less of you," she walked circles around him.

"Do you want to be publicly executed? Then by all means, be my guest. I will personally hang the rope. Do you not understand knighthood is something that has to be earned? You must save the king's life or complete a dangerous quest."

"What if I did complete a dangerous quest?" she asked.

"What?" He almost laughed.

"What if I completed a dangerous quest? Would you knight me then?" She was solid in truth. Despite knowing she would later regret what she said, she continued to open her mouth. She needed to prove to herself that she could do this.

And to his ignorant ass too.

"Eldora, don't be stupid." Sir Henderson furrowed his eyebrows.

"Come on, think of the most impossible, gut-wrenching mission you could possibly dream of. Something no other knight would ever dare to do. And I will do it." She was taken back by her own words. What was she actually agreeing to? Whatever, it didn't matter. Whatever it was, she could take it.

He paused and thought for a moment. "There is one quest that no knight has ever completed successfully. But it's pointless. It is very unlikely you would even survive."

"Well then, *great knight*, you have nothing to worry about." She felt proud knowing she would not back down from this conversation without a fight. God, her friends were going to hate her for this.

"Do you even hear yourself? Do you think the king would agree to something like this? I do not know much about whatever far away land from which you washed up, but clearly you don't know how things work here in the Five Kingdoms." His tone made it apparent that his patience was growing thin.

"Then talk to him. What, are you afraid?" she stepped closer. She could feel his breath on her face. She watched him flare his nostrils and gnaw at the inside of his cheeks. He was not happy with her, and she loved every moment of it.

"Fine," he gave in. "I speak with King Kay first. But do not get your hopes up. Meet me in the Throne Room tomorrow morning. And Eldora," he paused. "Don't say I did not warn you." She could tell he meant that.

"Fine. See you tomorrow, then."

"Ahem." He cleared his throat and gestured to the bow that was tightly wrapped between Elle's fingers. She rolled her eyes and placed it in his leather glove.

"Knock, knock." Elle peeked her head through the entrance to Luna's room.

"Hey, Elle. Come in." Luna was sipping a cup of tea near the fireplace.

"Oh, Luna. You're just living your best life here, aren't you?" Elle mocked, sitting on the seat across from her. Luna's room was by far the nicest of the four.

"I mean, I can't complain," her voice softened. "You know I never had anything like this back home," she stared down at her cup.

"Yeah. Yeah, I know." She fidgeted in her seat. "I'm sorry I didn't mean…"

"Hey, it's okay," Luna interrupted. "I know."

Luna was one of the strongest people Elle knew. Although she would never admit it, part of Elle always wished she were more like her.

"How are you holding up?" Luna asked, "After today and everything."

"I'm fine," she lied. She hated her for bringing it up. "I never thought I'd say this, but I already miss Iris. Kinda weird not hearing constant complaining and smartass comments all day," she admitted.

"Yeah, I miss her too. A lot. But I guess we're gonna have to get used to this, right? Being apart from each other, I mean." Luna had not looked up from her tea.

"What do you mean?" Elle tilted her head.

"College, Elle." Luna finally met her eyes.

"Oh. Right." Until now, the thought hadn't even crossed Elle's mind. She had been so caught up in this new world, their old lives had slowly begun to slip from her worries. Luna was right. In a few days, they would have to go home, and everything would change.

"Are you ready? For college?" Elle asked, twiddling with her thumbs.

"I suppose so. Aren't you?"

She wanted to say, "*To be honest, Luna, I have no idea. You know, I spend so much of my life trying to put on a brave face. I know I have to be brave for my friends and my family back home so I can take care of everyone. I'm supposed to be the strong one. I figured, if I can convince everyone else I'm fearless, then maybe I'll believe it too. And honestly, most of the time it works. I sorta, fake it till I make it, so to speak. But with this...Luna I'm terrified.*"

But, "Why wouldn't I be?" was all she could manage.

"Yeah, thought so. I mean, if anyone could handle being on their own it's you," Luna said.

But that was far from the truth.

"I think I'm gonna head to my room. Feeling a little tired," Elle lied through her teeth.

"Oh, okay. Goodnight, Elle," Luna said, taking one last sip of her tea. She got up and quickly left the room.

Elle never cried. Sometimes she'd go weeks, even months, without shedding a single tear. If she ever did, it was always in private. Always.

She rushed into her room, promptly shutting the door behind her. *You're okay,* she told herself. *You're okay, you're okay, you're okay.* She repeated it over and over again in her head like a prayer. Why was she reacting like this? This was so embarrassing. She was so weak.

Her back slammed against the door as she slid to the ground. She pulled her knees into her chest and tried to hold her breath, knowing Luna was still right next door. She covered her hand over her mouth as the warm tears slowly trickled down her cheeks.

IRIS YUKI

I ris felt weird watching her friends leave her in the middle of the Elderen Wood. Although this was her decision, it tugged on her heart. She knew they'd be reunited and heading home soon enough.

Home. *Ugh, college,* she remembered. *I guess this is just a taste of what's coming. Damn, we really are a bunch of codependent idiots.*

Iris followed Marjorie up the long spiral staircases, into the city above. The breeze was strong, but felt warm and pleasant. Iris could almost see Camelot through the trees. This comforted her. Her friends were not too far away after all.

There were many women, young and old, in Castemaga, Iris noticed. *Witches.* Magic flowed from their hands and illuminated the world around her. She smiled, realizing she was a part of this now.

Majorie brought her to a small room that sat at the top of the tallest tree. It was much different than her room back in Camelot. The ivy and tree bark coated the walls in a tangled, but beautiful mess. There was no wardrobe overflowing with precious gowns. Instead, there was only a small dresser, filled with two or three dresses. A tiny bed, fitted with dark green sheets, laid in the center of the room. It was small and cozy.

Majorie drew her attention to the dresser, "There are a few things here you may wear. You might find them more comfortable than those palace gowns. Much easier to move in, I think."

Iris walked to the dresser and opened the top drawer. She pulled out a black, velvet dress. It looked much like the dresses she saw all the other witches wearing. It ran to her ankles and had long, flowy sleeves. On the back, there was a draping hood attached. It was clean and simple. Just the way Iris liked it.

"This is freaking perfect. Thanks, Marjorie," she smiled.

"You are quite welcome. I will allow you to settle in and get comfortable for the night. I do not wish to overwhelm you. We will talk tomorrow. If you need anything at all, I am just across the way." She pointed to the swinging bridge. "I do hope you make yourself at home, Iris. We are happy to have you here," she smiled.

"Thank you."

Marjorie left the room, disappearing across the bridge.

Iris let out a breath she did not realize she was holding in as she untied her corset, slipping out of the tightly fitting dress. It pooled on the wooden floor as she reached for the velvet dress. Brushing against her bare legs, it was soft. She stretched her long arms into the sleeves and gently pulled the hood over her head.

Marjorie was right. This was much more comfortable.

Adjusting to this new world was difficult. No technology. No screens. No distractions. A part of her found peace in that. Normally, at this point in the day, she'd be buried deep in her couch watching reruns of *Supernatural* on the CW. Now, her reality was much different. Better even.

In her small room, directly across from the bed was a square window. It was framed by twisted branches. Snug in her cozy new dress, she sat on the window sill. She rested her head on her knees and watched the sun swiftly sink into the trees. As the sun drifted lower and lower, the glowing balls of magic gleamed brighter and brighter. While they rose in the air, Iris watched them. Her eyes filled with their magical light.

She giggled as one light moved closer and swirled around her. It moved like it had a personality of its own. Iris reached out, wondering what it would feel like to touch it. She stretched her arm, barely skimming the light with her fingertips. She gasped as a tingling sensation ran up her arm.

Over the past few days, Iris had learned that magic was tangible—that it was not just a thing, but a feeling. It weighed heavy with purpose and life. It sent chills down her spine and made all the little hairs on her arms stand up straight. It made her invisible. Powerful.

Oh, what the hell, she thought as she watched the lights flicker against the pink sky.

Iris again extended her hand, this time with her palm facing upwards. She closed her eyes and let out a deep breath. She focused all her feelings and energy and directed it to the palm of her hand. She wasn't exactly sure what she was supposed to do, but she tried to follow her instincts. She focused on how she felt lifting those books back in Camelot.

The darkness from her eyelids started to fade. She blinked her eyes open and watched as her own ball of light blinkered in her hand. It was just like the others swirling around her. Well, perhaps, bigger and brighter.

"I did it," she smiled. She lowered her hand, letting the light join the rest in the sky.

She pulled her legs into her chest, resting her head back on her knees. The sun was almost gone now, allowing the magical flares to take on their strongest form.

I could get used to this, she thought, as her friends became a distant memory.

Iris rubbed her eyes as she looked around her unfamiliar settings. Waking up not knowing where you are is not the most ideal thing. "Where the hell am I?" she yawned. She looked out the window and saw she was miles above the ground. "Oh, right," she muttered. "Almost forgot."

She just about panicked when she noticed there was no mirror in her room. How on earth was she going to get ready without a mirror, or even a brush for all that matter? *Shit, maybe I didn't think this through.*

She ran her fingers through her hair, combing it out to the best of her ability. Its length and thickness made it tangle easily. She could only imagine what it looked like right now. No, literally. She could only imagine.

She slipped on her boots and walked out onto the bridge. *You look fine. No need to worry. No one here even knows you. Doesn't matter. No one has freaking mirrors here, anyways. Everything's fine.* She repeated these thoughts over and over again in her head as she spiraled down the staircase.

Marjorie was standing amongst a crowd of other women, who were dressed very similarly to her. They turned their heads at the sound of Iris's boots crunching the leaves beneath her feet as she ran towards them. "I'm here!" she yelled.

"Ah, Iris. I had almost thought you'd forgotten. It's nearly midday," Majorie chuckled.

"Dammit, is it really? Sorry, I sorta have a bad habit of not waking up when I'm supposed to. My mom hates me for it," Iris responded. To be fair, there were no alarm clocks in the Elderen Wood, so this was hardly her fault. What was she supposed to do?

"Do not apologize. You are here now," Marjorie gestured to the rest of the women, "Would you please excuse us? I need to speak with Iris alone."

They left one by one, leaving just the two of them.

"Iris, please have a seat," Marjorie guided her to a concrete bench that, much like her room, was covered with ivy. The two sat down. "Do you know why you're here?" she asked her.

"Well, I'm assuming it's something to do with my magic?" Iris tried her hardest to not use a sarcastic tone. It certainly was a challenge.

"Yes, indeed. I see great potential in you, Iris. I believe it's important you understand what you are truly capable of. Do you understand?"

"Uh, I think so," Iris nodded, although she wasn't sure.

"You will work alongside Maeve. Her goal is to help you grow to your full potential. I think you two will get along well. Oh, look! There she is now," Marjorie pointed.

A girl, no more than eleven or twelve, was approaching them. She was clothed in a similar dress to Iris, but instead of black, hers was a luxurious dark green that sat nicely against her tan skin. Her wavy raven hair that reached her shoulders bounced as she walked towards them. As she drew closer, Iris could see a large scar that ran along her cheek.

"Iris, this is Maeve."

Maeve extended her hand to Iris, "Hello, Iris. Nice to meet you! I cannot wait to help you on this new journey." Her little voice was filled with enthusiasm.

"Um, hi," Iris shook her hand. Great, now she was going to be trained by a kid.

"Well, you two have much to do, so I will be off. Iris, if you need anything at all, just ask Maeve. She knows where to find me," Marjorie said, leaving Iris alone with the girl.

"Well, this is exciting, isn't it? Follow me!" Maeve said with a large bubbly grin. She grabbed Iris's hand and pulled her along. Iris was already getting irritated with this girl. Her overflowing, positive energy was far too exhausting.

"Yea, sure," Iris's voice was monotone, "So, where exactly are we going?"

"Where all the young witches go to practice their magic! Well, you are not exactly young. Not to say that you are old! But you are older than me, and I have been practicing magic since before I could talk," she spoke so quickly Iris could barely keep up with what she was saying.

"Gotcha. So, uh, you're a witch then?" Iris asked, trying to create small talk as they walked.

"Of course! Everyone in Castemaga is. It is the home of the witches, you know."

"Right," is all she could say.

After a few more minutes of uncomfortable silence, they stopped at the foot of a large clearing. The vibrant grass stretched across the earth about a mile long. Yellow flowers seasoned the field with their bright colors. "This is where we will begin," Maeve said.

"So, what is it that we'll be doing exactly?" Iris asked.

"Come here," Again, Maeve grabbed her hand and dragged her out into the clearing. No one had given Iris a straight forward answer since the moment she stepped through that stupid door.

"Will you stop doing that?" Iris tore her hand from her grasp. "I can walk perfectly fine without you yanking me around like that."

"Oh, sorry. Habit, I suppose. Now, how is your movement of objects?" They stood in the center of the field, surrounded by trees on all sides of them.

"Um, I don't know. I was able to levitate a cup and a few books," Iris shrugged.

"Very well then. We will start with this." She gestured to a rock the size of a dog, "Oh! Let me draw a face on it, so it looks like a tiny person. This will be so fun," she giggled.

"No, Maeve. We really don't need to do that," Iris rolled her eyes.

But with the wave of Maeve's fingers, a little smiley face appeared on the rock.

"And now you've done it," said Iris. Magic was really capable of all sorts of things.

"Okay! Oh, what should we name him? Christopher? Edward? Oh, I know, Charles!" Maeve said, far too enthusiastically.

"Is naming the rock really goddamn necessary?" The day had barely begun and Iris had just about had enough. *This is so stupid.*

"Iris! Language! And, absolutely necessary. Now, come on. Lift Charles into the sky!"

Iris thought she was going to roll her eyes so much they'd fall out of her head. Trying her best to ignore Maeve, she slowly raised her hand and pointed it at the rock. At the moment, she was lacking confidence. After all, rocks are much heavier than books. What if she wasn't able to do this? She did not want to embarrass herself in front of this kid.

Snap out of it, she tried to clear her mind.

She focused heavily on the rock, completely letting go of anything else. Other thoughts and feelings soon became irrelevant. Her surroundings blurred and Maeve's voice faded away. Soon it was just her and the rock.

Although she would never admit it to Maeve, that dumb smiley face was actually helping. She focused all her energy on it and slowly began to raise her hand. She watched steadily as the rock followed her movements. Although it was barely hovering on the surface, it was working.

"You did it! You lifted Charles!" Maeve celebrated.

Iris snapped out of it, causing the rock to fall back down to the ground. "Hey, you distracted me! Maybe don't yell in my freaking ear next time!"

"Sorry, sometimes I can get a little too excited."

"You think?"

"Go on. Do it again. I promise I will be quiet," Maeve batted her eyelashes. Iris didn't believe her.

This time Iris moved more quickly through her movements. Within seconds, the boulder shot up into the sky, much higher than it had before. Knowing that Maeve would react to her smile, she tried to hide it. She held the rock in the air for a few minutes, then gently brought it back down to the ground.

"YOU DID IT!" Maeve released the scream she had been holding in for the last five minutes.

"Yes, I did it," Iris covered her ears. "But there's no need to scream!"

"Oh, sorry," Maeve whispered. "But I'm so proud of you!" She ran up to Iris and wrapped her arms around her so tightly she could hardly breathe. She nuzzled into Iris's chest, clearly with no intentions of letting go.

"Hey, kid. There's no need for that. You gonna be giving out hugs after every single thing I do?" Iris asked, genuinely concerned. She was never much of a hugger.

"Perhaps," Mave said, still not letting go. Iris grabbed onto her arms and physically pried her off of her.

"Okay, that's enough. So, I lifted the rock…"

"Charles," Maeve interrupted.

Iris sighed, "I lifted…*Charles*. What's next?"

"Hm. Are you able to deflect objects?"

"I don't know. I've never tried."

"Well, then. Let's find out." Maeve walked across the clearing, leaving a large space between her and Iris. Next to Maeve's feet was a pile of chopped up wood. Maeve levitated two rather large pieces into the air. And very quickly, she sent them hurling towards Iris.

Iris panicked and dropped to the ground. "Dude! Now, hang on a minute! You didn't tell me you were gonna throw stuff at me! Jesus, how 'bout a little warning next time? And can we start with just one, maybe?" God, this girl was going to get her killed.

"What did you think deflecting objects meant? Get up! Be ready this time!" As per her request, Maeve lifted *one* piece of wood into the air.

Iris jumped back on her feet and took a deep breath. She dug her feet into the ground and tensed the muscles in her arms. Her eyes fixed on the wood as Maeve made a move. As it cut through the air, she held out her hands in front of her. She tried not to overthink it.

Just move it out of the way. Plain and simple.

With a quick movement of her hands the wood tore in half straight down the middle, splitting it into two. It was loud and violent, throwing splinters everywhere. She gasped as each half of wood dropped on either side of her. Her own strength stunned her.

Across the clearing, she could see Maeve jumping for joy.

LUNA AMBRIS

G lowing embers and murky ash rained from the sky. The sky was dark, but the glowing orange flames lit Luna's surroundings. Where was she? Encompassing buildings and structures crumbled around her, dispersing into nothing but piles of hot rubble. Among the debris was a flag bearing the Pendragon crest.

This was Camelot.

Her feet began to move quicker than they ever had before. "ELLE! AMAYA! IRIS!" Her eyes searched desperately for her friends. But there was nothing. Not a single sign of life.

Not able to keep up with her feet any longer, she stumbled to the ground. She wept in the dirt and ash, feeling hopelessly afraid. The sound of a roaring blaze grew louder. She slowly lifted her head and blinked the tears out of her eyes.

The Elderen Wood was a sea of flames. Not a single tree stood untouched. Somewhere in the distance, Luna could hear the faint screams of her friends.

Suddenly, her eyes shot open at the sound of her name ringing in her ears. She was confused when her eyes were met with Liana's. Her confusion only increased when she noticed that it was still dark outside her window. "Liana? What's going on?" She sat up in bed, still feeling disoriented from her dream.

"Luna, I'm sorry to wake you. I need your help, my dear" she whispered in a panicked tone. Her voice was shaky and uncertain. Something was wrong.

"What happened? Are my friends okay?" Her mind whirled through all the worst possible scenarios. Did something happen to Iris? She knew they never should've left her alone in the Elderen Wood. What were they thinking? Or maybe it was Elle. She was always getting into trouble. Maybe she took something too far this time. Or was it Amaya? Had Luna not been there for her?

"No, your friends are fine. I will explain on the way." Liana was already halfway out the door. *Oh, thank God.* Luna sighed in relief, pulling herself out of bed. She hurried out the door, still shoeless and clothed in her nightdress.

The corridor was dark, dimly lit by a few candles that faintly burned. Every door was shut, each room filled with people tucked away in their dreams. The moonlight spilled through the cracks in the walls reacting with both Luna and Liana as they touched it. She would never get used to this.

"Liana, where are we going?" Luna quickly trailed behind her, trying to keep up with her incredibly fast pace.

"Something's happened. A few knights were ambushed in the Elderen Wood. They are fighting for their lives and I need your help healing them. I cannot do this on my own."

Luna felt a lump forming in her throat. This was serious. This was life or death.

"I will help in any way I can," she responded.

They reached a door that Luna had never seen before. It stood alone in a dark corner, seemingly separate from the rest of the castle. When they rushed inside, Luna could see it was some type of infirmary. There were dozens of shelves overflowing with small glass bottles. Like the rest of the castle, it was dimly lit with candles spread amongst the room.

In the center of the room were two tables that held the men screaming out in pain. Luna noticed Sir Henderson was there, watching over them. "Luna! Liana! Please help, quickly," he begged.

Luna rushed to the man with an open gash in his leg. His pants were ripped to shreds, drenched in massive amounts of blood that spilled onto the floor. She winced, seeing the bone peering through the broken skin. She took a deep breath and placed her hand on the open wound. It took everything in her power not to vomit.

The man screamed out in pain, sweat pouring down his face. "You're going to be okay," she said, although she doubted he could hear her.

Compared to healing herself or Amaya, this was much more challenging. The injury was life threatening, and it was difficult to concentrate in such an environment. The blood chilling screams ripped through the air, making Luna sick to her stomach. She felt tears welling in her eyes as the stress swelled through her body. She couldn't do this.

She desperately looked to Liana, who was healing the knight bleeding from his head. Luna shook her head, letting a single tear fall down her face. "I can't do this," she panicked.

"Luna, yes you can! Just focus on the healing, like I taught you."

Luna nodded and quickly whipped away the tear. This man needed saving and she was his only hope. She closed her eyes and imagined his skin sewing itself back together. She focused on the pooling blood fading away to nothing. She tried to ignore his screams and fixated on her own breath.

In. Out. In. Out.

He's going to be okay.

I can do this.

His screaming began to ease as her hand tingled. *Almost there.* She felt that recognizable warmth shooting up her arm. It was much more intense than before, and almost made her lose her focus. She chewed hard on the inside of her mouth, forcing herself to concentrate. Her heart was pounding loudly in her ears.

Suddenly, it was quiet.

She carefully opened her eyes and moved away her hand. Just like she had been envisioning, his leg was perfectly healed. Luna practically collapsed on the floor in relief.

"You did well, my dear." Liana closed the door behind her, allowing the men to rest.

"Liana, you said those men were attacked. Is everything okay?"

"It was most likely some loathsome bandits looking for a fight. You do not have to worry about anything, Luna, I assure you."

Luna nodded. Part of her did not feel at ease, but she trusted Liana. She filed her concerns in the back of her mind and went to bed.

ELDORA PEREZ

Elle paced around her room as the sun trickled through her window. Inevitable regret filled her mind as she awaited her meeting with Sir Henderson and the king. God, why did she have to open her stupid mouth again? Oh, well. It was too late. One thing Elle would never do was go back on her word.

It seemed neither Luna nor Amaya noticed that Elle had left her room. Chances were, they were still sound asleep. Sometimes waking at dawn played in her favor.

As she approached the throne room, she recalled the wary whispers she heard coming through those heavy, metal doors just a few days ago. She remembered how fearful she felt when the knight wrapped his hand tightly around her arm and warned her not to get involved. *Never again.*

She tried to tuck her curls behind her ear to make herself look more presentable. The few short days of being away from shampoo and running water had taken a toll on her hair. It was matted and frizzy beyond belief. Whatever. She did not have time to worry about her hair. She took a deep breath, pushing through the doors.

King Kay stood there, his arms crossed and his brows furrowed. He was speaking to Sir Henderson, who stopped talking when he saw Elle standing in the doorway. He faintly smiled in contrast to the king who kept his cold exterior.

He returned his attention back to Sir Henderson and nodded. Elle watched and waited. Then without a word, he left the room.

"Eldora," Sir Henderson gestured towards her.

She quickly entered the room, holding onto the hem of her dress so she wouldn't trip. She strode through the long, stretched room, holding her head high. No matter how nervous she was, she was not going to let it show. With many years of practice, Elle knew exactly how to mask her fear.

"So, what did the king say?" she spoke quickly.

"Eldora," he spoke softly, his voice riddled with fear.

"Well?"

"He agreed to your terms but…"

"Yes, I knew it!" she interrupted, "Bet you're feeling pretty stupid right about now."

"If you wish to undertake a suicide mission then I will not stop you." His doubts about her survival were evident. "But you need to promise me, you'll be careful."

"Yeah, yeah. I promise."

"Well then," he began. "In order to retrieve knighthood, you must embark on a journey outside of Camelot to the Everen Cave and defeat the beast. You will be accompanied by me."

"You're kidding. Why do you have to come?" She groaned. It was already bad enough she was going to be risking her life to prove a point.

"This is not something you can do alone. Besides, if something were to happen," he paused, "I would need to alert your friends."

Elle's stomach turned.

"Fine. I accept this *quest*." She rolled her eyes. "When do we leave?"

"You must leave at once. There is no time to waste."

Her heart sank. She would be leaving her friends today. What about Iris? She couldn't bear the thought of not saying goodbye to her. Maybe she shouldn't be doing this.

"Can I at least say goodbye to my friends?" she pleaded. *God, they're gonna kill me.*

"Of course. We'll leave at noon," Sir Henderson spoke softly, his voice full of pity.

"Thank you," she said out of breath as she ran through the doors. Her mind was searching for the right words to say to Luna and Amaya. Sincerely, she was more nervous to tell them what she did than about the quest itself. *There's no way this doesn't end with Amaya having a panic attack.*

It dawned on her that she had no idea how long she would be gone. It seemed the likelihood of her returning home was slipping further and further away from her grasp. What if her friends left her behind? No, they would never do that. She needed to focus. What was she going to say to them? They probably were not even awake yet. *Great,* she thought. *Good morning, besties, I'm leaving and might not return.*

She could back out of it. It would be so easy.

No, she couldn't. Then they would get the last laugh, and that was not going to happen. Besides, how bad could it really be?

When she reached the guest chambers, she gently knocked on Luna's door. She was not planning on telling Amaya alone. After a moment, a very tired Luna cracked open the door.

"Elle? What's going on?" she yawned. "Sorry, I was up all night. Long story."

"Hey, sorry to wake you. There's, uh, something I need to tell you. You and Amaya," her voice was shaky.

"Yea, Elle. Of course. What is it?" her voice was genuine.

"I wanna tell you together. Come on," she gestured toward Amaya's door.

The two quietly entered the room to find a sleeping Amaya all snuggled in her bed. She looked so peaceful and relaxed. Elle would hate to ruin that. Unfortunately she had no choice. "Amaya? Hey, wake up," Elle said, gently.

Amaya rubbed her eyes and shifted in the bed. She was taken back at the sight of her friends standing over her bed. "What's going on?" Concern rang through her voice.

Elle sat down on the bed and Luna joined her. "I did something stupid," she began.

"Why am I not surprised? What is it this time?" Amaya rolled her eyes.

"So, I sorta got into this fight with Sir Henderson and I maybe, sorta challenged him to knight me?" she awkwardly smiled, not wanting to go into any more detail.

"Okay, so what's the problem?" Luna asked.

"Well, uh, to be knighted you sorta have to go on a dangerous quest or whatever. And I may have possibly agreed to that." She sat, anxiously awaiting their response.

"What do you mean *dangerous quest*?" Amaya abruptly sat up in bed. Elle didn't answer. "Elle, what do you mean *dangerous quest?*" she repeated, more emotion in her voice this time.

Elle stared at her hands in her lap avoiding eye contact. "I have to go to the Everen Cave and slay some beast," she said quietly.

"Elle, what makes you think you can do something like that? In case you forgot, we're from Southern California, not Middle Earth. You're gonna get yourself killed," Luna insisted.

"So that's it then, You're leaving?" Amaya sounded like she was going to cry.

"Listen, I'm sorry. I just wanted to show ignorant people like Henderson that women can do just as much as men. I'm sick of being told otherwise. I know it was stupid." Her head fell in her hands, "But I feel like I need to do this."

"So, you're doing this to prove a point?" Amaya's tone shifted.

"Typical Elle. You know, you've always been so brave and stood up for what you believe in. I've always wished I were more like that," Luna said.

No, you don't.

"Lou, I think you're confusing braveness with stupidity," Amaya commented. Elle shot her a menacing glance. "Sorry. Iris isn't here to say brutally honest remarks, so someone has to do it."

"Oh no! Iris! You're gonna leave without telling her!" Luna exclaimed.

"I know," she paused. "But don't worry, I'll be back soon. It'll all be fine. The thought of Sir Henderson calling it a "suicide mission" rang through her head like a loud bell.

"You cannot expect to go walking into the Everen Cave in a lady's dress, I hope?" They stood on the training field, while Sir Henderson was packing supplies for their journey.

"Well, what else do you suggest? It's not like I have many options here," Elle responded. Sir Henderson held up bulky chainmail that was twice Elle's size. "This is a joke, right? There is no way I'm wearing that thing. It's huge!"

Sir Henderson ignored the words coming out of her mouth, and began to slip it over her head. It was heavy when it hit her shoulders, immediately weighing her down. Because Elle was the smallest in the group, the shirt hovered inches above the floor. The metal rubbed abruptly against her skin when she moved. It was by far the most uncomfortable thing she'd ever worn.

"I look ridiculous," she glared.

"No, you look very noble," Sir Henderson was clearly repressing a laugh.

"How do you expect me to shoot an arrow with this thing? It's so heavy, there's no way. I need to wear something else," she pulled the chainmail over her head and tossed it on the floor.

"I guess you can look in the armory for something you believe would be a better fit. But I will say, this is probably your best option, so do not come crying to me when you cannot find anything."

"Oh, trust me," she said. "*Anything's* better than this." She returned to the castle and headed straight towards the armory.

She pushed open the door to a room heavily blanketed with metal. Every corner of the room was filled with some type of weapon or armor. Unfortunately, it seemed like Sir Henderson was right. Her eyes met nothing but different variations of bulky metal armor and chainmail. Her eyes traced the walls, searching for anything that wasn't three times her size.

Just when her luck was running out, her eye caught sight of a wooden chest hidden beneath a pile of swords, maces, and rusty spears. Watching the dusty atmosphere that surrounded the chest, it was evident that it had not been opened in a long time. She carefully lifted the lid, coughing as the dust swirled in the air.

At first glance, it appeared that the chest was filled with nothing but more chainmail. However, Elle began to sift through the metal, her hand came across something smooth. Something leather. She pulled it out of the chest and held it firmly in her hands. It was a brown leather vest, fashioned with laces. Her eyes widened with curiosity.

She reached her hand back down towards the bottom of the chest. Once again, she felt the smooth leather beneath her fingertips. But instead of another vest, her eyes were met with a matching leather armguard. *I wonder,* she smirked.

She lifted her arms and slipped the vest over her dress. Her first attempt to fit it wasn't perfect, but she was able to secure the laces until it was snug against her body. She tied her hair back and pulled the armguard over her right arm. She reached for the quiver of arrows that was gently laying against the chest and fastened it tightly against her back.

She walked back out to the training field with her head held high. Nothing matched the adrenaline high of proving a man wrong. Without saying a word, she drew an arrow and knocked the apple right out of Sir Henderson's hand. He gasped, clutching his chest. "You have *got* to stop doing that," he said with a heavy breath. His lips parted and his eyes became fixed on Elle. Her new outfit clearly caught his attention.

"Told you I could find something better." She rolled her eyes.

"I stand corrected," he stuttered. He placed his sword in his sheath and secured the last of the supplies on the horses.

Suddenly, laughter filled the courtyard. The rest of the knights surrounded them, giggling and pointing fingers. The man who threatened Elle outside the Throne Room stepped forward to speak, "Does this dainty twat actually think she's going to be a knight?" The men roared with laughter.

"I could take you any time, any place." She gripped her bow a little tighter.

"Okay, that's enough," Sir Henderson stepped in front of her. Although it annoyed her that he felt the need to protect her, part of her found it comforting. Not that she would never admit that.

"Henderson, come on. Let's be honest here. A girl can't be a knight."

"She has every right to be here as any of us," Sir Henderson insisted, taking a step closer to them. Elle almost gasped. Did he really think that?

The knights rolled their eyes and backed off. They were clearly intimidated by him.

He turned back to Elle and his voice softened. "Are you sure you want to do this, Eldora? It's not too late. We do not have to go…"

"I'm doing this!" she interrupted, "Don't think your pride can stop me."

"It is not my pride I am worried about," he took a step closer. "It's you."

Her heart began to beat a little faster as he towered over her, peering into her eyes with what seemed to be genuine concern. For one small moment, she almost considered taking his advice. But the moment passed.

"I'm doing this. With or without you. I'm going to say goodbye to my friends." She shoved him aside.

Amaya and Luna were waiting for her in front of the castle. Elle wondered if this was what it was going to feel like when they all went their separate ways for college. So filled with sorrow and hopelessness.

Unspoken words floated through the air, but not one of them opened their mouths to speak. Instead, they embraced each other, holding on like this was the last hug they would ever get. Elle could feel the rapid heartbeats of her friends pounding against her own chest.

It wasn't until Sir Henderson cleared his throat that Elle released her grip. "I'll be back. And that's a promise," she said with truth in her voice. Elle did not care whether she believed that or not. As long as they did, she would be okay.

"You better. Three is an unlucky number," Luna said.

Amaya didn't speak, but she didn't have to. Her eyes said everything Elle needed to know.

AMAYA BROOKS

Amaya bit her tongue as she watched Elle leave Camelot. Another piece of her perfect family just drifting away like leaves in the wind. Luna squeezed her hand. "It's gonna be okay," she whispered. "She'll be back. They both will."

"I never imagined Camelot would become the place that tore us apart," Amaya's eyes glazed over.

"Hey, it's not tearing us apart. Amaya, we're literally in one of your mother's stories right now. We only have a few days left. Let's try to enjoy it while we can, okay?"

"You're right," Amaya sighed. "I'm sorry."

"Don't apologize."

"If Iris were here she'd probably tell me to stop acting like I'm in a soap opera." Amaya faintly smiled.

"Oh, she would never let you hear the end of it. You're lucky it's just me. You just need to get outta your head. Why don't we do something fun, huh? Come on, we've barely been outside the castle walls in the past few days."

"Okay," she agreed. Luna was right. She usually was. "What's your big idea, then?"

Luna's head turned as she pointed to a big wooden sign that read "Gawain's" in bold yellow letters. "A tavern is always a good place to start," she smirked.

Amaya was welcomed with the strong smell of musk and ale as she opened the creaky wooden door. Wall to wall, the tavern was bustling with people. It seemed to be primarily townspeople, particularly men, with the exception of a few knights. They pushed their way through the large bodies and reached an empty table in the corner of the room.

The room was dimly lit with large molten candles that swayed from the ceiling in metal casing. Amaya's eyes watched the room and the people that filled it. Laughter vibrated off the walls, echoing loudly through her ears. A rather muscular girl approached their table. Her hands were full of six tankards, while ale spilled onto the floor as she walked. Her face was full of freckles and her scraggly hair ran past her shoulders.

"Ladies," she said, lifting one brow. "Welcome to Gawain's! What'll it be?"

There was one drink Amaya had always been yearning to try but she nudged Luna, signaling her to speak first. "Hi, I'll take one tankard of, oh what's it called, *mead*?"

"Uh, make that two," Amaya finally spoke up.

"You've got it," she winked. "Say, I've never seen you here before. Are you travelers?"

"I guess you could say that," Luna responded. "We've been staying in the castle and haven't gotten out much."

The girl chuckled, "Now that's a laugh! Like King Kay would ever open his doors to strangers. What, does he tuck you in at night?

Read you a bedtime story?" Amaya glanced at Luna, unsure of what to say. Her laughter began to dwindle. "You are joking right?"

They shook their heads.

"That is very odd indeed," her tone shifted. "Where did you say you were from?"

"Um, very far from here. Outside of the Five Kingdoms."

The girl scratched her head and tapped her finger on the table. Suddenly, Amaya felt a queasiness seep into her stomach. Her expression worried her. She held her breath. Then the girl shrugged and said, "Well, then. You must be mighty fine guests if Your Royal Highness is letting you stay in his fancy castle. Two tankards of mead coming your way."

Amaya let out a deep exhale as she disappeared back into the tavern. "Well, that was weird, don't you think? I mean she has a point, Lou. Why is the king letting us stay with him anyhow? I mean, he doesn't even know who we are. Don't you find that a little concerning?"

"Yeah, I won't lie, it is kinda weird," Luna agreed.

"You know, I had a really weird encounter with the king the other day. I accidentally ended up in his private library and…"

"Hang on. You *what*?" Luna interrupted.

"Hey, I was lost and I saw books, I don't know what to tell you."

"You've been spending too much time with Elle."

"Anyways, that's not the point. The point is, he was acting really strange."

"Strange how?"

"He started talking about Arthur and something about how there are no such things as accidents." She felt a chill as she relieved the memory. "I don't know, something felt very off. Between that and what that man said? Something doesn't seem right, Lou. And yeah,

I know I worry about everything, but maybe this is something to worry about."

"I hate to say it, but you might be right."

"Maybe you should talk to Liana. See if she knows anything."

"I don't know, Amaya. I don't think it's a good idea to get involved."

"Come on, Lou! It feels like everyone has been leaving us in the dark the whole time we've been here. Don't you think we deserve some answers?"

"Yeah, yeah, I guess you're right." Amaya sensed her hesitation when she spoke.

"I can try to talk to Edmund, too. He's his servant, he must know something."

The scraggly haired girl returned slamming the two tankards of mead down in front of them. Amaya flinched as some of the mead splashed on her face. "Er, sorry 'bout that," she said. "I didn't catch your name."

"I'm Luna and this is Amaya," Luna answered for them per usual.

"Luna and Amaya, what lovely names such as yourselves. The name's Wren. I run the place."

"Nice to meet you. So, why is it called *Gawain's*? Why not *Wren's*?" Luna asked.

"Gawain was my father. He practically lived at the tavern," she laughed.

"Sir Gawain?" Amaya asked, recognizing the name from her mother's stories. She felt a glint of excitement.

"The one and only. God rest his soul. He was a good man. An honorable man. I just wasn't cut out for that kind of life. The life of a noble. Figured I'm more useful in a joint like this. These here are my people."

As she watched Wren's unabashed happiness, Amaya smiled a bit. After seeing nothing but despair in the streets of Camelot, she was glad there were still some small pieces of joy that shone through the darkness. It gave her hope.

"Enjoy the mead, ladies." She left with a wink.

Amaya held the large, metal cup in her hands and lifted it to her lips. While she wasn't exactly sure what she anticipated, she never imagined it would taste this good. It was bubbly, sweet, and tasted like honey. Far better than anything she had tried back home.

"No wonder everyone was drunk during the Middle Ages. This stuff is freaking fantastic!" Mead ran down her chin as Amaya took another big sip.

"Okay there, crazy. I don't wanna have to use my magic to heal you when you get alcohol poisoning," Luna said.

"But isn't that what friends are for?" Amaya teased.

IRIS YUKI

I ris felt a large weight crush her feet at the end of the bed. Opening her eyes, she saw Maeve, who was grinning from ear to ear. Iris threw the covers over her head and groaned. As she began to close her eyes again, she was hit with the cool air as Maeve pulled the blanket onto the floor. "You know you can't hide from me."

"I sure as hell can try," Iris said, her face buried in her pillow.

"I guess you're okay with missing breakfast then," Maeve smirked, inching towards the door.

"Wait. Breakfast?" Iris sat up quickly. Though Iris had only been in Castemaga for a short while, Maeve already knew her weaknesses. Iris hated that.

She pulled herself out of bed like her body weighed a thousand pounds and dragged her feet with every step. She followed Maeve across the bridge and down the windy wooden staircase. When they reached the soft grass, Maeve shoved a small bowl full of murky brown liquid in Iris's hands. "Eat up."

"Now what the hell is this?" Suddenly, she lost her appetite.

"Rabbit stew," Maeve said with a mouthful. "No complaining. It's good, now eat up! We can't have you training on an empty stomach."

Iris was beginning to miss the glorious castle feasts and baked goods. Oh, well. She closed her eyes and scrunched her nose as she shoveled a spoonful into her mouth. To her surprise, it wasn't half bad. "Luna would be shaking in her boots if she knew I was eating this," she said under her breath.

"Luna?" Maeve questioned.

"She's one of my best friends. She's a vegetarian."

"What's a veterinarian?" Maeve asked.

"*Vegetarian*, and it's someone who doesn't eat meat."

"Tell me more about your friends." Maeve's voice was stern yet enthusiastic.

"Okay, um. Well, there's Luna. Probably the kindest person I know. Smartest too. She loves the stars. She's studied them a lot. Drives the rest of us crazy. Then there's Elle. Talk about driving us crazy. She is incredibly stubborn and headstrong. She's a fighter and will always stick up for us. And then there's Amaya, who loves so strongly I swear someday it's gonna get her killed," Iris's voice softened. "It's just been the four of us for as long as I can remember. They're a crazy bunch of idiots, but I wouldn't trade them for the world."

Iris stared down at her rabbit stew, a bit terrified of how vulnerable she had just let herself be in front of Maeve. Maeve's silence made her uneasy. "Why the sudden interest in my friends anyways? Come on, I can never get you to shut up." Iris gently nudged her.

"Look around. Do you see anyone my age? I've been surrounded by grown-ups my whole life. I've dreamed of what it would be like to have just one friend."

The look on her face pulled on Iris's heartstrings. "Why aren't there any other children?"

"During the Great War, all the male sorcerers were slaughtered. I was not supposed to be born. My father was a bad man who tried to take over Castemaga and hurt my mother." Her eyes grew glossy.

"Maeve, I'm so sorry. What about the kids in Camelot? I'm sure they'd love to be your friend," Iris said, attempting to comfort her. For such a magical place, The Elderen Wood and Camelot had such a dark history. It was almost ironic.

"I'm not allowed to leave Castemaga. I did once, a long time ago." Her hand ran over the scar that braised her face, "There are bad people out there who want to hurt me. People like the man who hurt my mother. I'm not strong enough to protect myself." Iris was shocked at the maturity the weight of this young girl's voice carried.

"But you will be one day, won't you?"

"It's a little more complicated than that. My mother is Marjorie, the protector of the Elderen Wood. I'm her weakness. The bad men can use me to get to her. So, I have to stay here, not just for my sake, but for the entire wood's sake."

Iris couldn't imagine what it must be like to carry that burden at such a young age, and with no one with whom to share it. She began to see Maeve in a whole different light.

"Hey, well lucky for you, we're looking for a fifth member of our crew, and you might just be tough enough to fill the spot." Iris winked.

Maeve's eyes lit up, "Really?"

"Really. Just don't let Luna know you murdered rabbits for breakfast," she teased. Maeve threw her arms around Iris, practically tackling her to the ground. This time she didn't hesitate or push away. She reached out her arms, and held her tight.

"I wonder what your mith is." Maeve pranced on top of rocks as they made their way back to the open field.

"Mith?"

"Your special skill. Every witch has their own unique ability. We call them miths."

This was the first Iris had heard of this. "What is your mith?"

"I can turn people's eyes into stone," she prided herself. "I've only done it once. Miths are usually only used in emergency situations. It's our way of protecting ourselves."

"Holy shit, Maeve. Turn them to stone! Remind me not to piss you off. So how do I find my mith? It's not like I can test it on you. No matter how much I want to," Iris said out the side of her mouth.

"Hey!"

"I'm kidding, I'm kidding."

"You'll have to discover it on your own. When you're in danger it will come to you. Like an instinct."

"Why didn't witches use their mith things during the Great War? I think turning people's eyeballs to stone would have really come in handy."

"They did, but a witch can only withstand so much. It requires all our energy. If you're injured, it's pointless."

Magic was so much more complicated than Iris imagined it being. Iris felt like she'd never be able to understand it all, even if she tried. She wished it were like *Harry Potter* where she could just flick a wand in the air and say some fancy words. God, it would be so cool to have a wand. "Well, it's not like I want to put myself in emanate danger, but now I'm curious."

Maeve stopped walking, causing Iris to bump into her. "Iris, you need to be careful. I don't want you to get hurt."

"Okay, okay, don't worry. I won't do anything I shouldn't."

That was mostly true.

LUNA AMBRIS

Luna pushed through the heavy doors into Liana's library. Liana stood gazing out the tall glass window with a cup of tea in her hands. "Ah, Luna. What can I do for you, my dear?" She placed her cup down on the table, standing before Luna.

"I was hoping we could talk in private. It's kinda a sensitive matter." Her words were slightly slurred together due to the large amount of mead still coursing through her system.

"What is it, my dear?"

"What do you know about King Kay? I may just be in way over my head, but something seems off with him. Since you're part of the Royal Court I figured you might know something. And I don't…"

She was interrupted with the loud slamming of the door and Liana's hand covering her mouth. "Shhh, keep your voice down! Do you have a death wish?" Fear flooded Liana's eyes. Luna felt a tight pinch in her chest. She had never seen Liana like this before.

She felt instant regret, remembering something her mother always told her. "Keep your head down and don't cause trouble," she would say.

"I'm sorry, I shouldn't have asked," she whispered, her voice shaking.

"No, I apologize, my dear. I did not mean to frighten you. But speaking unkindly about the king can get you in a lot of trouble. I don't want to see you hurt, Luna." Liana shut the doors behind her, making sure they were sealed shut. She poured Luna a cup of tea and offered her a seat. Luna noticed her hands were shaking. "Have a seat."

"If he's such a cruel man, why is he letting us stay here? It doesn't make any sense."

"That's a question to which I do not hold the answer. I've wondered that myself. When you first arrived I thought, maybe he does have a heart? But I fear there is another reason." She sighed.

"What do you mean?"

"I wish I knew, my dear." She leaned in closer. "All I do know is that I do not trust him. I think he's hiding something. Ever since the death of Arthur, Camelot has not felt like home. He will never be the king Arthur was and he knows it."

Luna felt a great sense of importance knowing Liana trusted her with this information.

"Should we be worried? My friends and I?"

"I cannot say for certain." She pulled out a small wooden box and placed it on the table. Inside it was a dagger and a small holster.

"Wear this under your dress. You never know when you might need it," Liana said, placing it in Luna's hands. The handle was a royal blue encompassed with little specks of gold. It was small, but sharp. Sharper than any knife she'd ever held before.

She lifted her dress and securely fastened the holster around her thigh. She slipped the dagger into position and covered it with the flow of her dress. In all honesty, she had never felt cooler.

"Luna, there is something you should know. Being a Mage, you will be targeted. You are a creature of magic, therefore the enemy sees you as a threat. I should have told you before, but I did not want to frighten you. You must be prepared for anything."

Luna furrowed her brows, "I thought the war was over? That all magic was now protected by Camelot?"

Liana sighed, "I fear the war was just beginning. There are dark times ahead, my dear. When I close my eyes I see destruction. I see pain and loss. I see the Camelot we once loved crumble to nothing but scorching ash blowing in the wind."

Luna recalled her dream. The chilling sounds of her friends' screams echoed through her mind. Her body shivered. Was this more than just a bad dream? She opened her mouth, yearning for answers, but did not speak in fear of the truth.

"Is there something I can do?" she asked, not knowing what else to say.

"I'm afraid not, my dear. This is not your concern. It is unfair to burden you with such things and I apologize."

But it was too late. They were becoming a part of Camelot just as much as anyone else there. Luna wondered if it was a mistake going through that door. Perhaps they should have made more of an effort to reopen it and just gone home. But there was no point in pondering such things now.

AMAYA BROOKS

Amaya collapsed on her bed, allowing the blankets and pillows to engulf her. She would've fallen asleep right then and there if it weren't for the loud sound of her creaking door. She shot up and a familiar voice spoke. "Sorry, I didn't mean to startle you."

Edmund.

"Edmund! Where have you been? I haven't seen you in ages."

"Been busy running around for the king." He stepped into the room. "You've been at the tavern haven't you?"

"Maybe. Sit," she said, gesturing next to her. "Edmund, can I ask you something?" He nodded. If anyone was going to give her answers, it was him. "What happened in the Great War? It's been mentioned many times, but no one seems willing to tell us what happened."

Edmund stayed still, wrapping his arms around himself. She could almost hear his heart beating against his chest. He took a deep breath, gently closing his eyes. Amaya's mind flooded with regret. "You know what, forget it. I shouldn't have asked."

"My parents were killed during the war." The words spilled quickly from his mouth. His eyes met Amaya's. This wasn't her time to speak. She sat and listened.

"My mother was a witch and my father was a sorcerer," he continued. "I barely knew them. I was so young. You know, it's so unfair. The only memory I really have of them is watching them being burned

alive. I was hiding in a hay bale, just watching. I couldn't do anything."
Amaya watched the guilt overtake him as he scrunched his nose with
frustration and dug his nails into his arms.

"Hey, it wasn't your fault. You were just a kid, Edmund." She
pulled her paperclip out of her pocket and handed it to him.

"What is this?"

"It's something I use to calm my nerves back home. Just fidget
with it in your hands. It's saved my fingers over the years." This was
true. She lost count of the times she'd torn her skin around her fingers,
even drawing blood a few times.

Edmund released the grip on his arms and accepted the paperclip. "Every year we celebrate the war, but it's just a constant reminder
of everything I lost. Everything we all lost."

"Have you been here at the castle all this time? Just on your own?"

"Not exactly. After I lost my parents, I didn't know where to go
or what to do. So, I hid in the Elderen Wood. It was there that Merlin
found me."

Merlin. That was the first time Amaya had heard that name
since being in Camelot.

"He was searching for all the surviving witches and sorcerers,"
he continued. "That's when I learned I was the only sorcerer left. So,
Merlin took me in and began raising me as his own. We lived in the
woods for a while, just the two of us. At first, it was perfect. We had
each other and that was enough. The more I grew, the more I began
to learn why we never left the Elderen Wood. Merlin believed that
Arthur was going to return. He became obsessed with it."

Amaya remembered this from her mother's stories. *The Once
and Future King.* Arthur would return to Camelot when they needed
him most.

"Merlin loved me, I know that," he paused, "But he loved Arthur more than anything."

Oh.

"Arthur started the Great War all for him, you know. Merlin showed him the beauty of magic and Arthur realized the world needed to change. So, he fought for magic. And he died for Merlin."

This was the part of the legend that had been missing from her mother's stories. It all made sense now.

"But then Arthur consumed his mind and drove Merlin mad," Edmund continued, "He became irritable and restless. He started disappearing for days at a time. I never knew where he went or when he'd return. Something terrible happened one night. Bandits found our camp and I was all alone. I had my magic to protect me, but I was just a boy. I was so scared; I didn't know what to do. Thankfully, Merlin heard my screams and came just before it was too late. It was that night he decided to take me to the castle. He made a deal with King Kay and I've been here ever since."

"Well, what happened to Merlin? Did he just leave you here?" Amaya asked.

"The day he brought me here, he promised me he'd return. But one thing I learned at a young age is the world is filled with broken promises," he paused, "I don't know where he is. There's stories that he got tired of waiting and used Excalibur to take his life. But they're just stories. Truth is, he's probably somewhere deep in that wood, still madly searching for a man who will never return."

Amaya knew he didn't mean that. She could tell, deep down, Edmund knew Arthur was coming back. But loss and grief can change the way one views the world. Her heart ached for him as she understood his pain. Losing one parent was bad enough. She couldn't imagine losing three.

"You know, I never knew my dad," she said. "My mom said he left when I was just a baby. She says I remind her of him," she scoffed. "My whole life, she's always been so distant from me, like she's built this wall between us that I just can't break down. To her I'm this constant reminder that he's gone. For so long I thought it was my fault that he left. I would worry she was going to do the same to me," she reached for his arm, meeting his eyes. "What I'm trying to say is, it's not your fault Merlin left."

Edmund smiled like those were the words he'd been waiting to hear his whole life. Amaya felt that piece of herself that had been hurting begin to heal. "So, what was Merlin like, anyways? Super old? Long beard? Big, point hat?"

Edmund threw his head back in laughter, "What? No, Merlin was younger than Arthur! No beard, and definitely no hat."

Well, that's one thing the stories got wrong. She wondered what other parts of the legends were fabricated.

"Okay, another question. So, you're a sorcerer. Do you ever use your magic?"

"Not since Merlin left. It reminds me of him. And my parents."

Amaya nodded in understanding. Edmund's eyes shifted, a slight smirk creeping across his face. "Would you like to see?"

"Only if you want to," she smiled.

Edmund lifted his hand to the star-painted sky. She watched his palm illuminate with warm light. Just above them, the shape of a small dragon formed from a flurry of glowing balls of light. Against a dark night sky, its wings moved in slow, fluid motions. She lifted her hand and reached towards its benevolent glow. When her fingers met the dragon, light sprayed into the air like fireworks.

With a low hung jaw, she watched the sky swirl and dance with magic. She glanced at Edmund, who was smiling brighter than the sun. She might not have gotten answers about King Kay that night, but she had done something far better.

ELDORA PEREZ

E lle had only been on a horse once in her life. It was Iris's sixth birthday party when Luna got sick and threw up all over her horse. She didn't remember it being so uncomfortable. Despite having only been riding for a few hours, Elle felt like she had the back of an 80-year-old man.

"Do you want to take a break?" Sir Henderson asked, clearly observing her struggle.

"No, no. I'm totally fine. I could do this all day," she lied, straightening out her back. Sir Henderson smiled, rolling his eyes. "Oh, shut up."

"I didn't say anything."

"Yeah, but you were thinking. So, stop that," she pouted, eyes fixated on the path.

"You know, you're going to have to talk to me at some point. You can't just be silent the entire trip."

Elle lifted her eyebrow, keeping her mouth shut. She didn't have to do a damn thing he said.

"Alright, fine. I will just continue talking to myself. Pretend you're not even here. I'm simply strolling through the woods, just me, myself, and I. I love the peace and serenity of being alone. I can do and say anything I want. What a luxury, what a..."

"For the love of everything holy, please stop," Elle interrupted.

"Sorry, Eldora. You either talk to me or I talk to myself," he smirked. She knew exactly what he was doing. Before she could open her mouth to speak, her attention turned to a rustling in the trees.

Sir Henderson's head shot back at her. "Bandits."

Elle gritted her teeth as she remembered her experience with King Caradoc. She relaxed as the weight of her arrows pressed against her back. She'd be ready this time. She gripped the bow tightly in her hand and nocked an arrow into place.

She held her breath, waiting for Sir Henderson's signal. He quietly drew his sword, staying as still as possible. Elle gripped her bow tighter as the sound of the bandits grew louder. In an instant, three men on large horses appeared in front of them. Elle held her breath.

"Now!" Henderson yelled as he charged towards the men. Elle was hit with the realization she had never shot an arrow from horseback before. She squeezed her muscles tightly as the horse moved beneath her. With the bandits approaching quickly, Elle drew back her arrow.

The movement of the horse made it difficult to aim. She closed one eye and focused on the man as best she could. Upon release, the arrow tore through the air like a strong man ripping a piece of paper. It grazed the bandit's face, burying deep into the tree bark behind him. His brows turned inwards as his eyes focused shifted to Elle.

Trying not to panic, she reached for another arrow and quickly nocked it into place. He was directly in front of her now. A missed shot would mean the end of the line for her. She filled her lungs with air and drew the arrow back. Without hesitation, she let go.

A direct hit from the arrow knocked the rider off his horse. After exhaling in relief, Elle's moment of peace vanished within seconds. Standing behind her was the second bandit. Before her shaking hands could reach for another arrow, the man thrust his sword up against her neck. A sickening smile swept across his face, exposing his rotting teeth.

"Now, why's a pretty thing like you dressing like a man?" he asked, nodding at her armor. Elle felt sick to her stomach. Without thinking, she spat right in his face. A low growl came from the depths of his throat as he gritted his teeth. She gasped, realizing what she had just done.

Growling, the man released her and drew back his sword. Elle shut her eyes and braced herself. *When my friends find out I'm dead, they're gonna kill me.* But when the bloodcurdling pain of sharp metal didn't come, Elle opened her eyes. There was Sir Henderson, standing over the man's now impaled, lifeless body.

He rushed to her side, his eyes filled with concern. She shuddered as his fingertips grazed her neck. "Are you alright?" he asked. "Did he hurt you?" Her heart began to beat a little faster.

She pushed his hand away. "I'm fine."

"Now let's see, this makes it the second time I've saved you?" he smirked. God, she hated him so much, but he was right. He'd saved her life more than once. But this was the last time, she'd be sure of that.

"Yeah, yeah, yeah. If your head gets any bigger, you're gonna fall off your horse. Let's keep going." She saw him smile out of the corner of her eye.

"It was a good shot though. For no experience on horseback, I mean." He sounded genuine.

"Yeah, well, not good enough," she pouted.

"You cannot be so hard on yourself, you know." Elle hated how he could see right through her. She bit her tongue.

"You don't know anything about me," she said, taking the lead.

"Really? I know you're stubborn as an ass. You would never admit you were wrong. You underestimate the danger you put yourself in. You think you are better than me for some reason..."

"Okay, you're done," Elle interrupted.

"I wasn't finished," his tone shifted. "I know you care a lot about your friends. That you feel the pressure to protect them. I know you're strong. Maybe even stronger than me. And if anyone is capable of actually completing this quest, it's you."

Attempting to conceal her smile, Elle bit the inside of her cheek. Her hands that were tightly wrapped around the reins suddenly felt sweaty. She avoided his eyes and gazed off into the trees. She didn't dare open her mouth in fear of what she might say.

The journey was silent for a while after that. Elle focused deeply on the rustling of the leaves and rushing sounds of water. Even her own breath became a prominent sound in the mixture of acoustics. She felt on higher alert than usual, jumping at any sudden noise. She hoped Sir Henderson didn't notice.

Sometimes she'd catch him staring at her out of the corner of her eye. She tried to ignore it, but his stolen glances grew more and more irritating. *Screw him and his stupid big, green eyes.* She swore they were going to end up lost if he didn't keep his eyes on the path.

In an attempt to distract herself, she filled her mind with thoughts of her friends. She wondered what Amaya and Luna were filling their time with back at the castle. She hoped they were doing okay without her. She wished to see Iris somewhere out there in the woods. She missed her sarcastic comments and the way she pushed Elle's buttons. She almost felt bad for all the witches at Castemaga who were having to put up with her.

IRIS YUKI

I t was far past sunset and Iris was getting restless. She paced around her room, combing her fingers through her hair. "Screw this," she whispered, grabbing the black cape that lay at the foot of her bed. She wrapped it around her shoulders and threw the hood over her head.

She carefully made her way across the bridge and tiptoed down the stairs. She let out a deep breath as her feet hit the ground. She held onto the cape, pulling it in tightly around her body as she moved.

"And where do you think you're going?" a voice came from behind her. Iris jumped.

"Maeve," she whispered, turning to see the young girl standing in front of her with her arms crossed. "What are you doing awake?"

"Couldn't sleep, and I saw you sneaking around from my window. Where are you going?"

"Listen, I'm just gonna pop into Camelot real quick and visit my friends. They won't even know I'm gone," Iris grabbed her shoulders and turned her to face the stairs. "Now back to bed." Maeve cleared her throat, leering back at her. "What?"

"How were you planning on finding your way there and back?"

To be completely honest, Iris hadn't thought of that. She had just blindly followed her impulsive thoughts, head completely empty. She flashed Maeve a sarcastic smile. "Now, I don't suppose you know that spell your mom cast for me before, do you?"

Maeve smugly shrugged her shoulders. "It's possible."

"Okay, what do you want?" Iris rolled her eyes.

"Take me with you," she said, bouncing up and down.

"Maeve, you know I can't do that. Your mom would have me killed. Or worse. I'm sorry, I really wish I could."

Maeve's shoulders shrunk as disappointment spread across her face like a bad rash. "Yeah, I know," she spoke softly. She gently turned to face the brooding woods that stared back at them. Maeve slowly lifted her hand, closing her eyes. Iris watched the ground beam with light, stretching deep into the trees.

Maeve's extended hand turned into a fist. Despite Iris's gaze, Maeve was silent. She had never seen Maeve so quiet and stern. Iris could sense her sorrow, but knew there was nothing she could do. She couldn't risk her safety like that. Not after hearing what had happened.

Iris knelt down to be at her level. "I'll be back tomorrow, okay? Thanks for everything. I couldn't have done this without you," she winked. The corners of Maeve's mouth slightly turned upwards in response. Iris got back on her feet and started following the path, leaving Maeve behind.

Iris had never been a fan of the dark. Not that anyone should be a fan of the dark and anyone who says otherwise is a psychopath. But, walking through a dark forest in another universe by yourself in the middle of the night was a whole other level of scary.

Thankfully, the light from the path provided some relief, but it wasn't enough. Surrounding her were dark, ominous shadows that felt like eyes watching her. The trees sounded like ghosts crying in the wind and the moon poured down a menacing glow.

Wait a minute, she thought. She held out her hand and faced her palm to the sky. She remembered her first night at Castemaga when she was able to create a ball of light. Maybe she could do it again. She concentrated on her hand as she tried to remember how it felt.

Chills shot down her arm, causing all her little hairs to stand up. She directed all her energy to the palm of her hand. In no time at all, a ball of illuminating energy began to form. The more she focused, the more it grew, brightening all that surrounded her. A small giggle escaped her mouth, feeling overwhelmed with joy and pride. She would never get used to this.

As she walked, the light followed. It trailed alongside her like a poor, lost puppy. She felt comfort, knowing she had this power sitting at the base of her fingertips. It gave her meaning, a sense of purpose.

She looked up at the moon and the stars as she continued her journey to Camelot. They reminded her of Luna. "If Luna were here she'd be telling me a bunch of BS about how the position of the stars tonight are impacting my mood or something," she mumbled to herself. The thought of this made her smile.

She could see the dire silhouette of the city buried deep in the rocky mountains. Camelot was so beautiful. No bustling cars. No light pollution or neon signs. No large billboards advertising car insurance. She wondered if her home once looked like this. Not overcome with pomp and circumstance, just simply existing.

That's what a home should be.

After arriving at the city's gates, she realized she had no plan. Iris was notorious for not thinking things through. She glanced down at her hands. "Alright, let's see what I can actually do," she whispered. Standing at the foot of the castle, she gazed up at Luna's window. Well, good thing she wasn't afraid of heights.

She placed her hands at her side and clenched her fists. Levitating herself shouldn't be that hard, right? It was just like levitating an object, which she had done a million times. Except this time, she was the object.

She pressed all her energy into the ground, clenching her fists even tighter. Her stomach dropped when she felt her heels peel off the earth. She instinctively shut her eyes. A weightless sensation washed over her body as her feet dangled in the air.

Although afraid to open her eyes, Iris looked down at her feet. *Shit.*

She, Iris Yuki, was floating through the goddamn air. She tried not to panic, in fear of plummeting to the ground. She controlled her breathing and watched Luna's window come further into sight. *Luna's gonna lose her goddamn mind.*

She stopped in front of the rose-colored glass, seeing Luna buried in the massive pile of blankets. Iris knocked on the window. "Luna! Luna! It's me!" she yelled. Luna shot up in bed and frantically searched for the source of the sound. Iris waved in the window, feeling very pleased with herself.

Luna's jaw fell to the floor when she saw her friend. She rushed to the window and pried it open. "Are you here to take me to Neverland?" she asked. The moonlight fell through the open window, hitting Luna's skin. Iris's eyes widened as a fantastic, blue light started tingling of Luna

"Holy shit, Luna, you're glowing!"

"And you're floating in the sky," Luna said, helping Iris in the room.

"Camelot's one hell of a place, isn't it?"

Luna pulled Iris into a tight hug, practically tackling her to the ground. "I missed you."

"Yea, yea, I missed you, too. Now, get off, you're hurting me."

"What are you doing here? Are you coming back for good?" Luna asked, sitting on the foot of her bed.

"No one knows I left. I just had to see you guys," Iris confessed, "Come on, let's go wake up the others!"

"Wait," Luna grabbed her arm, stopping her from taking another step. "There's something you need to know." Iris felt queasy, immediately assuming the worst. "Elle isn't here. She left yesterday on some stupid quest with Sir Henderson. We don't know when she'll be back."

Iris boiled with anger. Of course she was. Why couldn't Elle just be normal for one freaking second? Suddenly, her anger began to melt into sorrow. She collapsed down next to Luna.

"Iris?"

"She left? Without saying goodbye to me?" Her voice was so small.

"Iris, we didn't know when you'd be back."

Luna was right. She was the first one to leave. She couldn't blame Elle for this. But, it still stung a bit.

"Hey, but there is someone I know who will be thrilled to see you," Luna smiled.

AMAYA BROOKS

Amaya's heart nearly leapt out of her chest when she felt two strong hands shake her awake. When her eyes focused, she discovered that those two hands belonged to Iris. She must've been dreaming. "Dude, you look rough," the figure spoke.

Okay, definitely not dreaming. That was Iris, no doubt about it.

"That's what happens when you wake me up in the middle of the night," she smiled, shoving Iris off her bed, giddy with joy.

"Is that anyway to greet your long-lost friend?" Iris laughed. Amaya had missed those stupid comments.

"What are you doing here? And in the middle of the night?"

Iris pulled herself up off the floor and plopped down in between Luna and Amaya. "I snuck out. My teenage rebellion years aren't over yet."

"So, does this mean you're going back?" Amaya asked.

"Bro, don't ruin the moment," Iris said, climbing back onto the bed.

"So, Iris can fly now," Luna said, butting in.

"Can you phrase it differently, cause that just sounds stupid," Iris replied.

"Oh, what would you call it?" Luna rolled her eyes.

"Okay, can someone please explain?" Amaya asked. Iris stood up and walked over to the balcony. She opened the doors and stepped up onto the ledge. Amaya gasped when Iris stepped into the open air and levitated like a helium balloon.

Camelot had engulfed her friends, weaving them into a part of its story. It fascinated and terrified her all the same. Even Elle was on her way to becoming a full-fledged knight. Where did that leave her?

"Iris, get back in here, you're making me anxious!" Amaya yelled, reaching out for her. Iris jumped back in the room, laughing so hard she collapsed on the floor.

"So, you've learned a lot at Castemaga, huh? What is it like there?" Luna asked.

"It's freaking amazing, you guys. It's honestly impossible not to lose my goddamn mind every day. The stuff I can do is...incredible," Iris softly smiled, "I met this crazy kid. She's been teaching me about my powers. She drives me absolutely nuts, but she's fun to be around. She asks about you guys a lot."

For the next hour, the girls sprawled across the wooden floor, exchanging laughs and stories. Iris could make Amaya laugh so hard, tears would spill from her eyes. When things quieted down, Amaya glanced out the window and watched the dark sky begin to fill with warm morning light. She looked back at Iris, who had grown quiet. Amaya anxiously clutched her neck.

"Amaya, why are you gripping your neck like you're Will-freaking-Byers?" Iris groaned.

"You have to go, don't you?" Amaya said softly.

"I'm sorry," is all that left Iris's lips. Amaya watched as she stepped back out onto the balcony. Goodbyes started feeling like a ritual. But maybe that was a good thing. Because after years of worrying, she was starting to realize something.

Her friends would always come back to her.

IRIS YUKI

When Iris reached the border of the forest she realized there was one fatal flaw in her plan. The illuminated path was gone. To be fair, she never told Maeve how long she'd be gone or knew anything about how long the spell would last. The sun was already rising and she needed to come up with a plan quickly.

Her eyes scanned the trees, searching for anything vaguely familiar. Unfortunately, trees can only vary so much in difference. *I should've left a goddamn trail of breadcrumbs or something.*

"I knew you'd mess up your plan," a small voice from behind her spoke. Iris jumped out of her skin. Standing at the foot of the forest was Maeve, draped in a large black cloak with the biggest grin on her face.

"Maeve? What the hell are you doing here? Are you insane?" she grabbed her arm and yanked her closer.

"I followed you! Don't worry I didn't come into the castle. But I knew you couldn't do this without me," she held her chin high. Iris was two seconds away from smacking that smirk right off her face.

"So, you're down-right stupid is what you're telling me. Maeve, what if you'd gotten hurt? What if bandits came for you while I was in there? You were the one who told me there are bad people out there. Bad people who want to hurt you! I could've made it back on my own just fine. I don't need you."

Maeve's eyes grew watery. Her head sunk low and she wrapped her arms around herself. Iris might've taken it a bit too far. After all, she was just a kid. "I'm sorry, I didn't mean to yell at you. I was just worried, that's all. I know you wanted to help, and thank you for that. But we better get going right now before your mom realizes we're both missing."

Maeve's sorrowful look shifted into a smile. She raised her hand towards the trees and made the path appear once more. Iris could tell Maeve was proud of herself. She ruffled her hair and stepped into the forest.

"Were your friends happy to see you?" Maeve asked.

"Yeah, they were. I told them about you, you know," Iris playfully nudged her.

Mave perked up, "Really? What did you say?"

"Just that I met some really annoying kid who wouldn't leave me alone," she teased. Maeve pouted. "Come on, I'm kidding. They want to meet you."

Maeve looked up at her with her big eyes. "I would really like that," she spoke as if nothing had been truer.

The deeper they traveled into the woods the more cautious Iris became. She made sure Maeve's hood covered her completely and kept her close by her side. She jumped at every crunching leaf and falling branch. It was far past sunrise now and Iris feared Marjorie almost as much as she did the bandits.

Well, maybe she spoke too soon.

An arrow skimmed Iris' nose and slammed into a tree adjacent to her. She gasped and grabbed Maeve's wrist, quickly moving her feet. All she could hear was the sound of her own breath and beating heart.

Maeve resisted and tore her arm from Iris's grasp. "Maeve, what are you doing?"

Maeve threw her hood back on her shoulders and clenched her jaw. She whipped her body around to face the men. With a swift movement of her head the three men went flailing into the air and crashing down hard into the ground.

"Come on, let's go," she said, turning back around, pulling Iris along with her who barely had time to process what just happened.

"Holy shit," she said in between breaths. Over and over again, she repeated this under her breath until they reached Castemaga. They just about collapsed on the floor when they made it to safety.

"Iris? Maeve? Where have you been? I've been searching everywhere all morning!" It was Marjorie. Shit.

"We were just uh…"

"Maeve was just helping me out with some early morning training. Isn't that right, Maeve?" Unfortunately, Iris had no faith in Maeve's lying capabilities. This was not going to go well.

"Um, yes. That's right. We were up before sunrise!" *Okay, not too bad, kid.*

Marjorie paused for a moment. Her eyes shifted back and forth between the two of them. At least they were both here in one piece. Iris reminded herself, no matter what Marjorie could say, that's all that mattered. "Hmmm, very well then. But next time, please inform me. I was worried sick!"

"Yes, Mother," Maeve nodded.

Iris waited until Marjorie was just out of sight to release the breath she had been holding in all this time. "Good job, kid. I was worried you were gonna give us up there for a second."

"To be honest, me too. I've never lied to her before," she admitted.

"It only gets easier, my friend. Also, can we talk about what you just did back there? That was badass!"

"Really?"

"Yea, you've gotta teach me that. I'm ready to knock some bitches right on their asses."

LUNA ANBRIS

L una got a late start to her morning, still feeling drowsy from their late night with Iris. The loud rumbling of her stomach urged her to get out of bed. In her haste to get to the kitchen, she noticed the king pacing through the corridors. His eyes were shifty and he checked over his shoulder every few seconds, like he feared someone was following him.

As she observed his suspicious behavior, her hand laid gently against the dagger strapped to her thigh. She peered around the corner and watched him walk down the corridor. She noticed as he walked, he clutched something in his hands. It looked like a large brass key that was secured tightly around his neck with a rope. The knuckles of his hands turned white from holding it so tightly. This key was clearly very valuable to him.

He entered a room on the far end of the corridor, ending Luna's investigation as he tightly shut the door behind him. Luna assumed this was his private library that Amaya had told her about. What was in there that he had to keep locked away? She remembered Liana believed he was hiding something and this key must've held the answer as to what that something was.

Maybe I should tell Liana.

Completely abandoning her quest to find breakfast, she found herself back in the library. Learning from her past mistake, she made sure to shut the door behind her before saying a word.

"Hello, my dear," Liana said, sipping on her cup of tea. "Is something the matter?"

"I just have a quick question," Luna sat down. "What do you know about the key that hangs around the king's neck? I saw him earlier and he seemed very on edge, clutching it like it was his lifeline. I know you said you think he's hiding something, and I bet that key will tell you what that is!"

"I'm afraid I know very little. He's been wearing it ever since the passing of Arthur. I always believed it had something to do with him, although I was never quite certain. Luna, do you think you could find out more about this? If something is going on, I'd like to be one step ahead of him," she said.

"Oh, I don't know," she hesitated. "I shouldn't be playing Sherlock." Liana tilted her head, clearly not understanding the reference.

Right. I'm in Camelot.

"Never mind. I just don't know if that's the best idea. I mean, didn't you say he was dangerous?" Luna felt the gears of her inner turmoil turning.

Liana relaxed back down in her chair. "You are right, my dear. I apologize, I do not know what I was thinking."

ELDORA PEREZ

The sun was finally setting on what seemed to be the longest day ever. "We'll rest here for the night," Sir Henderson said while climbing off his horse. Elle mirrored his motions and securely tied up her horse next to his.

She sat herself down in the cool grass, attempting to embrace the fact that this would be her bed for the night. It's not like it was much different than camping back in Tahoe. It's funny how that seemed like such a distant memory now.

She watched Sir Henderson begin to collect firewood, which she should note, was normally her job back home. But she didn't interfere. She just sat back and smirked as he continued to scoop up leaves and twigs that wouldn't burn for longer than a few minutes. She rested her head back against the grass, allowing small twigs and branches to fill her curls. It was going to be impossible to get her hair back to its natural state.

"Oh, sure. Get all the rest you need," Sir Henderson snarked.

"Don't let me step on your toes," Elle smiled, crossing her legs.

Sitting across from her, he dumped his findings on the floor in a heap. He grabbed two rocks and began striking them against each other. Elle suppressed a laugh as she watched him struggle. She sat up and placed her chin in her hands, almost in a mocking manner. He glared up at her and continued unsuccessfully trying to create a spark.

"Okay, I've had enough of this." She got up and snatched the rocks from his hands.

"Hey!"

"Just be quiet and watch," she hushed him. She took the rocks and in one swift motion, sparks flew. Sir Henderson was silent. "And just so you know, this stuff is not gonna burn longer than ten minutes." She tossed the rocks by his side and sat back down. "So, aren't you a knight? Why don't you know how to do this stuff?"

"I do, I'm just not very good at this stuff," he admitted.

"Wow, the great Sir Henderson admits he's not good at something. My mind is exploding right now."

"Yea, my head's not as big as yours."

"Touche. So, how did you become a knight anyways? What was your big quest?"

"It's really a long, boring story but I saved the king's life. I never wanted to become a knight, you know. My mother actually forbade me. It's one of the very few memories I have of her. She would always say, "Evan, you're not allowed to turn out like your father." And yet, that's exactly what I did."

"Evan?"

"Oh," he fidgeted, "That was my birth name. When I was knighted, I started going by Henderson. My mother didn't want me to become Sir Evan, so I became Sir Henderson. I thought I could protect that piece of me. But truthfully, I think Evan died long ago." He let the truth spill from his lips like honey.

Elle had never seen this side of him before. It felt so genuine. She bit the inside of her cheek, trying to ignore the fact that her heart was beating a little faster than it should.

"So, your dad was a knight, huh? What was he like?" Although the intimacy made her uneasy, she yearned to hear more, wanting him to be vulnerable with her.

"Only the best in the kingdom. He was killed when I was only three, but he lives on through the stories people tell of him. The great Sir Lancelot."

Elle's back straightened and a small gasp escaped her mouth. "Wait, wait, wait. Your dad was *the* Sir Lancelot?"

"Yes, you've heard of him? His stories traveled outside of the Five Kingdoms?" He smiled like a kid in a candy shop.

"Very much so. He's quite famous where I'm from."

Sir Henderson gently smiled to himself, letting his curls rest softly over his eyes. Elle could tell he was very content with this knowledge. She'd be lying if she said he didn't look absolutely adorable at that moment. It made her angry.

"What is it like where you're from?"

"Very different from here."

"How so?"

"Well, people don't go around embarking on quests for starters. There are no castles, no knights, and certainly no great beasts. But the people aren't so different. Human emotion is universal, I guess." Sir Henderson's head twitched with fascination. Feeling a bit awkward, Elle cleared her throat. "Um, well I better be getting to bed. Can't slay a beast if I'm half awake."

"Right" he said, snapping out of his trance. "I will keep watch."

"Um, goodnight?" she mumbled.

"Goodnight, Eldora."

Elle couldn't help but smile as she drifted off to sleep with his soft voice still echoing through her mind.

AMAYA BROOKS

Amaya looked in the mirror and saw her bangs were now hanging heavy over her eyes. She had lost all track of time, not quite sure how long they had been in Camelot. The one-week mark that they'd all agreed on came and went, and no one even batted an eye.

She reached for the gold encrusted dagger that lay across her desk. She cut her bangs a thousand times at home, but never with something like this. But honestly, how hard could it be? And even if it turned out absolutely horrid, anything was better than hair in her eyes.

She steadied her hand and began slicing through her bangs like a lawn mower cutting through thick grass. The excess hair trickled down at her feet and tickled her toes. She evaluated her work and was surprisingly pleased with the results.

Amaya ran her fingers through the rest of her hair, studying its length. She paused for a moment, deeply considering what decision she was about to make. She shook her head in a "screw it" kind of way and placed the blade just above her shoulders. Camelot had woven itself into her friends. It was time it did the same for her. She tore the blade across her hair with almost no hesitation. She smiled, feeling the light bounce of her hair graze the tops of her shoulders.

Her smile faded as she saw her mother seep through her reflection. She looked like her more now than ever. Part of her felt guilty for not rushing home to return to her. But another, *bigger*, part of her felt like this is what her mother deserved after years of emotional distance and keeping her in the dark about her father.

Her father.

The thought of him haunted her like a ghost. She wondered if she looked like him. If she had his smile or his freckles. Would they have gotten along? Would he be proud of the person she was becoming? She didn't know why she cared so much about a man she'd never known, but she did.

She felt that all too familiar tingling sensation forming in her hands.

Not now, not now, not now.

She stepped out onto her balcony in hopes the fresh air would calm her body. She gripped the railing tightly, trying to focus her attention elsewhere. She needed something, *anything* to distract her mind. Her eyes fell to the streets of the city. They were flooded with malnourished families, sweaty and rotting in filth. Every last one of them was drowning in their own misery.

She inhaled deeply through her nose.

Her anxiety soon began to mutate into anger. How could King Kay stand idly by and watch his people suffer like this? It disgusted her. A coppery sensation appeared in her mouth as she bit down on her tongue. *This is not what Camelot should be.*

Each person moved through their routines like zombies. They dragged their feet with their eyes glazed over. Together they were like a machine, holding together the crumbling kingdom, while sucking the humanity out of them.

Standing in the center of it all was a little girl. Unlike the others, she stood still, gazing up at the castle. As if she was calling out to Amaya, her eyes locked with hers. Amaya felt this girl possessed a glint of hope. She nodded to her, almost like a promise. A promise that she would not be forgotten.

Just then, Edmund sprinted into the room, out of breath. "Edmund, what…"

"What did you do?" Edmund interrupted. His eyes were wide and sweat beamed down his forehead.

"What do you mean? What's wrong?"

"Amaya, I overheard the king telling the guards to keep a watchful eye on you."

The world went blurry for a moment. "I don't understand," she said with a shaky breath.

"I don't either. He must feel threatened. Amaya, you need to be careful. All the guards have been alerted and will be watching you. Promise me you will lay low?"

She nodded, feeling a small sense of comfort knowing Edmund cared for her so much.

"EDMUND!" A deep voice echoed through the castle.

"Wait, please don't go," she begged.

Edmund sighed, "You know I have to. I'll come back here tonight. I promise."

He left Amaya standing alone. What had she done?

LUNA ANBRIS

"Lou! We've got a problem," Amaya burst through the doors into Luna's room.

"Oh, hey. I was just looking for you. We need to talk," she paused. "Your hair! Amaya, I love it–"

"The king has ordered all the guards to watch my every move," Amaya cut her off, getting straight to the point. She sank to the floor and buried her head in her hands.

"Whoa, what do you mean?" Luna bent down to her level and placed a comforting hand on her back.

"I just ran into Edmund and he overheard the king."

Luna promised Liana she wouldn't get involved, but things were growing stranger by the second. Why would the king care about Amaya? "Okay, let's not freak out. I'm sure there's a very logical explanation for all this." Luna suggested.

"Maybe you can go and talk to him?"

"Amaya, he's the king. I don't think we can exactly question his decisions. That's how people end up in the freaking dungeons. We don't want to get into more trouble as it is." If Luna had learned anything from her parents it was to keep your head down and don't cause trouble.

"I guess you're right. Sometimes I forget where we are."

"It just doesn't make any sense. Why only you? Iris was a witch, Elle was becoming a knight, and Luna was a Mage. Amaya posed much less of a threat than any of them. Of course, Luna was not going to say this out loud.

"I don't know. It feels like he's had his eyes on me ever since the day we arrived," she admitted.

Luna knew she had to tell Amaya about what Liana had said. She had to tell her about her dream.

"He's hiding something. Not just from us, but from everyone. Liana thinks so. And I do too," her tone shifted and her voice softened, "Liana thinks dark days are coming. I know it sounds crazy but I had this dream the other night that the Elderen Wood was in flames and we were all in danger." Luna reached for Amaya's shaking hand, offering her comfort. "Listen, I know it sounds scary, but we're gonna get through this together, okay?"

Amaya squeezed her hand and nodded. "Yeah, together," she smiled.

"Why don't you just lay low? We don't want to get too far in over our heads here. I'll let you know if I hear anything else, okay?"

"Okay," she agreed.

IRIS YUKI

There was something off about Marjorie. Her behavior seemed tense and almost paranoid since Iris had returned from Camelot. She was quiet and isolating herself from the rest of the witches. Iris decided to confront her.

"Marjorie," she sat down next to her on a small, concrete bench that was covered in ivy. "Is everything okay?"

Marjorie smiled softly and took Iris's hands in hers. She sighed, "Iris, I confess, I do not often speak the truth. My job is to protect those who hold our gift and sometimes withholding information is necessary. Fear can breed chaos, and chaos and magic do not tread lightly together. But," she paused, "I will not lie to you."

Iris grew anxious. She could tell that whatever Marjorie was about to say was not going to be good.

"As I mentioned, my sense of your presence grew when you arrived. But it is more complicated than that. Not only did I feel such strong magic, but I felt…something else. Something I cannot describe. I feel as though everything is changing. Although I do not know what is going to happen, I know it will impact us all."

"Why are you telling me this?" Iris didn't understand.

"Because Iris. I feel a great power growing within you. I have not felt power like that since–well it does not matter, now. What matters is you understand of what you are capable. If the time comes, all will look to you. I feel that you are a part of something larger. You will have enemies, Iris. Enemies far crueler than you can ever imagine. I understand this is a burden of knowledge to carry and I apologize, but I fear time is something we do not have."

"What am I supposed to do? I don't think you understand, I'm not even from Camelot. I didn't even know magic existed until a few weeks ago! And now you're saying everyone's gonna count on me in a time of danger? You have the wrong person, I'm sorry. Shouldn't we be telling the king? He can probably do far more than I can." She crossed her arms.

"I do not trust the king," Marjorie whispered. "I never have and never will. He is not Arthur."

Iris panicked. She was about to break her one promise to Luna. "Look, apparently I'm not supposed to be telling you this, but I'm not just from outside the Five Kingdoms. I'm not from this world. Where I come from, magic, Camelot, witches, it's all just a bunch of bull shit!"

To Iris's surprise, Marjorie sat back and laughed. "I know."

"You know? What do you mean, you know?"

"Iris, I am a very powerful creature of magic. I could sense the shift in energy the moment you and your friends arrived. It wasn't just because of your powerful magic. It was something more."

"Why didn't you say anything?"

"I did not think it mattered. Where one comes from is less valuable than who they are."

"I guess you're right." Iris just wished she knew who she was. "Do you know why we're here? Is there a reason?"

"None that I can be certain. You don't need to worry about that right now. But I do need you to promise me something."

"Anything."

"Please watch out for Maeve." Iris could sense there was much more she wanted to say, but this was all she could manage. She felt a sense of guilt, thinking about the danger she put Maeve in. She wouldn't make that mistake again. She wouldn't leave Castemaga.

For Maeve's sake.

ELDORA PEREZ

Despite sleeping on dirt and sticks, Elle slept comfortably through the night. She woke up slowly, watching the tops of the trees sway in the wind as the sun crept into the sky. She glanced over to Sir Henderson, who was snoring so loud everyone in the Five Kingdoms could probably hear. *So much for keeping watch.*

She walked over to him and kicked his foot. As soon as his eyes opened, he frantically reached for his sword. He relaxed when his eyes met Elle's, releasing his grip on the handle.

She was standing over him, hands on her hips. "You know, I'd like to not be eighty years old by the time we reach the Everen Cave, so I suggest you get off your lazy ass and we get moving."

"Right, right." He stretched his arms and got himself on his feet. Elle felt a bit awkward, remembering how he had opened up to her just a few hours ago. She wasn't good with intimacy, whether she was giving or receiving it. Thankfully, Sir Henderson seemed unbothered.

She climbed onto her horse and braced herself for the long, uncomfortable day she had ahead of her. "How much longer till we get there?"

"We should be there by nightfall." He paused. "If you can keep up!" With a smirk on his face, he gripped the reins and abruptly took off. He zipped past her and weaved in and out of the mess of trees that stretched beyond eyesight.

"Hey, not fair!" Elle yelled, racing after him. Her lack of experience on a horse was quite evident. She held on tight, ducking out of the way of low hanging branches. The wind pulled back her curls and tickled her face.

Her eyes stayed fixed on Sir Henderson, who was just ahead of her. His movements were quick, yet smooth. The muscles on his back were tight and engaged as he cut through the air. He peered his head over his shoulder and flashed Elle a smoldering grin. She rolled her eyes, suppressing a laugh.

Suddenly, Sir Henderson came to a grinding halt. Elle came crashing by his side. "Ha! Told you I could keep up!"

But something was wrong. His eyes became wet and his lip quivered. An anxious look spread across his face as he scanned his surroundings.

"Is something wrong?" Elle asked.

"Uh, no. This is just," he paused, whipping away a tear. "This is the last place I saw my mother. We were sitting over by that waterfall and she told me to be brave. Then, she disappeared into the wood, and I never saw her again."

"Oh, I'm so sorry." Elle fiddled with her thumbs, unsure how to comfort him. "Tell me about your mother. But only if you'd like."

"Well, like I said before, I hardly remember her. I was so young when I lost my parents. And my mother was not around much. She was married to King Arthur. But they did not love each other, it was purely political. It was my father she loved, and he cared for her more than anything," he softly smiled to himself. "Did you know your mother?"

"Not as well as I'd like. She wasn't around much either. She and my dad worked a lot. I had to take care of my grandmother and little sisters pretty much all my life. But I never felt close with them either. Through everything, our relationship became much more professional, rather than family."

Elle realized she had never admitted this out loud before. It was always an unconscious thought that was buried deep inside her. Her blood relatives weren't her family. Luna, Amaya, and Iris. They were her family.

"Growing up too fast," he said. "I know what that's like."

Before she could respond he continued down the path.

⚔

They reached the far end of the forest, stopping where the trees met the valley. Miles of bare grass crashed into jagged rocks of the Everen Cave. "Let's stop here. When night falls, we don't want to be in the valley," Sir Henderson said, jumping off his horse.

"So, I know this is a question I probably should've asked a long time ago, but what is this beast anyway?" She tied her hair back and secured her horse to a nearby tree.

"It's a creature of dark magic who brought destruction and ruin to the Five Kingdoms long ago. If it weren't for Merlin, Camelot would not exist. He lured the creature into that cave and it has not bothered us since."

And there was a reason Elle had not asked this question yet.

"Wait, wait, wait. If it hasn't bothered you, why are we doing this? Wouldn't provoking it be a bad idea?"

"It's not that simple. His existence remains a threat to Camelot as long as he lives. He must be killed."

"What about Merlin, then? Can't he do something about it?"

"Merlin's been missing for ten years. I don't think he's ever coming back."

Regret greeted Elle like an old friend. Why was she doing this? "Okay, so you've tried defeating him in the past and no one's been successful so far?"

He avoided eye contact, "Uh, no," he paused. "Eldora, there's something I need to confess." Leaning in closer, his tone shifted. "The king does not plan on knighting you. He only sent you on this quest, because..." He sucked in his own words, almost like he was going to cry.

"Because what?"

But he did not respond. He shook his head, looking down at the ground. Elle took a step closer allowing the toes of their shoes to touch. She looked up at his sorrowful eyes and spoke gently.

"Evan, please."

His chin lifted in response to the name and a small gasp escaped his mouth. Even Elle was taken back by her own words. But she didn't regret it. It felt right.

"He told me to take you on this quest so you could be killed by the beast and never return. He knew it was impossible and I knew I couldn't convince you to back down, no matter the risks. I'm sorry."

Elle sat down, staring at her hands while trying to process it all. Deep down, a part of her knew this all along. However, hearing it out loud instilled a fear in her that wasn't there before. Maybe she was taking it too far this time.

"It's not too late to go back, you know," he said. "You don't always have to be so brave. It's okay to be scared. Hell, I'm scared! Going back won't change the fact that you're the strongest, most courageous person I've ever met."

All her life, she had needed to hear these words. Simple reassurance that being afraid didn't equal weakness. She felt hot tears begin to pour from her eyes. He sat next to her, testing the waters by placing his hand on hers. She accepted and squeezed it tightly.

"Everyone always expects me to be this perfect person. My family, my friends. They expect me to be the strong one so I can carry everyone else's burdens. But half the time, I'm so scared," once she started spilling, she couldn't stop. "I'm afraid if everyone knows how scared I really am, they'll think less of me. That I will just be this useless waste of space if I can't take care of everyone. And my friends," she paused, "God, my friends don't know how much I need them. They all think I'm the one who's going to be fine on my own, but truthfully, I think I'm the one who needs them most."

She almost instantly regretted confiding in him. What was she thinking? She braced herself for sarcastic remarks and smart aleck comments. Her body tensed.

But she relaxed when he said, "And you think that's weakness? Eldora, that's being human. You're allowed to be human sometimes. In fact, humanity looks good on you."

Elle cracked a smile, whipping her tears away. "You know, I like Evan a lot more than Sir Henderson," she said, shifting the conversation away from her.

"If I'm being honest, me too." He redirected his attention to the Everen Cave. "So, what do you think?"

She looked at the cave and felt her mind buzzing like it was filled with a million tiny bees. Her hands vibrated with adrenaline shooting through her body. She took a deep breath. "My head is not filled with a single coherent thought right now, so I think it's best I just sleep on it."

"Okay. Why don't you get some rest, then? I'll keep watch."

She nodded and rested her head on the soft grass as he stood. "Goodnight, Eldora."

"Oh, Evan. It's Elle. Call me Elle."

AMAYA BROOKS

Rain fell for the first time in Camelot that day. As usual, Amaya sat near her balcony, sipping on a warm cup of tea. She closed her eyes and listened to the soothing sounds of the rain tapping on the concrete walls.

She daydreamed about rainy days back home. Each raindrop held a memory that dripped into her mind as she listened to its patter. Due to Southern California's extreme drought, rain was always exciting when it came. The four of them would put on their rubber boots and splash around in the puddles that filled the streets. Amaya always wore her bright yellow rain jacket and pretended to be Georgie from *It*. Elle would roll down muddy hills and chase down a screaming Iris, while Luna would build little boats and send them floating down the gutter.

Her tea was growing cold and her mind restless. She placed her cup on the floor and peeked her head out into the corridor. She figured her need to lay low did not have to prevent her from visiting Edmund at work. She kept her head down and made her way to the kitchen.

Upon entry, there was no sign of him. *He must be running around for the king.* As much as she wanted to check in on Luna, she didn't want to bother her. She was with Liana doing important, Mage things.

So, she decided she was going to wander around the castle until she found Edmund.

The castle seemed busier than usual, most likely due to the rain. She squeezed passed the damp bodies, trying to ignore the strong odor of sweat and rain. Amaya hated how afraid she was to talk to people. It would be so easy to go up to any of the dozens of servants who filled these halls and simply ask if they'd seen her friend. But she couldn't, so she continued trailing through the halls and found herself in a lesser-known part of the castle. It was empty and filled with cobwebs. To her right was a dark staircase, faintly lit with a few torches. There was no way she was going down there.

She was about to turn around until a heavy set of footsteps began to echo through the halls. Panic set in as she realized she wasn't supposed to be here. Seeing the shadowy figure peering from around the corner, she rushed down the stairs. She had no clue where these stairs led, but she recognized that shadow all too well. It was King Kay. She knew if he saw her down here, it would not end well.

When she reached the bottom of the stairs, she was met with nothing but darkness. She reached for one of the torches that was hanging on the wall and illuminated the room. As her eyes adjusted to the low light, she found herself in a large, circular room. In the center of the room was a table. Amaya gasped.

The Round Table.

Arthur's Round Table was standing right in front of her. Just like in the stories, there was no head. It was a place where everyone could sit as equals. This was something Amaya had always admired about Arthur.

The table looked like it had not been touched in years. Sculpted from dark oak and blanketed in dust, it stood alone. The walls were bare, with nothing but crumbling rock and cobwebs.

She gently placed her hand on the table, tracing her hand over its smooth texture. She felt shivers rush up her arm as she pondered on all the wonderful things that might've happened at this table. The fate of the kingdom once lay here. She grinned, imagining King Arthur giving empowering speeches and great knights, like Sir Lancelot, heading his words.

The names of each and every knight decorated the table in fancy, blue letters. She felt proud, recognizing all but two of them. She finally reached Arthur's name, which was much bigger and dressed in red and gold.

Her hand stopped when her fingertips grazed what felt like a locked compartment right under Arthur's name. She tried pulling it open, but it wouldn't budge. Upon further inspection, she could see it was sealed shut with a large, steel lock. What was someone hiding in there? Was it Arthur's? Was it King Kay's? That could explain the key around his neck.

She jumped out of her skin as a deep voice interrupted her thoughts. "Interesting how I only see you in places you shouldn't be."

No. It couldn't be. She dropped the torch on the floor.

King Kay was standing at the bottom of the stairs. Amaya wanted to disappear. Her throat went dry.

"Listen, I can explain. I was looking for Edmund and I think I took a wrong turn and-"

"That's always your excuse, isn't it?" he said, stepping into the room. "Because to me, it seems like no coincidence I find you in my *private* library and now in Pendragon Hall, which is strictly. Off. Limits."

Amaya slowly backed into the wall, collecting cobwebs in her hair. He slithered towards her, clutching his hands in fists at his side. His chest expanded as his chin rose. "Tell me, *Amaya*," he spit out her name like it was a bad word. "What is your motive, hm? You think you can outsmart me?"

"No sir, I promise I didn't know! It was just by accident, I swear!" She panicked, holding her hands out in front of her. A single tear rolled down her cheek.

He was now towering over her, only inches away from her face. He reeked of ale and body odor, with dirt smeared in his beard. His key dangled between them. He leaned in close and began to whisper in her ear. "I know of what you are capable, Amaya. Do not think otherwise."

Her terror became mixed with confusion. What was he talking about? She opened her mouth to speak but was unable to find the right words. Instead, she picked up her feet and ran as fast as she could up the stairs.

She was too afraid to look back and kept her eyes fixated in front of her. All she could hear was the sound of her own breath and her beating heart. She should've listened to Edmund and Luna. She shouldn't have left her room. What was she thinking?

With a sigh of relief, she was back in the sea of servants, with no sign of the king. She decided looking for Edmund was useless at this point. With paranoia creeping over her shoulder, she returned to her room.

LUNA ANBRIS

Liana requested Luna join her on her morning rounds through-out the kingdom. It was something the Court Mage did daily; Delivering medicines, seeking new patients, and healing those who needed it.

It was fascinating how in a world with such little technology, almost any illness could be cured with a little bit of magic. The modern science and medicine of her old life didn't even come close.

To say Luna was worried about Amaya would be an understate-ment. She was assisting Liana heal a young boy with a nasty cough, but her mind kept wandering elsewhere. She already knew she couldn't trust the king. What if Amaya was in trouble?

"Is there something troubling you, my dear?" Liana asked.

"I'm just worried about Amaya. Do you think she'll be okay?"

"As long as she obeys the king's orders and stays out of trouble, I am sure everything will be perfectly fine."

Luna wanted to believe her. She really did. But a part of her couldn't let go.

"Go check on her," Liana smiled.

"Thanks, Liana. I'll be back as soon as I can!"

She rushed back to the castle, stomping through the mud and the rain. She felt relieved to find Amaya sitting in her room right where she had left her.

"Lou? I thought you were out with Liana."

"I was. I just wanted to check on you."

Amaya avoided eye contact while picking the skin around her fingers. "Lou, something happened. I was looking for Edmund and I might've, sorta, ran into the king."

"Amaya! Did we not tell you to lay low?" Luna should've never left her alone.

"I know, I know. I figured as long as I stayed in the castle, nothing bad would happen. But guess what? I found Arthur's Round Table! It's so beautiful, Lou. And you know that key King Kay has around his neck? I think it opens a compartment in the table. I can't be sure, but he seemed pretty upset I was down there. And the key seems to match the lock perfectly," Amaya was almost out of breath.

"Wait, slow down. So, you think he's actually hiding something in there? Are you okay? Was he furious?"

"I'm alright now. I was pretty shaken up for a bit, but I'm better now that you're here. I know there's something going on. He seemed so sure that I was onto him. He's hiding something big from us, I know it"

"Okay, meet me in Liana's library in one hour. I think she should hear about this."

Luna closed the door behind Amaya and made sure it was sealed tight. This was a discussion she did not want anyone to overhear. Luna pulled up a chair for Amaya and the three girls sat around the table.

"Amaya, you say you believe King Kay is hiding something in the Round Table?" Liana asked.

"Yes, I do. He thinks I'm up to something. I've never seen him so angry," Amaya admitted.

"Liana, does the king ever take off that key?" Luna asked.

"Only at night. Getting it would be impossible."

"Edmund!" Amaya exclaimed. "He's his servant. He would have access to his room at night."

"It would be risky. If Edmund were caught, he would surely be killed," Liana said.

Luna was beginning to realize how serious this was becoming. "Maybe we just forget about it. I don't want to put Edmund or any of us in danger."

"No! It's easy for you to say. He isn't out to get you! And Lou, look around. Everyone in this kingdom is miserable. Something needs to be done. I can't just sit by and watch it any longer."

Luna was shocked at how confident Amaya was becoming. She had always been the most passionate person Luna had ever known, but her mind often hindered her. She felt proud knowing Amaya was starting to see herself how Luna always had.

"You're right, my dear," Liana said. "I have been a coward, hiding in the dark for too long."

"Amaya, I don't know. What's your plan?"

Amaya leaned in, "Liana, do you have some sort of tincture that will put him in a deep sleep?"

"I do. I use it to treat different illnesses that require lots of rest."

"Perfect. You will deliver that to the king. Come up with some reason about why he needs to take it. That'll knock him out. Then that's where Edmund comes in. Once we have the key, we need to get in and get out, quick. I'll keep watch while Luna unlocks the compartment. Then, we need to get the key back to Edmund so he can place it back in the king's chambers before he wakes up."

"I think this might work," Liana nodded.

Luna feared this plan would only worsen the situation. But she didn't want to let Amaya down. It was the first time she'd seen Amaya so sure of herself. So, Luna tried her best to convince herself that this was the right thing to do. "You know, I've always wanted to do a heist."

"Then the game is afoot!" Amaya thrusted her fist into the air.

"Oh, shut up, Sherlock," Luna rolled her eyes.

ELDORA PEREZ

Elle woke, feeling the ground shake beneath her. It was small and subtle at first, but grew more violent with each shake. She couldn't figure out where it was coming from. It didn't feel like an earthquake. This was something different.

The violent shaking of the earth made her clumsy as she stood on her feet. She reached for her bow and nocked an arrow in place. Evan was still asleep, curled up in the grass. Elle rolled her eyes and shook him awake. "Sorry," he rubbed his eyes, "What's going on?"

"You don't feel that?"

As the ground began to tremble, his eyes widened. Quickly, he was on his feet with his sword in hand. "What do you think it is?" Elle asked.

"Let's just say, I don't think you can back down from this quest anymore."

Across the valley, a tall, dark figure came into Elle's sight. As anxiety blurred her vision, she couldn't quite make out what the figure was, but it was getting closer.

"It's the beast," Evan muttered with a shaking breath. "We need to go now!"

She gripped the bow in her hands and quickly followed him into the trees. Her senses heightened, causing her to hear nothing but her own breath and the booming of the shaking ground. She didn't dare look back over her shoulder.

To make matters worse, Evan was leading them right into a group of bandits. "Get behind me!" He unsheathed his sword and threw himself in front of her.

Towering over them on their vast horses, the men swarmed them. They were far outnumbered. Bracing herself, Elle gripped her bow.

Just as she drew an arrow, the men's attention turned to the sky. Their chins lifted as their jaws fell. Fear shrouded their eyes. There was a sudden gust of strong wind, almost blowing all the trees to the ground.

Evan turned to her, "What's going on?"

A dark shadow fell over them, sending shivers down her spine. Her fear was paralyzing her from looking up. She stood there, frozen, watching all the bandits run for their lives.

Whatever was blocking the sun dropped down right in front of her. The ground shook, sending a loud booming sound through her ears. Elle could see it for what it really was.

A dragon.

It was the size of a mountain, towering over all the trees in the Elderen Wood. Thick horns sat on top of its angular skull accompanied by a large set of nostrils. Two long, black wings, stretched from the center of its back. They were rounded at the top while curving down to a sharp point. Leather-like scales covered its body all the way down to its tail.

"COME ON, WE NEED TO MAKE A MOVE!" Evan yelled. But Elle stayed still, almost in a trance. She was so terrified, yet so amazed. A real-life dragon, right in front of her.

Now only a few yards away, it snarled its rows of jagged teeth. Elle knew she needed to run. But she didn't. Something was telling her to stay, almost like an instinct. She couldn't quite explain it, but something felt oddly familiar about this dragon.

The bandits screamed and yelled as the dragon unleashed its fiery breath. It positioned itself right in front of Elle, shielding her from the flames. Was it protecting her?

Evan grabbed her arm, yanking her in his direction. "What are you doing? Use your bow or something! You can't just stand here, it'll kill you!" he desperately begged. The dragon whipped around at the sound of Evan's voice.

It was now a few feet in front of them, staring at them with its jet black eyes. Evan threw his body in front of her and thrusted his sword towards the creature.

"NO, WAIT!" Elle screamed. But it was too late. The sword left his hand and hurled through the air, implanting itself the dragon's shoulder. The dragon winced out in pain. Just as Elle suspected, it grew even angrier. "Now look what you've done!"

The scales along its belly started to glow, as it took in a deep breath. *Oh, no.* "EVAN, GET BACK!"

Evan ran deeper into the Elderen Wood, but the creature was fixated on him. With its clawed feet, it stepped over Elle and stalked Evan like a predator. Fire spilled from his mouth, burning down anything that stood in its way. No matter how hard Evan tried, he could not outrun this massive beast. Elle watched him trip over his own feet and tumble onto the ground. The dragon had cornered him now.

Without thinking, Elle stepped in front of him, facing the dragon head on. "Your bow!" Evan suggested, but she did not reach for it. Instead, she yelled out a name that swirled around in her mind like it was waiting to be said.

"Astrea!"

With menacing eyes, the dragon's head lowered down to her. Elle's heart raced as she was inches away from death. She tried to remain calm and closed her eyes. She could hear Evan protesting behind her, but ignored his cries.

Following nothing but her own intuition, she lifted her hand and carefully stepped closer. She felt a lump forming in her throat, as a deep growl rumbled through her ears. Why wasn't she running? Like putting her hand over a hot stove, she delicately rested her fingertips on the dragon's leathery nose.

She was flooded with instant relief as the dragon leaned into her soft touch. Elle felt connected to the creature, like they were bound by invisible string. The feeling was that of old friends reuniting. "It's okay," she whispered. "I'm not going to hurt you. You were protecting me, weren't you?"

Evan rose to his feet. "How did you…"

"Evan, stay right where you are," Elle held her hand up, making sure he did not come any closer. She returned her attention to the dragon, "It's okay. We're not going to hurt you."

Elle nodded to Evan, as he carefully approached them, keeping his hands in front of him. His eyes were glued to Elle's, looking to her for reassurance. "Evan, meet Astrea."

He hid behind Elle, gripping onto her shoulders. "How did you know her name?"

"I can't even begin to explain it. It was like an instinct. My mind was just telling me what to do."

"In all my years, I've never seen anything like it. You probably saved my life, you know."

"Well, it was about time I returned the favor," she smiled.

Elle giggled watching Evan admire the dragon. He looked like a little kid in a candy shop. His eyes were wide and his grin stretched from ear to ear. "Here," Elle said, reaching for his hand and placing it on Astera's nose. Astrea hesitated for a moment, loudly breathing out of her nostrils, but slowly grew more comfortable.

"I always believed dragons were only capable of destruction. I never thought that they could be like this. No one in Camelot will believe it," he admitted.

"Well, maybe don't judge someone by their outward appearance," she smirked.

"Well played, Elle."

That was the first time he called her Elle. But it certainly wouldn't be the last.

AMAYA BROOKS

Amaya found Edmund in the center of the kitchen, covered in flour. Where had he been hiding earlier? His eyes lit up when he saw Amaya step into the room. "Your hair!"

"Oh," Amaya had almost forgotten. "Do you like it?"

"I love it! It suits you," he smiled, rolling up his sleeves.

"Thanks, magic man."

"Don't call me that!" He nudged her. It was so easy getting under Edmund's skin. Amaya found it quite fun.

"Listen, I've got a big favor to ask. We need to talk in private."

They stepped into a room adjacent to the kitchen that was filled wall to wall with large barrels of grain. Amaya made sure no one was listening, then began to explain the plan and how important Edmund was to its success.

"You're crazy. This is never going to work," Edmund protested. "You want me to steal from the king? *Me*? I can't walk two steps without tripping over my own feet!"

"You have magic. Now's the time to use it!" Amaya knew this would take some convincing.

"I can't believe you would even *think* about doing something like this! The king is after you, Amaya! You should be hiding or running away, for crying out loud! You're going to get yourself killed." His voice was angry and broken. She didn't recognize the boy standing in front of her.

"Edmund, I…"

"Why are you even still here? This isn't your home. All you've done is cause conflict since the moment you arrived."

Amaya felt her heart split into a thousand pieces. What was she supposed to say to that? So, she said nothing and left.

Maybe Edmund was right. She should just go home. Why did she even bother to try and be the hero? Running was easier. It was always easier.

The more she thought about it, the more it made sense. No one needed her here anyways. What did she have to give Camelot? She wasn't a witch. She wasn't a knight. She wasn't a Mage. She was just a scared girl. Like she'd always been.

And her friends? Elle and Iris were gone. They'd probably forgotten about her by now. Luna didn't need her. She never did. Her family had fallen apart. It would be so much easier for everyone if she slipped back through that door like she was never here.

So, she came up with a new plan. That night, she would escape.

Now came the hard part. Actually escaping. She had been told the guards were watching her, so she'd have to be extra careful. As the castle slept, she laced up her shoes and threw a cape with a large hood over her head. In her wardrobe was an abundance of old maps of Camelot and the Five Kingdoms. She grabbed one that bore recognizable landmarks.

Finally, she left a note for Luna on her desk. She hoped she would understand.

She walked out onto her balcony, taking in her favorite view one last time. For a moment, she considered staying. But the moment quickly passed. Placing the map between her teeth, she threw her legs over the railing and began to climb.

Thankfully, she was not afraid of heights because this was no walk in the park. Her sweaty palms gripped the stone as she transported herself down the side of the castle. She kept her eyes fixed in front of her, trying to ignore the sixty-foot plunge beneath her.

Her teeth clenched hard on the map as the cold wind pierced her back. The concrete stones were still wet from the rain, making this a lot more difficult than Amaya was intending. Her foot slipped only a few times, but she never fell.

As soon as her feet hit the ground, she started to run. There was not a single moment of hesitation in her movements as she tore through the kingdom. With the return of the clouds, the sky grew dark and gray. When the rain began to fall, so did her tears. Her sobs echoed through the Elderen Wood, like thunder accompanying the rain. The now soggy map shriveled in her hands, but it didn't matter. She just kept running and running.

She remembered the first time she set foot in the Elderen Wood. Its vibrant colors and magical nature felt like a swaddling blanket on a cold winter's day. But it was different now. The trees were gray and the birds no longer sang their sweet songs. Overshadowed by a veil of darkness, she felt lost.

The world was spinning around her as the adrenaline shot through her body like a drug. Her hot tears blurred her already impaired vision. Her feet were moving faster than they had ever had before. They were moving so fast she couldn't keep up.

She crashed face first into the dirt and mud.

Amaya was tired. Part of her wanted to lay in that mud forever and fade away until she was nothing but dust and bones. She closed her eyes and let the rain fall against her back and tickled her skin.

After laying there for what seemed like hours, she heard wet, squelching footsteps. She lifted her chin and saw someone standing over her, but she couldn't quite make out who.

"Amaya?" The mysterious person pulled her out of the mud and onto her feet. Squinting her eyes through the heavy rain, she realized this wasn't just any person. It was Iris.

Amaya collapsed into her arms and continued to sob.

Iris flung one of her arms over her shoulder and gripped her waist. Amaya leaned into the touch, allowing Iris to carry all her weight. She carried her up a set of wooden stairs that creaked every time they took a step. When they reached the tops of the trees, Iris gently laid Amaya down on a rugged mattress.

She wondered if she was dreaming. It was so dark, she could barely see. But then, from the center of Iris's palm grew a ball of light. She could see Iris's soft smirk that she missed so much. "Iris," she whispered.

"What were you doing out there?" Iris wrapped a blanket around her.

Amaya didn't respond. She was too tired to explain and relive it all. She pulled the blanket in tighter.

"Okay, we'll talk about it in the morning, then," Iris said.

Amaya closed her eyes and slept as if her world wasn't ending.

LUNA ANBRIS

Luna fell asleep before Amaya came back from talking to Edmund. It was almost midday and Amaya still had not come out of her room. Luna assumed the conversation must've gone poorly and figured Amaya was feeling down. She knocked on her door instead of barging in to give her some space. But, no answer.

"Amaya?"

No answer.

"Look, Amaya, don't be upset if Edmund said no. We'll figure out another way."

Still, no answer. She turned the knob and let herself in, where she found a completely empty room. Had she left early this morning without Luna noticing? Maybe she was with Edmund somewhere.

But then she noticed something out of the corner of her eye. A letter, sitting on Amaya's desk, addressed to Luna. It read:

Dear Lou,

I realized I was in way over my head with that plan of mine. I don't belong here like the rest of you do. I've caused nothing but trouble since the moment we set foot in Camelot so I think it's best I went home. Tell Iris and Elle I love them. I'm sorry.

Amaya

No, this couldn't be right. Amaya wouldn't leave without her. Would she? Luna thought she was going to be sick. With the note in her hand, she fled.

She found Edmund polishing armor in the training yard and began yelling for the whole of Camelot to hear, "What happened last night? What did you say to Amaya?"

Edmund sighed. "Okay, I might have said some things I regret, but that does not change my stance on this. I will not participate in this suicide plan!"

Luna threw the note at his head. "Amaya's gone, Edmund. Whatever you said to her…it drove her to the edge."

"No, no, no. I never meant for this to happen. I was just so worried about her and angry she was being so careless and I guess it came out wrong, but I never meant for her to leave. I was just scared, Luna. You have to believe me!" Luna could see his regret radiating off of him like the sun.

"I do believe you, Edmund. But that's the thing about Amaya. If she cares about you, she'll take everything you say to heart. Edmund, we have to do something. She's probably all alone!" Luna's rage turned to sorrow as she pictured her friend wandering the Elderen Wood probably scared and lost. She squeezed her eyes shut in an attempt to stop tears from spilling.

"Okay, don't worry. I will go search the wood tonight once the king is asleep. You stay here in case she comes back. If I can't find her, we just have to assume she made it home."

Luna didn't even want to consider the possibility of living in this world without Amaya. But, it was better than assuming her dead.

Edmund was gone, leaving Luna alone with her thoughts. Luna knew she had a long, restless night ahead of her. She couldn't live with the fact that Amaya would leave without her. She needed someone to blame. Something. Anything.

So, she blamed King Kay.

He needed to pay for all of it. Overworking Edmund. Locking Amaya in the castle. Treating his people poorly. Something in her snapped. Right then, Luna made a decision purely out of rage and spite. For the first time in her life, she was going to take a stand. She was going to get that freaking key, even if it killed her.

She knew where Liana kept the tinctures and potions, although she was not exactly sure which one was the right one. She sifted through the colorful bottles and settled one she had seen Liana give children who were suffering from nightmares. *This has to be it.*

She told the guards standing outside his door that Liana had sent her and this was a matter of medical emergency. Luckily, they recognized her and let her through. The king tilted his head in confusion when he saw Luna step into his room.

She noted the key resting on his nightstand.

"I'm sorry to wake you, your majesty. I've been sent by Liana to give you this tincture. Unfortunately, due to the rain, a serious illness is spreading throughout the kingdom. We need you in great health, sire," she lied. She held out the bottle that contained the deep violet liquid.

He took the bottle in his hands. "You are much more competent than your friend. You could teach her a thing or two," he said before drinking every last sip.

Luna almost laughed.

"I hope you have a restful night, sire," she smiled as his eyelids fell heavy over his eyes. She waited a few minutes, until she was absolutely certain he was asleep. Once she heard a small snore escape his mouth, she swiped the key from his nightstand and tucked it under her dress alongside her dagger.

"I may have to return in a little while, just to check on him," she told the guards as she was leaving, realizing she'd need an excuse to come back to return the key.

She wasn't exactly sure where Pendragon Hall was. This was the part of the plan where Amaya was going to be of great help. But she remembered Amaya said it was deep down in the castle. So, she went down as far as she could go. Any staircase she came across, she sent herself spiraling down. She reached a staircase that was unlike the others. It was dark, lit by only a few torches, standing in a seemingly abandoned hallway. *This has to be it.*

With a torch in hand, she rushed down the concrete stairs. She smiled when the glorious round table came into the light. She desperately searched the table, looking for the lock Amaya had told her about. She let out a small gasp when she saw it sitting there under Arthur's name.

She took the key in her hands and thrust it into the lock. A perfect fit. Her heart rate soared as she rotated the key and heard a clicking sound. The lock slammed against the ground causing sounds of metal to vibrate off the walls.

The little door to the compartment fell open revealing a small stack of papers.

That was it?

She sifted through the papers to find that they were letters from Arthur to Gwenevere. Why would King Kay have these locked up? It didn't make any sense. She tried reading one of the letters to try to understand it all, when a gloved hand tore it from her fingertips.

"You thought you could steal from me?" King Kay growled.

In his other hand, he grabbed her red hair, yanking her head back so she was forced to make eye contact, "You are going to wish you were fucking dead."

He gripped his hand tightly around Luna's arm and dragged her up the stairs. She kicked and screamed, but that only made things worse. She could feel the skin on her legs scraping and tearing against the ground. His grip tightened with each scream, no doubt leaving a ring of bruises.

She had no idea where he was taking her, but believed she would be dead by morning. She would never know what happened to Iris, if Elle survived her quest, or where Amaya ended up. That's what hurt most of all.

He practically kicked down the door to his chambers and dragged her body over to the fireplace. Making sure she was watching, he threw every last letter into the burning flames.

"Whatever you think you saw, just forget it. No one will believe you now," he laughed. But the thing was, she never figured out what he was hiding in those letters. All that and she had failed. She failed Camelot. She failed Amaya.

"Mage work is no longer necessary for you. There are no healers where you are going."

Luna kicked and screamed as the king dragged her by her wrists down to the deepest part of the castle. But the more she hesitated, the tighter his grip became. She felt her skin peel against the rugged, concrete floors. She cried out in pain.

The moonlight seeped through the cracks and crevices of the stone walls, causing her skin to glow, ever so slightly. It grounded her, temporarily easing her panic. But the moment was short lived. When they reached the dungeon, darkness swallowed them whole.

He threw her in an empty cell that was covered in filth. He slammed the door behind him and locked it shut. He disappeared without saying a word, leaving her alone in the cold dark room with nothing but a few rats to keep her company.

She should have never gotten involved.

AMAYA BROOKS

Amaya woke to Iris snoring in her ear. She felt a moment of peace in the familiarity before remembering all that happened that previous night. She stealthily slipped out of bed, trying carefully not to wake Iris. She couldn't handle a heart wrenching goodbye. It would be easier to just fade away.

She tiptoed down the stairs, trying to suppress its creak. When she reached the ground, the morning grass was cold and wet against her bare feet. She thought she was in the clear, but Iris proved otherwise.

"Now, where the hell are you going?" Iris was standing a few feet behind her, with her arms crossed and her eyebrows raised.

Bracing herself for the conversation ahead, Amaya stepped forward. "I'm going home."

"What are you talking about?"

"What are we doing here, Iris? This isn't our home. Come with me." She reached out her hand, but Iris didn't accept it.

"Why would you want to go back there?" Her voice was fused with confusion and frustration.

"Our entire lives are back there. What, were you just gonna stay here forever?"

"I mean, why wouldn't I? You don't understand, do you?" Iris clenched her fists.

"Iris, what are you talking about?" Amaya unconsciously started backing up.

"My whole life I've been lost. I've had no goddam idea who I was. Back there, through those doors? There's nothing for me. I can't go back to the endless repetitive routine of living up to the expectations of others. I was just gonna go to a stupid college, get a stupid degree in something I don't even care about, and waste away at a job I would probably end up hating. I can't do it, Amaya. But here, I've finally found a purpose. I know who I was meant to be. I can finally live for myself. And you just want to take that away from me? That's never going to happen."

Amaya didn't know she felt that way. She felt ashamed after all these years she did not notice her friend suffering right under her nose. But she couldn't imagine losing her friend to this place forever. So, all she said was, "That's it then? I'll just never see you again?"

"There's nothing back there for you, Amaya! We are all you have! I mean, your own mom doesn't even care about you!"

It was like being stabbed in the back with a sword. How could Iris say something like that? To use her relationship with her mother against her was crossing the line. Amaya was going back through that door whether Iris liked it or not.

So, she started to run. Iris screamed and yelled behind her, causing all the trees around them to collapse to the ground.

ELDORA PEREZ

" The king will have no choice but to knight me when I come soaring in on a dragon," Elle flicked her hair back, batting her eyelashes.

"Oh, no. We are not bringing her back to Camelot. Are you crazy? After she almost destroyed the entire Five Kingdoms?" Evan waved his hands in protest.

"She was probably just scared, Evan. With all those people throwing weapons at her?" She turned her attention to Evan's sword that was still lodged in Astrea's shoulder. "Of course she was going to defend herself."

Evan sighed, looking down at the ground. It was obvious he felt bad about what he'd done. "She's hurt. We need to get her to Luna," Elle continued. "I bet she'd be able to heal her."

"Okay, let's just say I agreed to this ridiculous plan. How do you plan on getting her there? It's not like she can read a map."

"No," she paused. "But I can."

"I'm not following."

Elle raised her eyebrows with a smirk spreading across her face.

"Nope. Nope. Nope. Not going to happen. Not in a million years," he said, catching onto her idea.

"Oh, come on! Don't you trust me?"

"Uh, no."

"Okay, at least you're honest."

Elle turned to Astrea and placed her hand against her cheek. "I'm gonna get you the help you need, but we're gonna have to work together on this, okay?" Like she was in agreement, Astrea lowered her head to the ground.

Elle approached with caution, making sure Astrea knew she could trust her. It astonished her how Astrea continued to treat her like an old friend. She looked at Elle like she knew her intentions were pure. Because of that, Elle had to be the one to help her.

She gripped onto the dragon's scaly skin and carefully climbed onto her back. It was surprisingly more comfortable than being on the back of a horse. She reached her hand down to Evan who was pouting with his arms crossed. And he said she was the stubborn one.

"Just take my hand!"

He shook his head.

"I guess I'll have to tell all the other knights you were too chicken to ride with me. Oh, well," she teased.

Evan groaned, taking her hand. She pulled him up and plopped him down behind her.

"Do you have any idea what you're doing?" he shouted in a panicky tone.

"Not a clue!"

Then, with a loud whooshing sound, they were high above the trees. The lush forest stretched for miles, creating a sea of green. It was the most beautiful thing Elle had ever seen. She could see Camelot tucked into the mountains in the distance. It stood out amongst the other kingdoms. While they laid on flat ground, Camelot was built right into the structure of the Earth.

The air felt fresh and crisp, filling up her lungs to capacity with every breath. The sun sat in a very blue sky. It always seemed to be bluer after it rained. Elle giggled with glee as Astrea soared higher and higher into its vibrant color. From way up high, everything looked tiny, making all her problems seem so insignificant.

"Evan, are you seeing this?" she yelled. But his eyes were sealed shut as he gripped onto Astrea's back for dear life. Elle laughed, "Come on, try this." She wrapped his arms around her waist, pulling his chest up against her back. Her breaths turned shallow. Evan forced his eyes open and screamed right into her ear. She winced at his booming voice but couldn't help but laugh.

He squeezed tightly as Astrea dove down and grazed the tops of the trees. Elle became hyper aware of his closeness, making it harder and harder to focus on anything but his touch. She could feel his heart beating against her back and his anxious breath in her ear. Although his skin was warm, the hairs on his arms were standing up straight.

She almost forgot she was riding on the back of a dragon.

"ELLE! WE AREN'T EVEN HEADING IN THE RIGHT DIRECTION! CAMELOT IS THAT WAY!" Evan yelled, causing Elle to snap out of it. He was right. They were going in the opposite direction of Camelot.

"Astrea! Go toward those mountains!"

Astrea made a sharp turn towards the kingdom. Evan buried his head in the back of Elle's neck. "Please just tell me when we get there," he cried.

As they reached the gates to the city, all eyes were on them. Heads turned and jaws dropped as they saw the great creature soaring through the sky. Elle waved to them and did her best to ensure that Astrea meant no harm.

She directed her to the training yard where she'd be able to land in the large open space. The knights scattered like ants, taking their weapons in hand. "STOP, IT'S OKAY!" Elle yelled, attempting to get them to stand down.

Astrea's feet met the ground with a large boom. The knights dropped their weapons in utter shock. Elle was going to love this. She chuckled and slid down the side of Astrea's belly. Evan followed.

The knights surrounded them with solemn looks plastered on their faces. Something was wrong. "You shouldn't have come back here, Henderson," one spoke.

Elle stepped forward, "If King Kay is gonna be upset he has to knight me, that's his own problem…"

"No, no, this isn't about that. Something's happened."

"What do you mean?" Evan asked.

The knight leaned in closer, "There have been rumors King Cardoc is going to try to take the Elderen Wood." Elle shuttered at the mention of his name.

"Another war?"

"That's the thing. King Kay told us to stand down."

"What, he's just gonna stand by and let it happen? That doesn't make any sense. Cardoc will burn it to the ground!" Evan exclaimed. The knight's silence answered his question.

"Oh my god, Iris," Elle mumbled under her breath. If this was really true, Iris was in trouble.

ELDORA PEREZ

Luna's bedroom was empty. So was Amaya's.

Elle searched every last inch of the castle, desperately looking for her friends. She found Edmund polishing armor in the armory. He was in an ill-lit corner of the room, hiding from the light. "Where are Luna and Amaya? I can't find them anywhere! I need to speak with Luna." She was desperate. Edmund's eyes stay fixed on the armor. "Edmund, answer me!"

The armor fell to the floor as his head fell heavy into his hands. "It's all my fault. I'm sorry."

"Just tell me what happened," she placed a comforting hand on his shoulder.

"I said awful things. Made the wrong decision. And now Amaya's gone and Luna's in the dungeon."

Elle's heart stopped. She feared the worst. "What do you mean Amaya's gone?"

"She just got up and left without saying goodbye. She said she did not belong here and she was going back home. Luna was heartbroken and tried to steal something from the king, but she was caught. Now she's rotting away in the dungeon and it's all my fault."

Elle should've never left. She wasn't there to look after them and look at what happened.

"Where's the dungeon? I need to talk to Luna," she said, taking her bow in hand.

Edmund hesitated. "It's on the far end of the castle, down six flights of stairs. But Elle, you need to be careful. Luna is now the king's enemy. He is not going to tread lightly around you. Especially now that you returned from a quest he never intended you to survive. Take off your armor and retrieve food from the kitchen. You can disguise yourself as a servant. The guards will not know otherwise. Elle, do not make the same mistakes as the others. I can't bear it," he begged.

"I'll be careful. I promise." But these were just empty words.

Elle did as she was told and grabbed a plate of stale bread and a small cup of water from the kitchen. She even doused herself in flour to make it more believable. The dungeon was guarded by three guards who stood tall and present. Elle took a deep breath and proceeded.

"Food for the prisoners," she said with confidence. The guards paused, carefully observing her. She bit her tongue but kept her cool. After a brief moment, they nodded and allowed her safe passage.

It was so dark, Elle could hardly see five feet in front of her. She wondered how long a person could survive down here like this. Almost every cell was filled with a tortured soul. She heard moans and cries as she slipped further into the darkness. Many of them banged against the steel bars and reached for the plate she was carrying.

It wasn't long before Elle noticed a particularly quiet cell. In the corner, a shadowy figure sat curled up in a ball. Though it was matted and dirty, the red hair attached to the figure was unmistakably Luna's. "Luna?" She crouched down and leaned up against the steel bars. "Luna, it's Elle."

Her head shot up and tears welled in her eyes at the sight of her old friend. "Elle," she cried, rushing to hug her through the bars. "You made it back," she sniffled into her shoulder.

"Told you I would, didn't I?"

Luna let go and whipped the tears away from her cheeks. "Does this mean you actually did it? You slayed the beast?"

"Well, not exactly. I may or may not have a dragon waiting for me outside."

"You know, I'd say I'm surprised but nothing about you or Camelot can surprise me anymore."

"You know, you are the last person I would expect to end up in a place like this. You're usually one to shy away from a fight."

"Yea, well I guess I was tired of letting people walk all over me," Luna confessed.

"I'm impressed with this new Luna. I like her," Elle smiled. She noticed her wrists were painted with bruises. Her legs were bloody and her cape was filled with holes. Above all, she looked so tired. Like she had no life left to give. "Oh, Lou. What happened to you? Why won't you heal yourself?"

"I can't. I'm too weak. And it doesn't matter what happened. What does matter is that you go find Amaya. I'm really worried about her, Elle."

"But we need to get you out of here," Elle whispered.

"We can worry about me later," Luna reached for her hand through the bars, "I need you to do this for me."

"Luna, there's something you should know. King Cardoc is planning on burning down the Elderen Wood and the knights have been ordered to stand down. That means not only Amaya is in danger out there, but Iris too."

"Then what are you still doing here?"

"Luna, I'm not leaving you here."

"I'm not giving you a choice. It's okay. I'll be okay."

Elle wanted so desperately to believe her. "We'll come for you. I promise."

"I know you will."

Elle left her friend alone in the dark.

IRIS YUKI

While Iris watched Amaya fade into the trees, she felt whips of instant regret creeping over her shoulder. *What if she never sees her again? That couldn't be the last thing she ever said to her.*

"Iris!" She heard a small voice yelled behind her. "What happened?"

Iris turned and saw Maeve standing amidst dozens of fallen trees.

Oh, no. What did she do?

"I–I don't know," she stumbled over her feet and her words. "I was talking to Amaya and I just got so angry. I didn't mean to do this." Maeve looked at Iris as if she didn't recognize her. That broke Iris's heart.

"You hurt the wood. We're supposed to protect it," Maeve whispered.

"Maeve, you have to believe me. It was an accident!" Iris's head began to spin, feeling terrified of her own power. She could've hurt someone. She could've hurt Maeve. She could've hurt Amaya.

Iris collapsed to her knees and wept, letting her emotions take control of her. Maeve rushed to her side and wrapped her little arms around her. They sat like this for a while, letting Iris's cries fill the silence. Maeve did not speak, allowing Iris to let out everything she had bottled up inside.

"I messed up," Iris spoke in between sobs. "I said something I shouldn't have and now she's gone. She's gone, Maeve."

Before Maeve could respond, an arrow skimmed Iris's shoulder causing blood to trickle down her arm. She quickly realized they were not in Castemaga.

Maeve was not in Castemaga.

"WE GOTTA GO!" She grabbed Maeve's arm and started running faster than she ever had before. She glanced over her shoulder and saw at least a dozen men on horseback on their tail.

Maeve tore her hand from Iris's grip. "We're never gonna outrun them! We need to stay and fight!"

"Maeve, we can't!" Iris said, remembering the promise she made to Marjorie. But the men were approaching faster. Unfortunately, Maeve was right. Iris felt sick to her stomach.

She tried to channel all the emotions she was feeling into her magic. She took a deep breath and directed the energy to the tips of her fingertips. She lifted a large boulder into the air and launched it at the men. Three of them went crashing down off their horses.

Maeve was throwing people in the air left and right with a simple flick of her head. It was rather impressive. *Okay, maybe we have got this.* More arrows took flight, slamming into the trees that surrounded them. "You know, it would be really helpful if they were all blind!" Iris yelled.

"I'm working on it!" While concentrating on the three men in front of her, Maeve's eyes grew dark as she clenched her fists down at her side. There was a brief moment of silence before she let out a loud scream, releasing her fists. Iris watched three men wail as the whites of their eyes cracked and crumbled into rock.

"Holy shit! Maeve, that was insane!"

Maeve was healed over, trying to catch her breath. She looked like life had been sucked out of her. "You better figure out your mith soon, cause there is no way I am doing that again."

Iris looked up at the remaining men who swarmed them like flies on old fruit. While they charged forward, Maeve was still struggling to catch her breath.

It was now or never.

Iris clenched her fists and focused on the men in front of her. She knew, whatever this was, it was going to take all the energy she had. The adrenaline of the fight fueled her magic. She stepped in front of Maeve, straining her muscles and clenching her jaw. She felt a warm sensation building in her arms, followed by tingling around her eyes.

The next part was a bit of a blur. It felt like she had stepped outside of her body and was watching the world like a ghost. She heard the cries of men grow louder as her strength dwindled down to nothing. She collapsed to her knees and tried to pull herself together.

What had she just done?

In front of her, the men writhed on the floor almost unrecognizable. Their oozing flesh was melting away like a popsicle on a summer day. It was a red, gooey, disgusting mess of bubbling blood. What was weirdest was the steam rising from their bodies. It was like she'd burned them from the inside out.

"Holy shit, Iris." Maeve's mouth hung open wide.

"Hold on, did you just say *holy shit*?"

"I mean you boiled their blood. That's the most powerful mith magic I've ever seen."

So, that's what she'd done. *Holy shit* was right.

"Iris?" Maeve gasped with fear in her eyes.

"What?" But then she felt it. A sharp, searing pain surging through her stomach. Blood spilled onto her hands as she gripped the arrow that was buried deep in her abdomen.

"NO, STOP!" Maeve pulled back her hand. "You have to leave it in there. It's the only thing stopping you from bleeding out. Come on," she covered her as they took refuge behind a tall tree.

Along with her own shallow breath, Iris could hear a strange crackling sound growing louder and louder. Her attention turned toward the source of the sound. She was met with tall, red flames that stood over her like the Devil himself.

It was too late. Castemaga was on fire.

"I will distract them so you can run," Maeve whispered.

"Are you insane? No, I will distract them," Iris insisted.

"Iris, it is unlikely that we will both survive this. You're too injured to fight. You have an arrow sticking out of you. Besides, you are much more valuable than I am. It's *you* we need alive, not me."

Iris clutched her stomach as the pain began to spread. "What about what you said before? They will use you to get to your mom."

"If Castemaga is on fire, then they've already taken her. This is our only chance. You are our only chance."

She could hear the footsteps and deep growls of the men drawing closer. They were running out of time. But she couldn't let Maeve sacrifice herself. There had to be another way. She tried to ignore the blood spilling onto her hands. "Maeve, please don't make me do this."

"You'll find me. I know you will." Maeve tore her body from Iris's grip and threw herself out from behind the tree. Iris wanted to scream and chase after her, but she couldn't let Maeve's sacrifice be for nothing. She placed her hand over mouth to guard her loud sobs and began to run.

Due to her loss of blood, the path in front of her was hazy. She could hear Maeve's muffled screams behind her. The ground was swirling, causing her to sway like an old drunken man. Branches and flames were all jumbled together in a churning mess. She pressed hard against her wound, biting on her tongue to stay quiet.

It was all happening so fast. The fire engulfed everything that was once alive. The once enchanting green was now a confetti of dark ashes that scattered in the air. Iris felt the heat of the flames against her skin. A cloudy haze filled her mind.

She dodged falling tree branches and burning leaves, feeling the thick smoke fill her lungs. Her adrenaline kept her moving and over-stimulated her senses. Her vision was distorted, making the dozens of witches feeling in chaos look like ghosts.

She stood in the center of Castemaga while the golden city that once stood in the trees crumbled to the ground around her. She screamed out, "MARJORIE!"

"She's gone," a voice said behind her. It was one of the witches Iris had seen once or twice. "King Cardoc's men have taken her." She grabbed Iris's arm. "We need to go, now!"

Iris resisted. "They took Maeve!" The pressure inside her finally gave way. Her screams shook the ground beneath her as she collapsed to her knees.

"I'm sorry, I really am." The witch's voice was sincere. "But you need to control your emotions or your magic is going to lead them right to us. Not to mention the arrow in your stomach. I promise, there will be time to grieve. But right now, we need to go."

Those words were the last she heard before she lost consciousness.

AMAYA BROOKS

Every tree looked the same.
Every leaf.

Every branch.

Amaya was hopelessly lost.

She was getting tired.

Hungry.

Thirsty.

She wanted to give up.

It was likely she would die before finding that stupid white door.

LUNA ANBRIS

Luna spent most of her time drifting in and out of sleep. It was a repetitive cycle of nightmares and waking dreams. She tried so hard to keep her eyes open, but she was growing weaker by the minute.

She clung to memories of her friends to keep her sane. She thought of the first time they met. It was the first day of kindergarten and Luna showed up to school wearing her dad's old shirt. Her hair was unbrushed and her shoes were far too big. Kids laughed and teased, calling her names.

She spent recess that day hiding behind the slide, wanting to disappear. But everything changed when a girl named Amaya came and sat with her. "I think your shirt looks cool," she said. "Can I play with you? The other kids weren't being very nice to me."

Right then, she became Luna's first friend.

Soon after that, Elle joined them. They noticed she was getting picked on by a rowdy group of boys and told her she'd be safe with them beneath the slide. Elle gladly accepted. A few days after that, they asked the girl who was always sitting alone under the old oak tree if she would like to join them. From that moment on, it was Luna, Amaya, Iris, and Elle against the world.

That was the beauty of their friendship. None of them fit in anywhere. They found safety beneath that slide and with each other. It was hard to believe that thirteen years had passed since then. But nothing had really changed. No matter where they were in the universe, together or apart, they would always be her home.

She was brought back to reality from the sound of Edmund's voice, "Luna. It's me," he whispered.

"Oh Edmund, I'm sorry. I know it was stupid of me to think I could get away with that on my own. I was just so mad and worried and I don't know what came over me."

"No, I am the one who should be apologizing. If it weren't for me, Amaya would still be here and none of this would've happened."

"That's behind us. Elle is going to find her and bring her back to us." She paused and lowered her voice. "I found something. In the drawer. It was a stack of letters from King Arthur to Gwenevere."

Edmund's eyes widened, "Goodness, Luna! Well, what did they say?"

"Unfortunately, King Kay tore them from my hands before I got a chance to read anything. Then he burned them all right in front of me. So, I guess it was all for nothing."

"It seems strange." Edmund scratched his head.

"What does?"

"That there would be so many letters between Arthur and Gwenevere. They were married, yes, but it was purely political. To my knowledge, they would never write to each other."

"There were dozens of them, if not more. There must've been a reason."

"A reason King Kay wants to hide from us. We have to figure out what that is, Luna."

"But how? He burned all the letters."

"I don't know. That can't be the only evidence. There must be something more." Heavy footsteps began echoing throughout the dungeon, making Edmund jump. "I'm sorry, Luna. I have to go. But I promise, we will get you out of here." Luna nodded and watched Edmund fade into the darkness.

Once more, she was alone.

AMAYA BROOKS

maya was so thirsty that the door had become inconsequential to her. The thought of water consumed her mind. Cold, refreshing water. Despite hearing the trickling sounds of a flowing stream, she feared her mind was playing tricks on her. At this point, what did she have to lose? So, she followed the sound, tripping over her feet and stumbling into trees.

Her heart just about leapt out of her chest when her bare feet met the cold splash of a small stream. She collapsed to her knees and cupped the water in her hands. She closed her eyes in relief as she brought the water up to her lips. Nothing had ever been so refreshing. She laughed, staring up at the sky while pouring the cool water over her face. She sat there for a moment and allowed the water to rush over her body.

Through the trees, Amaya could see the stream emptied out into a rather large lake that she had never seen before. Despite its distance, she could make out its glassy surface and sand filled beach. An object glistening on the shore caught her attention.

She pulled herself to her feet and followed the stream. The closer she got, the more the object came into view. The shimmering object was thrusted into something. Something made of stone. Her toes melted in the sand as she stepped onto the beach. The direct sunlight was warm on Amaya's face. It all reminded her of home.

The rays of the light fell gently onto the stone object like a spotlight. There was almost a sense that it was waiting there, just for her. Walking towards the stone, she could see that it wasn't just a pile of rocks. Almost like a statue, it appeared to be carved in the shape of a man. The man's face looked melancholic and afraid, like he was screaming out for help. Buried deep in his chest was the shiny object. She could now see it for what it was.

A sword.

Its rounded gold handle beckoned her. With not much thought behind it, she reached her hand out and tightly wrapped her fingers around the grip. Everything inside her was telling her to pull. So, she did.

Although it made no logical sense, the blade slid through the stone smoothly all at once. When the point left the statue's body, something weird happened. The stone exterior chipped away like old paint, exposing his pale skin. His limbs began making subtle movements, followed by a loud groan. Once the stone exterior completely vanished, the man tumbled backwards and fell off his feet.

He wore tattered clothing, much like the ones of the townspeople back in Camelot. He had dark hair that fell just above his eyes, accompanied by a thin, narrow face and rather big ears. He looked confused and disoriented, but when his eyes fell on Amaya, his face lit up with joy. "Amaya!" He jumped to his feet and wrapped his arms around her. Amaya stiffened. Why was this stranger hugging her and how did he know her name?

"Who are you?"

He let go. "I'm sorry, I almost forgot. I'm Merlin."

Merlin. Then that means—

A sudden feeling of heaviness filled her hand as she gripped the sword. Was she holding Excalibur?

In an excited tone of voice, he surveyed the beach. "Where's Eldora? Luna? Iris?"

Amaya's eyes blinked in confusion. "They're not with me. Wait, back up. How do you know who they are?"

Before Merlin could respond, an overwhelming aroma of smoke filled the air. Amaya's eyes looked up to the sky. A dark cloud seized the sky while ash rained down onto the golden beach. The Elderen Wood was on fire.

"It's already begun," Merlin said. "We need to get to Camelot, now." He grabbed her hand and started running into the woods.

"Wait! Wait! What's going on?"

"I will explain everything when we get there. You just have to trust me." He paused. "Your friends are in trouble."

She wasn't sure if she could trust him. Especially after everything Edmund had told her. However, if her friends were really in trouble, she could not leave now. She knew if she did, she'd regret it forever. So, with Excalibur in hand, she followed him into the flames.

ELDORA PEREZ

"Liana, I need your help." Elle burst through the doors of Liana's library.

"Eldora! Well, this is certainly unexpected. I see you have returned from your quest."

"I have and that's sorta why I need your help." There was no easy way of putting this. "Things didn't go exactly according to plan and there may or may not be an injured dragon in the training yard."

Liana took a step back and her eyes widened, "My goodness! I have never had the pleasure of healing a great creature. I will do everything I can."

"Thank you, Liana." Elle turned to leave the room.

"Wait, Eldora," Liana stopped her. "I need to speak with you about Luna." Her tone was solemn.

"Save it. I know what happened. I just went to see her, actually."

"My dear, please believe me when I say, I am so very sorry. I should have watched out for her. This is my fault." Liana's desperate manner reminded Elle of her previous conversation with Edmund. It was almost sweet to see how much they all cared for her friend.

"I do believe you. Don't blame yourself. This starts and ends with King Kay."

Liana quietly nodded. Elle could see she was frightened. Hell, she had every right to be. So, Elle did what she did best. "Liana, there's no need to be afraid. We are going to fix this. I'm going to find Amaya and Iris. When I come back, we will break Luna out and make everything right. I promise." More empty words Elle hoped would become true.

Liana squeezed her arm, "Thank you. Now let's go help your dragon."

Still there where Elle left him, Evan stood by Astrea's side while she slept. Elle pushed past him and didn't say a word. "And where do you think you're going?" Evan questioned.

"Liana's here to heal Astrea. And once she does, I'm leaving."

"Elle, you can't. The Elderen Wood is crawling with King Cardoc's men. If they see Astrea, they will kill her." He paused. "And you."

"Amaya ran away and I'm going to find her." Elle hated that even standing on her tippy toes, he still towered over her.

"This is suicide. I won't let you throw your life in danger like this. Not again." His voice cracked in desperation.

"I don't care. I'm not just gonna leave her out there." Elle's mind was made up. She had made a promise.

Evan grabbed her shoulders and forced her eyes to the forest. Her jaw fell when she saw black smoke dance on the top of the trees. It had begun. The Elderen Wood was on fire. Amaya and Iris weren't safe. "Then I'll go by myself," she said under her breath.

"Elle." Evan lifted her chin to meet her eyes. "Remember. It's okay to be scared," he whispered.

Her natural instinct was to lash out and defend herself. But the words did not leave her mouth. Instead, she took a deep breath and nodded. Evan cracked a small smile. "I'm coming with you."

"No, no. I can't ask you to do that. These are my friends and this is my decision. Besides, you've been ordered by the king to stand down. You'd be breaking the law if you came with me."

"Well, you know, this crazy girl once taught me that sometimes laws are meant to be broken," he smirked.

"Hmmm, she sounds smart."

"Sometimes. Most of the time she's just unbearable." He sarcastically rolled his eyes.

"Oh really? Cause you seem to be pretty smiley when she's around."

Evan's cheeks turned a deep red. "I'm good at hiding my suffering."

"Uh, huh. Sure," her tone shifted. "If we're gonna do this, we need to leave now. Before anyone sees us." Elle turned to Liana who had begun to heal Astrea. "No one must know about this. Can I trust you?"

"Yes, of course." Liana nodded her head.

"Please look after Astrea."

She nodded. "Be careful."

AMAYA BROOKS

When they reached the gates of the city, Amaya grew timid. "Wait. Merlin, there's something you need to know. I'm technically a prisoner of the castle. The king doesn't know I escaped. We can't let him see me."

Merlin almost laughed. "You think I can show my face freely in that castle? You're not the only one who's on the run," he winked. "Don't worry. I've got a plan. Follow me."

Amaya wondered if the stories were true. Maybe Merlin did try to take his life with Excalibur next to that lake because he grew tired of waiting for Arthur. But for some reason it didn't work, and turned him to stone.

They walked along back alleyways and snuck behind passing guards. It was obvious Merlin had done this many times before. Amaya tucked Excalibur under her dress. She didn't need to draw any extra attention to herself.

They reached a rusted gate along the back part of the citadel. Merlin fiddled with the bars and pried open the gate with his hands. "Let's go." Amaya followed him into the dark tunnel where she could barely see two feet in front of her. Their footsteps echoed with every step as they traveled deeper into the darkness. "Just a bit further now. Watch your step," he said.

In front of them was a steep staircase made out of aging, cracked concrete. It looked like it was on the brink of collapse. She held her breath and stepped onto the first block of concrete. She traced her hand against the course rock wall in an attempt to keep her balance. At the top of the stairs she could see a faint light growing brighter with each step.

When they reached the top, Merlin pushed the large barrel that was blocking the exit out of the way. They stepped into the room that was mostly empty except for a few barrels and sacks of flour. "Where are we?"

"An old storage room. Come on, let's go…"

"Merlin, stop! I'm not moving another step until you tell me what is going on!" She allowed Merlin to drag her back to the place from which she was trying so desperately to get away. He at least owed her this.

"I know you deserve answers. I promise you are going to get them. But right now we need to find Edmund."

"Edmund?"

"Yes. Amaya, please."

"Okay, I know where we might find him."

Amaya wondered how Edmund would react when he saw Merlin again. There was so much resentment and pain buried deep in their twisted history together. She hoped Edmund would be able to forgive Merlin somehow.

Merlin followed closely behind her as they tiptoed through the castle to the servant's quarters. Merlin froze when they reached the door. "What's wrong?"

"I'm not ready to face him," Merlin panicked. His eyes filled with sorrow and regret.

"You need to. He needs to know you're alive, Merlin. Listen, last I saw Edmund, he was unhappy with me too. But that doesn't mean I'm just going to ignore him for the rest of my life! We need to face our problems, head on." Amaya almost laughed hearing herself say these words out loud. Maybe Camelot was really changing her for the better.

He turned to face her, changing his tone. "You don't understand! I left him! How could I do that?" His words were broken up between cries.

"Talk to him," she said. She knew how badly Merlin hurt Edmund. But it wasn't something that couldn't be fixed. "Merlin, I spent years not knowing who my father was. I know what Edmund is going through. He feels like something is missing from his life. Like there's this empty hole inside him that can't be filled. Don't let him lose you forever."

Merlin was silent, but his eyes spoke a thousand words. She could tell he agreed with her words but was hindered by fear. She knew that feeling all too well. She reached for his hand and gave him a comforting squeeze. "You can do this."

After letting out a large breath, he nodded.

"Let's go, then," she smiled.

Edmund was sitting on his small, tattered bed staring blankly at the ceiling. Amaya slowly stepped into the room, leaving Merlin out in the hallway. When Edmund's eyes fell on her, his jaw fell to the floor. Before Amaya could open her mouth to speak, Edmund jumped out of bed and pulled her into a tight hug.

"I'm so sorry, Amaya," he cried over and over again, burying his head in her neck. "You do not know how sorry I am."

"Hey, it's alright. I'm the one who should be apologizing. I shouldn't have tried to force you to do something you didn't want to do. And I shouldn't have left like that."

Edmund released his grip and whipped away his tears. "No, this is on me. I never meant what I said. Camelot has been a little bit brighter ever since you arrived. I can't imagine it without you. Please never leave again," the words spilled from his mouth.

In light of everything, their fight seemed so small now. Amaya glanced down at the sword in her hand. "I don't think I'm going anywhere, anytime soon."

Edmund's eyes widened. "Is that…?"

"It is. There's someone here to see you, Edmund."

She held her breath as Merlin revealed himself. At first, Edmund was reactionless. He simply froze, not moving a muscle or saying a word.

"Hey, kid. You're so big," Merlin lightly chuckled through his tears. He wrapped his arms around himself and kept his distance.

"You…y–you," Edmund stuttered. His eyes grew watery and his eyebrows turned down as he pointed a shaky finger at Merlin.

"Edmund, I'm sorry. I was stupid and afraid. I didn't know what I was doing. I thought leaving was best for you. Now I realize how selfish that was. I just hope you can forgive me."

"You chose a dead man over me. Arthur was gone and I needed you." His words tore through the room like a sharp knife.

"You're right. And I will spend the rest of my life regretting that." Merlin took a step closer, reaching his arms out. Edmund resisted his embrace, squeezing his eyes shut like he was trying to pretend Merlin wasn't really there.

"It's okay," Merlin whispered. With a loud sob, Edmund collapsed into his arms. Amaya watched Edmund cling to him like he was his lifeline. Father and son reunited.

In spite of her happiness for Edmund, she couldn't help but think about her own life. She wondered if she'd ever get a chance to meet her father. She could only imagine the overwhelming emotions

Edmund was experiencing. She hoped, now more than ever, that the legends of him being the Once and Future King were true.

After emotions died down, Merlin got down to business. "There will be time for catching up later, but right now, we need your help. Do you know where we could locate the king?"

Edmund leaned into whisper. "He's been missing since yesterday. One of the knights claims they saw someone leaving the citadel in the middle of the night. A few knights went out searching for him, but I haven't heard a word."

He was running. Just like the coward Amaya knew he was.

"Just as I thought," Merlin said. "It looks like it's time for an announcement. Edmund, I need you to gather everyone in the stone courtyard. And I mean everyone. Knights, maids, servants, townspeople. Everyone."

"Would you like to tell me what's going on?" Edmund asked.

"Oh, you will see." Merlin shot a smile at Amaya. "Just trust me."

IRIS YUKI

I ris woke up slowly. She felt weak, and was almost unable to sit up. As her vision adjusted to the light, she looked around. It was dark and smelled like mold. Wet rock surrounded her in every direction. She had no freaking idea where she was. If she learned anything in high school, it was that waking up in a place you don't recognize with no memory of the night before is never a good thing.

"You're awake," a quiet voice uttered.

"What happened? Where am I?" She winced at the aching pain in her stomach. *Shit.* Why did it hurt so bad?

The woman placed a hand on Iris's shoulder and slowly lowered her back down. "You need to take it easy. You are not healed yet."

Iris looked down at her tattered dress and blood-stained hands. She quickly started to remember. "Maeve," she whispered.

"Yes. I'm afraid Maeve is gone. As is Marjorie and almost every witch from Castemaga. I was able to escape, along with only a few others. You are lucky I found you. I am Lorelie."

She didn't deserve luck. She had failed Marjorie. She had broken her promise. And now the Elderen Wood was dying.

"I'm Ir…"

"I know who you are," she interrupted. "Right now we are some-where deep in the Elderen Wood. We need to get you to Camelot immediately. You need Mage magic."

Mage magic. Luna.

Her body relaxed a bit at the thought of her friend. Just seeing Luna, Elle, and Amaya would be all the healing she needed. God, she hoped they were alright. "Well then, what are we freaking waiting for? Let's get moving," Iris said, trying to get on her feet.

"Whoa, whoa, whoa. Did you just forget what happened out there last night? We cannot simply go prancing through the forest! We need to be smart about this or we will be killed."

"I thought you said I need a healer immediately?"

"If you're dead, a healer won't be of much help."

Iris was too weak to argue. She couldn't help but think about the danger that was growing stronger. She could still smell the smoke in the air. Those flames would carry evil to each and every kingdom within the Five Kingdoms.

"We will travel in groups of two. It will be much easier to stay hidden in small numbers. Iris, I will stay with you. We will leave last so the others can greet any danger before it reaches us. We will leave at sundown. This will give us an advantage over those without magic."

Iris clutched her stomach and allowed her eyes to flutter shut. Blurry images of her friends filled the darkness. She remembered her fight with Amaya. She saw flashes of her hurt look after Iris had said something she shouldn't have. *There's nothing back there for you, Amaya! We are all you have! I mean, your own mom doesn't even care about you!* Her stomach turned queasy, realizing those might've been the last words she ever said to her.

Iris's eyes slowly opened. The sky that was once filled with a thousand stars was now clouded by a towering mass of smoke. Even the moon could not break through its thick shroud. Is this really what King

Cardoc wanted? To strip this world of its magic and beauty? What kind of monster would want that?

"Iris, it's time to go," Lorelei said. She reached for Iris's hand and pulled her to her feet. She was a bit wobbly at first, but leaned into Lorelei's support.

"Camelot better be freaking close, cause this is a very unfortunate situation we've got going here." Lorelei said nothing, telling Iris all she needed to know. She had one hand wrapped around Iris's waist and another out in front of her illuminating the way.

Iris was struggling to keep her eyes open. "Iris, you need to stay awake. You can do this," Lorelei kept repeating. But Iris was tired. Last time she felt this exhausted, she was twelve years old taking a red eye to Japan to see her father.

She floated in and out of consciousness, feeling bad knowing Lorelei was probably carrying her dead weight. But she couldn't help it even if she wanted to. Lorelei occasionally whispered muffled words that Iris could not make out. She must have been really delusional because she swore she could hear Elle's voice.

ELDORA PEREZ

"This is the last place we want to be in the dark," Evan said as the sun drifted beneath the trees.

"Listen, I told you not to come with me. So, if you're going to bitch about it, I don't want to hear it." Elle rolled her eyes. But she couldn't lie, she was extremely grateful he was there.

Like they were superglued together, Evan was connected to her at the hip. He almost stepped on her foot a few times, but did not shy away. His eyes were shifty and his hands were jittery. "Wait," Elle said. "Are you scared of the dark?"

"I most certainly am not!" He jumped back, creating a space between them.

"Hey, you're the one who said it's okay to be afraid," Elle smirked.

"But that does not mean I am afraid of the dark." Elle said nothing and raised her eyebrows. Evan let out a loud sigh. "Fine, okay. I am afraid of the dark," he admitted.

Elle chuckled.

"Don't laugh!"

"No, it's just…I think it's cute." She felt her cheeks growing warm. Evan ducked his head, failing to hide his smile. "Would it help if I held your hand?"

Although it was meant to be a joke, Evan slipped his hand into hers, interlocking their fingers. "Yeah, it would," he smiled.

Elle was extremely flustered and practically rendered speechless. She cleared her throat and continued walking like nothing happened. It was undeniably hard to ignore the fact that this was the first time she had ever held someone's hand before. Her palms grew sweaty as she could feel his pulse in his fingertips. It was something so simple yet so intimate. She tried to not let it bother her, worrying that he would be able to feel her increasing heart rate.

Elle quickly released Evan's hand when she heard rustling of leaves. "King Cardoc," Evan whispered. He quietly drew his sword as Elle reached for an arrow. They stayed glued at the hip as they tiptoed forward.

Elle squinted her eyes, unable to make out the two shadowy figures that were hiding in the distance. Their silhouettes were without weapons or armor. Elle lowered her bow. "Evan, stand down. I don't think they're soldiers," she whispered. She took a step forward and dropped her bow on the ground. "We aren't going to hurt you! We're from Camelot!" She called out to them.

Evan grabbed her arm and pulled her back, "Are you mad? What do you think you're doing?"

"When are you gonna learn to trust me?"

"When you stop being an impulsive idiot."

"Evan, you need to accept that that day will never come."

In the corner of her eye, a bright blue light caught Elle's attention. She could now see the shadowy figures were two women. One was slumped over, drenched in blood. The other was holding the ball of light in her hands. *A witch.*

Elle dropped everything and rushed to meet them. "Are you from Castemaga? I'm looking for my friend, maybe you can help me," she said desperately out of breath. The woman looked so tired and afraid. Elle's eyes shifted to the bleeding girl. Something seemed familiar about that long black hair. "Iris?"

When the girl lifted her head up, Elle was met with Iris's droopy, tired eyes. She collapsed into Elle's arms, almost pulling her down to the ground. Elle felt like she could hardly breath. "Iris, what happened?"

"Castemaga was attacked," the other woman spoke. "We were lucky to get away with our lives. We are traveling to Camelot to seek shelter and aid from a Mage," she turned to Evan, "Are you a Camelot knight?"

"We both are," he said. Elle tried to hide her smile.

"Very well, then. We could desperately benefit from your company."

"Of course. We shall leave right away," Evan said, scooping up Iris into his arms.

Elle grabbed his arm and pulled him aside. "What about Amaya?" Elle was not going to choose between the two of them.

"Iris needs a healer. We will get her back to Camelot and then continue our search for Amaya." His voice softened, "Elle, look at her. She needs help now."

Elle's eyes drifted to her friend who was limp in Evan's arms. Besides the deep red that stained her hands, her skin was colorless. Elle rested a soft hand against her face. Iris's whole body was trembling like the world had frozen over. Her eyes remained open, but there was no life behind them. It was like her soul had been torn out of her body. She was unrecognizable.

Evan was right. They needed to get her back.

"Okay. Let's go," Elle whispered, her eyes still fixed on Iris.

I'm sorry, Amaya.

IRIS YUKI

Iris drifted in and out of consciousness, seeing flashes of blurry trees and mutated faces. She was in someone's arms, but she wasn't quite sure to whom the arms belonged. Although it was hazy, she could see Elle's curls bouncing next to whomever was carrying her.

She thought she might just be hallucinating. That her mind was just filling in the gaps of the empty faces. "Elle," Iris mumbled softer than a whisper. A gentle hand rested on her face. Iris closed her eyes, choosing to believe it was Elle who reached out to her.

People think dying is like slipping into darkness. Into nothing. It is actually quite the opposite. When she closed her eyes she saw blue skies and pink trees. Everything was warm and welcoming, like a fireplace on a winter's day.

It would've been so easy to just let go.

Iris never feared death. That's because she never felt like she had anything for which to live.

Caught between life and death, she was finally starting to realize this wasn't true. Her mind focused on Elle's gentle touch. *Elle. Luna. Amaya.* She saw flashes of their life together. All this time she had been searching for who she was when it had been staring her right in the face.

She was the one who pushed Amaya to do things she was afraid to do. She was the one who kept Elle on her toes. She was the one who listened to Luna's rants about the world. Her friends had given her a purpose. They made her who she was—Iris. She needed to live for them.

So, she would fight, and she would fight hard.

When she opened her eyes, Elle was smiling right back at her. "Hey," Elle said with a breath of relief.

Iris could hardly believe Elle was standing right in front of her. It felt like a dream. Her memory was foggy. "What happened? Where the hell am I?"

"You're in Camelot. You're safe. Liana was able to heal you and you're gonna be okay."

Iris felt her muscles relax, realizing the once burning pain in her abdomen was gone. She was alive and safe. "Liana? What about Luna? I figured she'd be tripping over her own feet to help me," she teased. Elle didn't respond. "What's wrong?" Iris's stomach turned and twisted.

"Luna's in the dungeon, Iris."

This didn't make any sense. What could Luna have possibly done to end up in a place like that? "Luna? *Our* Luna? The same girl who wouldn't step on a spider cause she was afraid it had a family?"

"I know. I didn't believe it either. Oddly enough, I'm proud of her. She finally stood up for something," Elle smiled.

"She learned that from you, you know."

"Considering the fact that her actions got her thrown in the dungeon, I don't know if I should be taking that as a compliment."

"It is." And it really was. "Elle, I really messed up." Iris changed the subject.

"You mean besides getting impaled?"

"Yes, Elle. Besides getting impaled. A couple days ago, I ran into Amaya in the Elderen Wood."

"YOU WHAT?" Elle looked like she'd seen a ghost. "Is she okay? Where is she? Why isn't she with you?" She was talking so fast Iris could hardly keep up.

"Okay, slow down. She told me she was running away and that she felt like she didn't belong here. We got into this stupid fight and then..." Iris hesitated, sinking into her regret. "Then, I just let her go. I didn't even chase after her. I just watched her run." She felt a warm tear roll down her cheek.

Elle was silent.

"Yeah, I know. Blame me all you want, okay?"

"No, Iris, I wasn't gonna do that."

"Sure you weren't." Iris dropped her head in her hands.

"Whatever. We can't change what happened. What matters is finding Amaya and getting Luna back."

"And Maeve," Iris added. She felt shivers trickle down her spine remembering Maeve's screams as those men dragged her away. She clenched her jaw tight.

"Who's Maeve?"

"This kid I met in Castemaga. It was my job to protect her and I failed. Those bastards have her now and I'm gonna slit their throats if it's the last thing I do." Iris gripped the table tightly.

"Um, Iris?" Elle had fear in her eyes.

"What?" Iris looked up and saw everything in the room had lifted off the floor and was flailing through the air. She gasped and relaxed her hands, causing everything to come crashing down with a large thud.

"Did you mean to do that?" Elle asked.

"No. No, sometimes I just get so riled up and things sorta happen." Iris realized she desperately needed to learn to control her emotions. Someone was going to get hurt.

"Geez, Iris. I knew you had powers, but I didn't realize you were this powerful."

"Neither did I." It terrified her.

"Well, maybe we can use that to our advantage." Elle began pacing back and forth. "Okay, let's think. We need to find Amaya, break Luna out of prison, and rescue Maeve from who knows where. Even with your powers, there's no way we can do this by ourselves."

"I don't know, Elle. I think I could single handedly take over the entire Five Kingdoms. I might be the most powerful creature in all of Camelot." Iris smirked.

Elle raised an eyebrow. "Right, and remind me. Who's the one who got impaled with an arrow?"

"Okay, whatever. We'll be stronger in numbers or whatever. What about that knight of yours? Is he still following you around like a little lost puppy?"

Elle smacked her on the arm. "Shut up. He's not *my* knight." She looked down and fidgeted with her thumbs. It was clear something was up.

"Holy shit, Eldora Perez. You like him!"

"Oh my god, I do *not*. You're being ridiculous." She pulled her curls away from her face, still avoiding eye contact. Iris could see right through her.

"This is insane. I never thought in a million years you'd actually fall for someone. Let alone some manly man like him. You need to tell me everything," Iris giggled. Talking about something as stupid as boys with Elle was comforting. It almost felt like the world wasn't ending.

"We are not having this conversation right now." Elle rolled her eyes. "Yes, he can help us. *But*, you better not speak a word of this to him or it will be the last thing you do."

Iris smirked at her empty threat. "Take me to your lover boy and let's get this party started."

Elle shot her a dirty look and opened the door.

"Hey, Elle?" Iris said just before they stepped into the corridor. Elle turned to look at her. Iris's voice was soft and her eyes were genuine, "Thank you for saving me."

Elle's face melted into a smile. She placed her hand on Iris's shoulder and gave it a small squeeze. It was good to be back in Camelot.

When they reached the Throne Room, Elle seemed perplexed by the group of knights surrounding the door. "What are you all doing out here? Is there something going on?" Elle asked them. Iris recognized Sir Henderson as he stepped forward to speak.

"We're not sure. We were told there's going to be some sort of announcement."

"Who told you this? The king?" Iris asked.

"No, Edmund." His tone changed to a whisper, "Apparently the king is missing. There has been no sign of him anywhere."

"Do you think he's been captured?" Elle asked him. Iris found it strange seeing Elle interact with him so easily considering last time she saw them speak, Elle was ready to rip his heart out.

"No, I don't think so. Hopefully whoever called this meeting will give us some answers."

"The king is missing, you say?" Iris smirked. She had an idea.

"Oh, no. I know that look," Elle said. "What are you thinking?"

"If the king isn't here, who's to say I can't simply go into the dungeon and, I don't know, maybe free a certain someone?"

"Well, it will still be guarded," Sir Henderson said.

"Please, a few guards don't scare me. In case you haven't realized, I'm sorta a really powerful witch or whatever." She brushed her hair off her shoulder.

"She's gotten a really big head ever since she's been to Castemaga," Elle said to him.

"Elle, maybe you should go look in the mirror sometime."

"She has a point," Sir Henderson agreed. Iris already approved of this guy.

"Why are we even having this conversation?" Elle threw her hands up in the air. "Iris, go get Luna and meet us back here. But be careful!"

In order to get a clear view of the guards, Iris carefully rounded the corner. They sat, backs against the wall, staring straight ahead like there was not a single thought in their heads. *This should be easy,* Iris thought.

She began waving her fingers through the air, like she was playing an invisible harp. The men's eyes grew droopy as their heads slowly tipped down. Soon, their bodies completely collapsed forward. Iris chuckled when they started to snore. *Idiots.*

She grabbed the hem of her dress and ran through the dark halls of the dungeon screaming out for her friend. Yells and moans came out of every cell, as hands reached out through the rusted bars. Through all the overwhelming sound, she could hear a familiar voice. She desperately followed the sound, yelling at the top of her lungs. Her eyes fell on the tangled mess of red hair that spilled through the cell bars as a desperate arm reached out for her. Luna.

There she was, just as Elle said she would be. She was beaten, bruised, and had one foot in the grave. "Stand back, Luna. I'm gonna get you out of here." Luna quickly backed up into a corner while Iris extended her arm out. Energy shot all the way down through her finger tips and with a bright flash of light, the lock crumbled to the ground.

Iris ripped open the cell door and embraced Luna with her whole heart.

"You're back," Luna said with a shaking voice. She sounded so broken.

"Told you I would be." Iris released her grip, "Let's get you out of here, okay?"

"Okay," Luna smiled. Her tears drew lines through the dirt that coated her face.

AMAYA BROOKS

Amaya stood at the center of the Throne Room watching people flood through the open doors. So many eyes were falling on her. She felt like she was going to vomit. Her lack of knowledge of Merlin's plans only made things worse. "I don't know if I can do this," she told him.

"You have nothing to worry about. Just let me do the talking," he said.

People were squished, shoulder to shoulder, wall to wall. Everyone from child to man alike were whispering amongst each other, no doubt wondering what was going on. The knights were the last to enter the room, shutting the doors behind them. When she saw Elle standing amongst them, Amaya let out a breath she hadn't even realized she was holding in.

All eyes turned to Merlin when he stepped forward. The crowd fell silent. A genuine sense of shock filled the room as jaws fell and eyes widened. "No, you are not seeing a ghost," Merlin began. "It is me, Merlin. I have returned." The faint murmurs resumed. "And I am sorry. For years I left you in the hands of a monster. He has been lying to you. Abusing you. And now, he has abandoned you. You see, the man you know as King Kay, is in fact, not Kay at all."

Amaya held her breath as Merlin finally spoke his truth.

MERLIN

Although Camelot was saved, Merlin's world crashed and burned around him. What was the point of any of it? He failed to save the one person who mattered most and now he was gone. Arthur was gone. The worst part of it all was Merlin didn't have time to grieve or mourn. The war was over. But something much worse was only just beginning.

Rumors were spreading that Mordred was searching for Gwenevere. Killing Arthur wasn't enough. He wanted every piece of him wiped from the face of the Earth. He always envied Arthur, believing he deserved to be king. He almost hated Arthur more than magic. When he betrayed Arthur and sided with King Cardoc, Arthur was heartbroken. His own nephew had turned against him, just like so many other people in his life.

Merlin never understood how Mordred learned of the baby. Outside of Arthur and Gwenevere, Merlin was the only one who knew Gwenevere had given birth to an heir near the end of the war. Unfortunately, Arthur never met this child. While he was away on the battlefield, Gwenevere sent him countless letters describing her. This was the only piece of her he ever had.

Merlin knew it was his duty to keep Gwenevere and the child safe before Mordred could get to them. There was only one safe place of which he could think. One place where Mordred would never get to them. A place where the young child could grow up safely.

So, deep in the Elderen Wood, he created a portal. A portal to another world.

Gwenevere resisted and begged Merlin to come with them. But how could he? If Arthur were really going to return like the prophecy said he would, he had to stay. "Merlin, please do not make me do this," she had said.

"I'm sorry. It's the only way." He felt guilty sending them to this unknown place, but convinced himself it's what Arthur would have wanted. *He would want his daughter safe.*

For a while, Merlin believed Mordred was dead. The Five Kingdoms finally seemed to be at peace. Merlin spent most of his time taking care of a young, orphaned sorcerer. He truly cared for Edmund like his own son. By giving him a purpose and distracting him from his past, Merlin was able to cope with his deep-rooted pain.

But Merlin learned trying to outrun his past demons was impossible.

At first, he thought he was just paranoid. Late at night he would hear voices and see shadows. It was all in his head, he told himself. Unfortunately, soon the shadows became all too familiar. "Morgana," he whispered into the dark. She stepped into the moonlight.

"Where is the child?" she asked.

"You're working with Mordred, aren't you?"

"My business is my own."

"Morgana, don't let him deceive you. He is not on our side."

"There is no *our* side, Merlin!" Morgana and Merlin had never seen eye to eye. Like many, she despised Arthur. She believed the throne was rightfully hers. Although she and Merlin were both creatures of magic, Merlin's loyalty and love for Arthur built a wall between them.

"I'm just trying to protect you."

"You've never cared about me. Only him." Arthur. "If you are not going to help us, then I have no choice." Her hand lifted into the air, gleaming with a growing red hue.

"Morgana, stop this," Merlin threatened. Her aim shifted to the small sleeping boy in the corner of the room.

"If you even think about making a move, I will end his life right now. It's you or him."

Merlin watched Edmund snug under the covers, tucked away in his dreams and relaxed his clenched fist. He didn't have a choice. Morgana smirked.

She began reciting spells that Merlin knew to be dark magic. His insides tingled, like an itch he could not scratch. It grew painful and burned. He bit down on his tongue hard, so he would not wake Edmund.

He collapsed to the floor and gasped for air once she released her hold on him. When he looked up, she was gone. At first, he could not quite figure out what she had done to him. But he could feel something was wrong.

Something inside him was empty. *Oh, no.* That was it. His magic was gone.

Merlin never knew what Mordred promised Morgana to win her over. About a month after her little visit, word of her death spread through the Five Kingdoms like wildfire. *Mordred must've gotten what he wanted.* Merlin tried to warn her.

Life without his magic grew weary. Thoughts of Arthur began consuming his mind once more as he searched for something to fill the void. As much as he tried to deny it, he had turned a little mad.

He began to feel unfit for looking after Edmund. He only wanted what was best for him and Merlin was not that person at the moment. He knew many great people in Camelot and thought this would be a safe place for him to grow up while Merlin got better.

Merlin lost a part of himself when he handed Edmund away to the staff of the castle. Why was he always sending away those he loved? He wanted to reach out and take Edmund right back home to the Elderen Wood. But he didn't. He hoped he could forgive him one day.

In light of their old friendship, Merlin felt it best to bid King Kay farewell as he left the kingdom. He always admired Kay and thought he would make a fine leader. But something felt different. This Kay was not the man that Merlin once knew.

Could it be?

He pondered for a moment, but ultimately brushed off his suspicions and faded back into the trees.

AMAYA BROOKS

People's heads turned and looks of confusion were scattered throughout the room. Amaya watched the world around her turn blurry. She felt like a ghost thrown out of her own body.

Merlin continued. "Mordred has been disguising himself as Kay all this time and now he is hiding. Allowing King Cardoc to take the Elderen Wood and destroy all magic as we know it."

With a loud thud, the wooden doors flew open. Standing in the doorway were a very disheveled Luna and Iris. Their eyes fell on Amaya as they joined the crowd. She tried to keep her composure.

Merlin continued. "All because he is afraid." Amaya bit her tongue as Merlin turned to her. "Afraid of that girl right there."

The room grew noisy as the focus shifted to Amaya. She wanted to crawl into a hole and never come out. She searched the crowd for her friends and found comfort in their eyes. She could hardly believe that they were all between the same four walls again.

"She is the only one who can stop him. And that is because…"

Amaya braced herself for whatever words were about to slip from Merlin's tongue.

"She is Arthur Pendragon's one and only heir."

LUNA ANBRIS

Time stood still. The hundreds of bodies that were shoveled into that room yelled and screamed. Not a soul believed it. To be honest, neither did Luna. How could it be true? Amaya wasn't even from this world. How could Amaya, her Amaya, be a Pendragon?

"Quiet down! Quiet down! I'm sure you all have questions." the man spoke.

Everyone began yelling all at once. "We need proof!"

"How do we know you're telling the truth?"

"Arthur didn't have a child!"

"Are you even the real Merlin?"

Merlin, Luna thought. So that's who this man was.

Poor Amaya was collapsing in on herself standing in front of all these people. Luna only wished she could've been by her side up there.

Merlin continued. "During the great war, only weeks before Arthur's death, Guinevere gave birth to a daughter. Aside from them, I was the only one who knew of Amaya's existence. After killing Arthur, Mordred set out to kill Gweneviere as well. In doing so, he discovered Arthur had an heir who would stand in his way. So, I sent both of them far away where he could never reach them. But now, Amaya has returned to take her place on the throne."

As Luna heard the name "Guinevere" she was reminded of the letters she found. Maybe this is what King Kay, or Mordred, was trying to hide. Although Luna was beginning to believe the impossible, the crowd still needed some persuasion.

Merlin remained quiet and nodded his head at Amaya. In response, Amaya unsheathed a beautiful sword and held it high in the air. Many people gasped. Luna didn't understand.

"Long standing members of Camelot should recognize this sword. The very sword that Arthur used in his final battle. The sword he pulled from stone that was made just for him. I enchanted Excalibur so that Arthur could be the only one to wield it." He paused. "Or a direct heir."

Luna could sense a shift within the crowd. People's uncertainty morphed into excitement. They began to cheer and chant, while Amaya held the sword proudly. Luna couldn't help but smile.

"Don't you see?" Merlin continued. "A war is coming. King Cardoc has already taken control of the Elderen Wood. He will come for Camelot next." He reached for Amaya's hand and lifted it into the air. "This is your queen. She will lead us to victory! Long live the queen!'"

Everyone joined in on the chant. "Long live the queen! Long live the queen! Long live the queen!"

Luna didn't know what to make of all this. Amaya wasn't just Amaya anymore. She was a part of something greater. This must have been how Amaya felt all this time watching her friends weave into the fabric of Camelot. She understood that now.

"None of this makes any freaking sense," Iris yelled over the chanting.

"I don't know. I mean, it could be possible."

"You really think Amaya is Arthur's kid? Come on, Luna. Be real."

"Look around, Iris! I'm a Mage. You're a witch! You have powers! You literally broke me out of prison with your mind."

Iris rolled her eyes, "Yeah, I guess you're right. I just can't believe it."

"By the looks of it, neither can she. We should go see if she's alright. Where's Elle?"

"She's over there with her boyfriend." Iris pointed to the knights.

"Boyfriend? How long was I in the dungeon?"

"She and Sir Henderson seem pretty close if you ask me," she winked. "ELLE! LET'S GO!" Iris yelled across the room.

"I'm sorry. I was just talking to the knights about all this. I mean, can you believe it? Our Amaya is the rightful queen of Camelot."

"Yeah, we're on our way to see her majesty or whatever and you're coming with us, so let's go," Iris said, grabbing Luna and Elle by the wrists and pulling them out the door.

AMAYA BROOKS

Amaya gripped the concrete wall and tried to slow her breath. Merlin was lying. He must've been. He just needed someone to fill the role of the hero. That certainly wasn't going to be her. How could it be?

"Amaya?" Merlin placed a hand on her shoulder.

"Just leave me alone."

"Amaya, I am sorry for telling you this way."

"Well, it isn't true. It just isn't."

"I got so sick and tired of waiting for Arthur, I sort of lost myself. I knew if I impaled myself with Excalibur, I would turn to stone. That way I would not have to endure the agonizing pain of waiting for him anymore. The only way someone could bring me back is if Arthur, *or a direct descendent,* pulled the sword from my body. I left that door there knowing one day you would find your way back, as you were always intended to."

Feeling faint, Amaya dropped the sword. *No, no this isn't true.*

"Merlin, you have the wrong person. My mother would've told me. She would have told me!" Her voice cracked in despair. She knew the words coming out of her mouth were lies. Of course her mother wouldn't tell her. She never told Amaya anything. Now she was starting to understand why.

Merlin cupped Amaya's face in his hands. "I know it's you, Amaya. When I look into your eyes, I see him. I see my Arthur."

Something inside her shifted after hearing those words. *I have my dad's eyes.* She tried to suppress her smile. The pieces of her life started to fit together like a puzzle. Her absent father. The way her mother was obsessed with Arthurian legend and withdrew herself from the world. How the Truckee River magically seemed to change overnight. And the sense of familiarity Amaya had been trying to deny ever since that first day in Camelot.

King Arthur was her father.

She hated her mom at that moment more than she ever had before. How could she keep something like this from her all these years? Maybe they could have been closer if her mom just opened up to her and shared her pain. Although this felt like a wound that would never heal, she also pitied her. She must have been so lonely leaving everything she knew and loved behind. Maybe someday, Amaya could bring her back.

She took a deep breath, trying not to become too overwhelmed. "Why would Mordred do this? Why go after Kay?"

"After he killed Arthur, he knew he would never be able to inherit the throne after what he'd done. I believe he consulted with Morgana le Fey. She used dark magic to change his appearance. He killed Kay and took his place. And you've been right under his nose."

Shit.

"I should have stopped him." His voice was shaking. "But Morgana stole my magic. Without it, I felt helpless. So, I ran. I hid. But I knew it was him. I was so foolish. I should have done something." Tears poured from his eyes.

"Hey, it's okay. You couldn't have known. Don't blame yourself," she spoke softly. Part of her wanted to hate him. For abandoning

Edmund. For abandoning her. But she couldn't. She now saw he was just a broken man with a broken heart.

"Enough about me. Are you okay?" Merlin asked.

"I just need a moment to catch my breath." That was an understatement.

"Amaya, there's something else. When Morgana stole my magic, it became her own. I can only assume when Mordred killed her, it then became a part of him. I believe if he is killed with Excalibur, it will return to me."

Amaya tried to piece it together. "So, why am I holding the sword then?"

"Amaya, that sword was made for a Pendragon. You have to be the one to wield it."

A Pendragon. Being referred to as a Pendragon felt like squeezing into new jeans that didn't quite fit. She wondered if she'd ever get used to it.

Amaya snapped out of it when she realized what he just asked of her. "Wait, you want me to kill someone? No way. Not happening. I'm not a murderer."

"If you don't do this, Camelot will fall. It will bring down you and your friends with it." He took a step closer. "Amaya, this is *your* kingdom. Your people. Don't let him take that away from you."

My kingdom. Years of playing princess and projecting herself into fairytales felt all too real now. Amaya felt her mind and heart playing tug of war. She felt like every moment in her life had led her here, backed into a corner with nowhere else to go. She couldn't kill someone. She just couldn't. But she also knew she couldn't let Camelot fall. She couldn't let Mordred win. Not after everything he had put her family through.

"Okay. I just need some time to think."

"I'd love to give you all the time in the world, but I can only give you until tomorrow. The Elderen Wood is burning, Amaya."

As she walked back to her room, Amaya avoided the crowds that filled the hallways. She had just about made it to the stairs when someone tapped her on the shoulder. "Hi, Amaya."

It was Edmund. Although she was unsure why, seeing him broke the dam that was holding back all her emotions. She threw her arms around him and let it all go. "I guess sorcerers and Pendragons always find each other," he said.

There was something so comforting in that sentence.

"Look what I found." He pulled a small piece of paper out of his pocket. It was torn and burned on the edges. On it read "Amaya."

"What is this?"

"When you left, the king—I mean Mordred—burned everything that was in the drawer of the Round Table."

"I don't understand."

"This was in that drawer, Amaya. They were letters from your mother to your father. About you." Amaya took the scrap of paper in her hands. "I found it near his fireplace just moments ago. Now we know what he was hiding. *You.* You were the answer we were searching for all this time."

She almost laughed. She knew there was a reason she was drawn to whatever was in that drawer, but she never would've imagined it was this. "Why wouldn't he just burn them the moment he found them? Why take the risk?"

"I do not know. He must've had a reason."

Even if he did, it didn't matter now. Her head hurt far too much to try to figure it out. "Walk me to my room?"

"Always."

LUNA ANBRIS

Amaya was sitting on her balcony, peacefully gazing at the kingdom. Exactly where Luna knew she would be. Her head didn't turn as they entered the room. She didn't even flinch.

"Amaya? It's us," Luna said quietly.

"Your highness?" Iris teased.

"Shut up." Elle smacked her on the arm.

Amaya's head quickly turned. "Am I dreaming or are all of you actually standing in my room right now?"

"That would kinda be a boring dream if you ask me," Iris said.

Amaya grinned from ear to ear, throwing herself onto her three friends. They all wrapped their arms around her, surrounding her with warmth and love. Once again, the universe felt balanced.

"I missed you guys so much," Amaya mumbled into their arms. "I couldn't have gotten through all that without you guys there."

They broke the hug but stayed close. "So, is it all true? Are you really Arthur's daughter?" Elle asked.

"At least that's what Merlin says. It's all been so weird. I haven't had time to process it all. To be honest, I still don't really know what's going on," Amaya admitted. It seemed like she did not want to talk about her newly discovered family history.

"Well, that makes four of us," Iris said. "Listen, Amaya, about what I said I…"

"It's forgiven."

"Amaya…"

"No, really. I know you didn't mean it. There's too much happening right now for us to be at each other's throats. We need each other now, more than ever."

"Spoken like a true queen," Luna smiled.

"Lou! What happened to you?" Amaya gasped, pointing to Luna's cuts and bruises. Luna had almost forgotten.

"This bitch got herself thrown in the dungeon," Iris chimed in. "But I rescued her of course."

"Lou, is that true?" Amaya's eyes flooded with sorrow.

"Yea, I sorta went through with your crazy plan by myself when you left. Long story short, the king, I mean Mordred, caught me. Needless to say, he wasn't happy," Luna spared her friend the stomach churning details.

"Merlin didn't tell me that! Lou, you could've gotten yourself killed."

"After you left, I was just so angry. I didn't want to let you down. I got into the drawer. It was letters between, um…your mom and dad." It felt weird referring to Arthur and Guinevere this way. "He took them from me before I could read them, but I can only assume they were about you."

"I know. Ummm, Edmund told me. He found this. I guess one piece escaped the fire." She held out the burnt paper with her name on it. "I can't believe you did that for me. I mean look at what he did to you." Amaya's eyes filled with tears. Luna placed a hand on her shoulder.

"Hey, what matters now is that I am okay. We all are. And we're here to support you in whatever comes next."

Amaya smiled, letting out a sigh. "I think what comes next is bedtime. I'm exhausted. It's been a long day." The three girls agreed and turned to head to their bedrooms. "Wait. Do you think you could all sleep in here tonight? I would feel a lot better knowing you guys are close."

"It sure has been a while since our last sleepover. And it's not like the maids can get mad. You are the queen now," Iris reminded her.

Elle, Iris, and Luna pulled their mattresses off their bed frames and dragged them into Amaya's room just like they'd done as kids. Amaya too carried her mattress down onto the floor so they could all be together.

The girls laid in a circle with their heads turned in towards each other. It all felt so familiar. The room was dark except for the faint moonlight that spilled into the room, lighting up Luna's skin. It wasn't long before they were all fast asleep. The four of them had been through so much in the past few days alone. Resting in the comfort of each other's company was like a cure to their sorrows.

Luna couldn't speak for the others, but she slept better than she had in weeks that night.

ELDORA PEREZ

Elle woke up to the snoring, drooling sight of her friends. She rolled over and saw the sun rising over the smoke-filled sky. In all the commotion and excitement, she had almost forgotten about Astrea. In a quick, panicky motion, she threw on her boots and ran to the training yard.

She fell to the ground in relief when she saw Evan standing in the middle of the yard with Astrea. "What are you doing out here?" she said out of breath.

"I've been coming to check on her every once in a while. I know you've been preoccupied with everything happening with your friends, so I thought I would keep an eye on her for you."

Elle almost kissed him right then and there. "Evan, you didn't have to do that. How is she doing?"

"She's doing great. I think she's starting to like me." Astrea blew a puff of smoke down on him, messing up his curls. "Or not."

"Sure seems like it," Elle laughed. "So, how are you doing? After learning all that about your mom?"

"I'm okay. I mean, it's good to know why she just disappeared. Now I understand. I just wish it didn't have to be that way. But more importantly, how is Amaya doing?"

"I think she's doing okay. A little overwhelmed. Wait—Evan, do you know what this means? Amaya is your sister!" How did she not realize this before?

"You're just putting this together now? I always knew I was the smarter one," he teased.

"Why didn't you say anything?"

"I don't know. Everything was happening so fast. And I didn't want to overwhelm Amaya any more than she already was. But, I don't know. It's comforting knowing that I'm not completely alone."

"You were never alone, Evan," Elle whispered under her breath. She quickly changed the subject before he could register what she had just said, "You should talk to her! She grew up with your mom, you know. In fact, I knew your mom!" It was weird to think about. All this time, Amaya's mother had a child in another world. And that child was Evan.

"What was she like?"

"I think that's a question you need to ask Amaya." Evan seemed nervous to do so. He looked down at his feet and fidgeted with the buttons on his shirt. "Hey, it's gonna be okay. Amaya is the sweetest human being that I know. She'll be more than happy to have a brother, I promise." She lifted his chin, forcing his eyes to meet hers. "Remember…it's okay to be scared."

"You've given me all the courage I need," he smiled before disappearing into the castle. Elle's heart grew warm. What was happening to her?

Her attention turned to Astrea, who stood tall over her. "Sorry for leaving you. Things got complicated. Turns out my best friend is the queen. But you know what that means?" She placed a hand on

Astrea's scaly cheek. "You don't have to hide anymore. We're going to set things right."

For once, Elle felt like these weren't just empty words. She meant it.

AMAYA PENDRAGON

Dreams were nothing in comparison to Amaya's waking reality. It almost felt like when she closed her eyes, she was slipping back into the truth. Behind her eyelids laid the harsh reality that was her real life. When her eyes opened she was living and breathing in a dream. A wonderful, crazy dream.

She was still tangling in a mess of blankets when there was a knock at the door. Knowing Iris nor Luna would get up, she pulled herself out of bed with the covers still draped around her. She cracked the door open and saw Sir Henderson standing timidly in the corridor.

"Sir Henderson? Are you looking for Elle? She isn't here right now."

"No, I was just with her actually. I came to speak with you." He tugged on the back of his neck.

"Oh. Okay." Amaya dropped the blankets onto the floor and closed the door behind her. He sat down on a small velvet bench that was propped up against the concrete walls. Clenching her nightgown in her fists, she sat beside him. "What do you want to talk about?"

"Amaya, there's no easy way to say this," he began. Amaya felt a lump forming in her throat. How much more life altering news could she take? He kept his eyes steady straight ahead, avoiding Amaya's gaze. "Guinevere was also my mother."

Amaya didn't understand. "What do you mean? How—how is that possible?"

"Before her political marriage to Arthur, she was in love with Sir Lancelot. My father. They had me a few years before the war. Then I lost my father and mother all at once. I never understood why my mother disappeared. Until now."

Suddenly, Amaya felt guilty. "Oh Henderson, I'm so sorry. I can't imagine what that must have been like for you."

"Call me Evan. It's what my—our mother—used to call me."

Our mother. "I don't know what to say." It was a crazy thought. Two siblings growing up in different worlds, while the same blood coursed through their veins.

His tone shifted as his eyes met hers. "What was she like?"

Amaya sighed. "She didn't talk much. We did not have the best relationship. It always seemed like her mind was elsewhere. Now I think I understand why. I can't imagine what that must've been like for her being ripped from her home like that. For years she told me stories and tales of the great King Arthur and Camelot. She told me about your father as well. I never knew they were more than just bedtime stories." She reached for his hand. "I'm sure she missed you very much."

"You think so?" His voice cracked as the tears slipped from his eyes.

"Of course. I think that's why she was so lost. She left a part of herself in Camelot. For so many years I thought it was my fault. I thought I had done something wrong. Maybe I was just a reminder of everything she once had. I'm sorry. She would still be here if it weren't for me."

"No, do not apologize. If I've learned anything, it's that some things are bigger than us. Mordred would have killed you. Both of you. And if that meant sending you away, then I wouldn't change a thing. If you're anything like our mother or your father, then I know you will be the greatest ruler this land has ever known. I will humbly serve by your side until the day I die."

Amaya always believed family is not defined by blood. But that didn't mean blood could not be family. It was comforting to know that a piece of her mother was right here in Camelot. The piece of her mother that was not broken.

"Thank you Sir—I mean Evan. She would have been proud of you, you know." Amaya didn't know how she didn't see it before. He had her rounded nose and loose curls. His eyes even lit up the same way when he smiled, like their mother's.

"I just wish I could tell you about Arthur. I am sorry you were never able to meet him."

"It's alright. In a way, I feel like I have. Through our mother's stories. Even just being here, it's like I can feel him with me."

Evan lightly chuckled.

"What?"

"Nothing, it's just…I know exactly what you mean," he smiled.

IRIS YUKI

The Royal Court gathered around the Round Table. According to Amaya, this table was famous. It was where Arthur and his court would gather to have meetings, just like this one. It was the first time that Iris truly realized they were now a part of something bigger. They were going to war.

A map of the Elderen Wood and the Five Kingdoms sat in the center of the table. "If we travel up the river and cut across the Lake of Avalon, we should make it to Cardoc's kingdom in no more than two days," Sir Henderson said.

"How do we know he's there? Who's to say his men aren't still scouring the forest?" Elle asked.

"We've been searching for the king—uh, I mean *Mordred*, for the past two days and there has not been a sight of them. We believe after capturing the witches and setting fire to the wood, they retreated back to their kingdom," another knight said.

"Mordred is with Cardoc, I know for sure. He's repeating his same cowardly motions as before," Merlin said.

"It sounds like a trap. They are obviously expecting us to come and rescue the witches. Are you sure this is the best idea?" Elle asked.

"What choice do we have?" Iris slammed her fist down on the table. "A little girl is trapped there because of me. As are dozens of others who are counting on us! I will burst down King Cardoc's freaking door myself, if I have to."

"Iris, no one is saying we're going to abandon them," Amaya said. "We just need to be smart about this. Iris, I need you and Edmund to lead the army into the city. You're gonna have to use all the magic you've got to bring down those gates. Once we're inside, our goal is to find the witches. Leave Mordred to me."

"What should Astrea and I do?" Elle asked.

"Who's Astrea?" Amaya asked.

"My dragon."

"Elle, since when did you get a dragon?"

"Okay, we clearly all have a lot of catching up to do. I'm a witch, Amaya's a queen, Luna's a mage, and Elle rides freaking dragons. The details are unimportant right now." Iris firmly planted her fist on the table. Her friends shot her a strange look. Why couldn't she care about something every once in a while with everyone being weird about it? "Shut up."

"Okay, we head out at first light. We need anyone and everyone who can fight. We'll be stronger in numbers," Merlin said.

Iris lifted an eyebrow. "Let's show these sons of bitches what we're made of."

Morning came with a chill in the air. The unspoken truth of what they were walking into weighed heavy on them. It was the first time in who knows how long Iris actually woke up on time.

From head to toe, everyone was covered in metal armor of all different kinds. Each person was accompanied with a weapon of some sort, either draped on their backs or held tightly in their hands.

Wearing nothing but her black silky dress, Iris stood out amongst the crowd with empty hands.

There was one other person who was unlike the rest. Out of the corner of her eye, she noticed a boy in tattered clothing, fidgeting with something that looked like a paperclip in his hands. "So, you're a sorcerer then?"

Edmund jumped. "Oh. Yes, I suppose."

"It'll be nice to have another pair of magic hands out there."

"I really don't think I will be much help. My magic is rarely used." His posture was poor and uncertain.

"Don't sell yourself short. I didn't even know I was a witch 'til a month ago." She placed a hand on his shoulder. "We can do this. Okay?"

Edmund's fearful eyes softened into a smile. "Thanks, Iris." He paused. "What do you think about Amaya being queen?"

"I think it's freaking nuts. I think it makes no freaking sense." She laughed softly under her breath. "But at the same time, it makes perfect sense." She didn't know how else to explain it. It just felt right.

"I always knew there was something special about her. From the moment I met her, I felt something inside of me intertwining myself with her. Like my lost, broken soul needed mending. When I spoke to her, I knew she would be the one to mend it."

"Shit, Edmund," Iris smiled. "I think you might be right about that."

Just then, large trumpets rang through the air, catching everyone's attention. It was time to move out. Iris took a deep breath, preparing to cross the threshold.

Walking through the Elderen Wood wasn't what it once was. The air was thick with nauseating smoke and the fairies had gone dark. The charred branches crunched beneath her feet with each step. Everything that was once so green and full of life was withering away.

In the distance, she could hear the roaring of the flames that continued to engulf every last inch of the forest. The ashes fell from the orange sky like rain, tickling her nose. Iris felt like she was walking through the apocalypse.

And it broke her freaking heart.

No one said much as they continued their journey. What was there to say? Iris wasn't normally one to wallow in silence. This time she couldn't bring herself to speak. She knew cracking a joke would just upset her friends.

That was the last thing she wanted to do right now.

When the sky turned dark, they settled in for the night.

LUNA ANBRIS

Amaya squeezed in between Luna and Iris, trying to warm herself by the fire. Funny how everything started with the four of them huddled around a campfire. Things always had a funny way of coming full circle.

"There's someone to whom you haven't been properly introduced. Merlin, come here!" Amara gestured to him. He came and sat across from them, gazing over the flames.

"Guys, this is Merlin. Merlin this is…"

"Luna, Iris, and Eldora." He finished her sentence. How on earth did he know their names already?

"How did you know that?" Elle asked.

He sighed. "There was a part of my story that I left out. I was waiting until I could tell all of you. Together."

She felt Amaya instinctively grab onto her hand. "Merlin, what are you talking about?" Amaya asked.

"When I sent you away, I was really worried. I had promised Arthur that I would look after you. I needed to find a way to protect you. Make sure you were safe. So, using my magic, I created Eldora, Iris, and Luna," he turned to them. "I gave you each a piece of myself and placed you in that world with her. So, no matter what happened, Amaya would never be alone."

Luna's mouth went dry. She searched for the right words but they were nowhere to be found. She felt Amaya's hand go limp.

"Camelot will fall without the four of you. Yes, Amaya is important, but the three of you are equally so. When I lost Arthur, I lost a piece of myself. A piece that I'm afraid I will never get back. I did not trust myself to look after Camelot anymore. I have passed that task to you."

"Why should we even believe you?" Iris asked.

"You should have discovered your abilities by now. Iris, I gave you my magic. Eldora, you have my strength. And Luna, you have my healing powers. You must have noticed you were far more powerful than anyone else in Camelot."

"That would explain things, I guess," Luna mumbled.

Iris jumped on her feet, "So, we're not even fucking real? You're just dumping your work on us cause your fucking tired?"

The others stayed silent.

"You are just as real as the rest of us. You just came to be in a different way. That does not change anything." Nevertheless, it felt like everything had changed.

"Holy shit." Iris collapsed back down, dropping her head in her hands.

"So, that's it then? We were just made to do *your* work?" Luna recognized Elle's angry tone. This was going to get ugly, quick.

Merlin grew timid, "I—I am sorry, I did not think this would upset you. You were not meant to feel this way."

"You didn't think this would upset us?" Iris stood back up and stepped towards him, "You just tell us that our entire life has been a lie and you didn't stop for a moment and think that we might be a little upset?" The earth began to shake beneath their feet. "Sorry, there goes my all powerful, Merlin magic," she spit.

"Iris, stop," Amaya spoke up.

"No, you don't get to say a word." She returned her attention to Merlin. "And you don't get to tell me who I am. I get to choose who I want to be, and you are goddam lucky that I love these girls more than anything. I'm not doing this for you or some greater purpose. I'm doing it for them."

Before Merlin could respond, someone called for him. "I am sorry, I have to go," and he vanished into the crowd of soldiers.

Everyone was silent. Luna still had not spoken a word. She didn't know what she was feeling. Hurt? Fear? Anger? Maybe all three mixed together.

"Guys?" Amaya's voice was almost a whisper.

"I just need a moment." Iris's gaze was locked on the burning wood. Elle stayed quiet, but Luna could only assume she needed a moment as well. They all did.

Luna reflected on her childhood, looking at it through a completely different lens now. She finally understood why she felt like a fish out of water all those years. She was plucked from her world like a weed in a garden. She felt a single tear slip from her eye. It wasn't because she was sad or scared. There was no word in the English language to describe what she was feeling. It was like all the positive and negative emotions crashed into each other, making a big mess in her brain.

She knew she couldn't dwell on the negatives. Not at a time like this. Sure, her entire life had been a lie. *But* that lie had given her the three most amazing friends anyone could have asked for. And if Merlin had not sent Amaya away…she might have never existed.

Slight sniffling interrupted her thoughts. "I'm so sorry," Amaya whispered.

"What are you apologizing for?" Luna asked.

"This is all because of me. You heard him. I mean, you were all basically forced to become my friend. Was any of this ever real?"

Luna's heart cracked in two. "Hey, no one's saying that."

"I meant what I said, Amaya," Iris agreed. "I don't give a shit what anyone says, okay? No one chooses my path but me. We may have all been destined to end up here, or whatever, but we chose each other. We chose this family. Trust me, if I wanted to abandon all of you, I would have done it a long time ago."

Luna rolled her eyes. Of course, Iris couldn't get through a serious moment without cracking a joke.

"She's right," Elle said. "This doesn't change anything. We always knew our friendship was special. Now we know why, that's all. That doesn't change the fact I want to rip Merlin's head off his shoulders, but that's beside the point."

"We all have every right to be angry," said Luna. "All of us, including Amaya, have been lied to our entire lives." She paused, feeling the moonlight dance on the surface of her skin. "We are a part of something bigger now. Like Iris said, we're doing this for each other."

Amaya collected herself, straightening her spine. "Okay. For each other. For Maeve. And for anyone who's suffered at the hands of Mordred."

ELDORA PEREZ

The red flames of the burning wood illuminated the kingdom in an eerie manner. Elle felt the hairs on her arm begin to rise. She wasn't sure if it was from the slight chill in the air, or the blood curdling fear that was filling every inch on her body. Probably a little bit of both.

She looked down and noticed her hands were shaking. Normally, she would try to hide this from others. Now, things were different. She held her hands out in front of her and looked to her friends. She let the truth drip from her tongue for the first time. "I don't know what's going to happen. I don't know if I'm strong enough to make it out of there and I hate myself for it. I don't know if I will be able to protect all of you and…it terrifies me. I know it's stupid."

Elle braced herself for judgment and humiliation from her friends. She was certain they wouldn't take her seriously. She feared they would simply laugh and brush it off. She would never be taken seriously.

Instead, Luna said, "Hey, don't put that pressure on yourself. None of us are prepared for this. I we don't make it out, we at least go down fighting. That is not your fault. Elle, we're all terrified."

"Yeah, I'm pretty sure I just shit my pants," Iris laughed.

"And you know me, I'm scared every waking moment of my life," Amaya said.

"We're all in this together, okay? No matter what happens," Luna assured her.

Elle collapsed with relief into her arms. She let go of a breath she had been holding in for who knows how many years. Her three friends surrounded her with warmth and love. *What was I so worried about?*

"Did you think we were going to say something different?" Luna asked.

"I don't know. I've just always felt like you would think less of me if I weren't the fearless girl you thought I was," she finally told her truth.

"Elle. We don't love you because you're brave. We love you because you're Elle. Whether you're scared, brave, sad, happy, it doesn't matter. We love everything that comes with it," Luna smiled.

"Have I ever told you guys that I love you," Elle mumbled into their embrace. Although meant to be a joke, she feared it was true. Saying such things would require vulnerability, which Elle opposed, of course. Or at least, she used to.

"To be honest, I can't say that you have," Iris said.

Elle removed herself from the hug so she was looking at each friend right in the eye. This, right here, was probably the bravest she'd ever felt. "Well, I do. I love you." To think it took going to another world to say so.

"We love you, too," the others said in unison. Whatever worries she had were subsided by the comfort of her friends. She just hoped it would be enough.

"I hate to break this up, but we need to move," Merlin said, stepping in between them.

"Of course Merlin's here to ruin another moment," Iris rolled her eyes.

Amaya interjected, "Come on, he's right. It's time to go. Iris, you stay up at the front with Edmund and Lorelie. Use everything you've got to take down that door. Merlin and I will be right behind you. Signal us when you're ready. Elle, take Astrea and fly overhead. Take down as many guards as you can. And Lou, you stay in the back with Liana and heal as many people as you can."

"But I wanna be up there with you guys. I want to help," Luna pouted.

"Lou, you will be helping. We can't do this without you. We need you back with Liana, where you'll be safe," Amaya said. "We meet back here when it's all over. Stick to the plan. Keep each other safe."

"Show Mordred he messed with the wrong crazy bitch," Iris smiled.

Elle ran back through the trees where Astrea was tucked away out of sight. Part of her felt guilty for pulling her into this. There was no doubt Astrea was as terrified as she was.

Elle climbed onto her back, gripping onto her scales, "We're in this together. You'll be alright. Once this is all over, you won't need to live in fear anymore."

She heard a faint voice calling her name in the distance. She squinted her eyes and peered through the thick of the trees. It was Evan, running as fast as his feet could carry him. "What? What's wrong?"

He stopped before her, seemingly out of breath. "Nothing, I just wanted to say good luck. Not that you need it." He softly smiled, scratching his neck, before turning to walk away. Elle felt a voice inside her screaming at him not to go.

After just a moment with hesitation, she called out, "Evan, wait!"

She held on to Astrea and leaned over, meeting Evan eye to eye. His eyes glistened with fear and vulnerability. A palpable nervous energy emanated between them.

It was now or never, she thought. "Thank you, Evan." She grabbed his face and closed the space between them.

The weeks of yearning poured out through her lips all at once. Before she could form a coherent thought, she pulled away. Evan stared at her in complete shock. He opened his mouth to speak, but said nothing but incoherent babbling. It was insufferable how flustered he was. God, she hated him.

Although there were so many things she wanted to say, all that she could muster up was, "Stay alive," before taking off into the sky.

IRIS YUKI

I ris would be lying if she said she wasn't a little excited to see what she was really capable of accomplishing. She had used her powers in dire situations before, but this was a whole different game. And now that she knew her mith, there was no way she could lose. Maybe she was a little too confident, but she didn't care.

She approached the city gates with Edmund and Lorelie on either side of her. Behind her was everyone else, out of sight and waiting for their signal. As expected, guards were stationed at the tops of the sealed gate. Their chins dropped and eyes followed their movements.

Two more guards stood in front of the gate, moving their hands to their swords. "State your business."

Iris bit her tongue, trying not to say some stupid joke. *Not the time or place.*

"We seek an audience with your king." She clenched her fists.

As the man's breathing deepened, he released his grip on his sword. He clenched his stomach and let out a blood curdling scream.

"WITCHES!" The guards scrambled on their feet, getting their weapons into place.

"Edmund! You two get that gate down! I will distract them." Iris needed another minute before she could use her mith again. She felt like she'd just been hit by a freaking bus. It was going to be a long night.

She turned her attention to the men running on top of the towers. With the flick of her chin, a few of the men went hurdling over the wall, slamming into the hard floor. She felt a rush of adrenaline surge through her body. She hoped it would give her some of her strength back.

There was nothing left of the large metal chains that secured the gate. Lorelie and Edmund had melted them away like they were marshmallows over a campfire. The gate came crashing down at their feet, revealing the entrance to the city.

They were in.

The signal. Iris conjured a ball of light in her hands and sent it into the sky.

"I'm gonna find Maeve and the others. You two stay here and take down as many people as you can." She grabbed Edmund's arm. "Make sure my friends are safe."

The city was mostly quiet. Iris figured it was the calm before the storm.

Although Iris had never been to King Cardoc's kingdom before, she knew exactly where to find the dungeon. *If you've seen one castle, you've seen them all.* The dungeon was always underground. Why was every castle always the same? Iris always found that stupid.

As she approached the guards to the main entrance, she had a decision to make. Was she going to distract them or harm them? She hadn't fully gathered her strength back yet, but she feared distracting them wouldn't be enough.

Maybe if she came up with a clever enough distraction.

There were plenty of things Iris did not know about her powers. She was unsure what the limit was or if the limit even existed. Messing around with things she didn't know seemed like a bad idea. But, hell, Iris was the queen of bad ideas.

She thought of something that would surely scare them out of their skin. Just enough so she could knock them on their asses.

She focused on them. On their mouths. Imagining them silent. Like a zipper running across their lips from one side to the other.

Suddenly, their lips started to fade. From their nose to their chin, it was nothing but skin. The men's eyes widened in fear. They tried to scream and cry, but they could not. Iris had erased their mouths. She almost laughed.

As the men panicked, Iris walked up the stairs towards them. They were so occupied with their missing feature, Iris walked right past them. Violence *and* distraction seemed to be the perfect combination.

Once she was inside, there was no time to waste. There was no doubt Mordred and King Cardoc now knew they were there. She needed to get Maeve out of there as quickly as possible.

She ran up and down empty corridors, searching for stairs that would lead her to the dungeon. Suddenly, something caught her attention. There were faint screams echoing from below. They weren't just any screams. They almost sounded like…

"Maeve?"

It had to be.

She followed the screams that continued to echo throughout the castle. It brought her to a dark staircase, draped in cobwebs and dust. She walked down the stairs, letting the darkness swallow her whole.

When she reached the bottom, she was met with three guards with their swords drawn. Taking a deep breath, she clenched her fists. Her vision blurred and her head spun. Even though she was weakening, she pulled strength from Maeve's cries for help. This time, distraction wouldn't be enough.

The guards writhed on the floor in agonizing pain while their flesh melted away into nothing. She shoved passed them and entered the dark hallway that seemed to stretch for miles. "MAEVE!" She continued to follow her voice, using her magic to illuminate the way.

As she approached the screaming emanating from a cell, Maeve's face came into the light. With whatever strength she had left, Iris tore open the cell door. Maeve was bound and covered in blood.

"I'm gonna get you out of here." Iris untied the rope around her feet and hands. Funny how breaking people out of prison had become somewhat of a routine for her.

"You found me. You actually found me." Maeve's voice was small and broken.

"Hey, I said I would, didn't I?" Iris's stomach sank seeing the terrible burns circling Maeve's wrists and ankles.

"I didn't think you would actually be able to pull it off," Maeve teased.

"Do you want to be freaking rescued or not? Cause I have no problem leaving you in this cell."

Maeve's laugh once irritated her, but now it brought her an endless feeling of relief.

She threw Maeve's arm over her shoulder and helped her to her feet. Maeve groaned in pain, struggling to keep her balance. They had hurt her. Bad.

"Where's Marjorie? And the others?"

Maeve was silent.

"Maeve, where are they?"

"I'm the only one left."

No, no that couldn't be true. "What do you mean?"

"King Cardoc...he killed them. He killed my mom."

Iris froze. That meant besides Lorelei, they were the only two witches left.

LUNA ANBRIS

Luna knew she was more useful staying back in the wood where she could heal people when it was all over. She knew that. But part of her yearend to be up there fighting with her friends. "It's for the best," Liana said, reading Luna's mind.

"I know, I know. It's just...I've spent so many years hiding. Playing it safe. I'm done with that! I should be up there with them."

"They cannot do this without you. If we go down, who will be left to save those who have fallen? If Iris, Elle, or Amaya need you, what will become of them if you're gone?"

She knew Liana was right. But she wished she weren't.

"Luna, I did not get the chance to apologize to you."

"For what?"

"For everything. For letting you get locked away in that awful place and doing nothing about it. I'm so sorry, my dear. I knew something was wrong for so long. I should have stood up to him! I should have done something!"

"Liana, this isn't your fault. I was the one who made the decision to steal that key, not you. It wasn't your responsibility to stop him. You can't blame yourself."

Liana's eyes softened. "You are a wonderful mage, my dear. Camelot is lucky to have you."

"Thank you, Liana. I won't let you down."

AMAYA PENDRAGON

Amaya ran her fingers along the deep grooves of the sword to ground herself. She tried to stay present in the moment, no matter how much she wanted to dissociate and launch her mind elsewhere.

At that moment, it felt like their plan was almost nonexistent. Find Mordred. Kill him.

Amaya had never even wielded a sword before. Mordred had years of training, fought in wars, and was strong enough to kill the great Arthur Pendragon. Merlin had told her, "When the moment comes, the sword will guide you. As it did Arthur. There's no need to worry, Amaya. You were born for this."

Of course, since she was Amaya, she was going to worry.

She couldn't decide if the prophetic nature of Camelot was comforting or not. After all, it was a prophecy that killed Arthur. But that prophecy also led her here. Being in Camelot had taught her that the world was not as black and white as she once thought it was.

Beauty can thrive in the darkness.

Sounds of clanking metal and screaming men rang through her ears. The world seemed to be moving in slow motion around her. It was like she was at the center of the universe, watching it all unravel in utter chaos. It felt like she was slipping into a dream. Amaya realized her toughest battle was not going to be Mordred.

It was herself.

Fighting against her mind that wanted to shut down and protect itself.

She focused attentively on the grooves of the sword again. She noted its rough texture and the weight it carried. She felt metal grow warm as her anxious hand gripped it tight. She counted each stair as she found her way through the castle.

One.

Two.

Three.

She focused on her breath. How the cool air filled her lungs like balloons. She allowed her worries to filter through her mouth as she slowly exhaled. Amaya repeated this over and over again as she trailed through the castle.

The sword. The stairs. Her breath.

The door to the throne room was wide open, inviting her in. She stepped into the room and saw Mordred holding a blade to King Cardoc's throat. There was blood seeping from his mouth and the whites of his eyes were showing. He looked like a madman.

"You're too late. I've already taken the Elderen Wood. Camelot will fall. Soon, I will have all five kingdoms within my grasp."

"The thing about people like you is you won't stop. You'll never be satisfied. You'll destroy the whole world trying to claim it. And you will take yourself out with it." She took a step closer, gripping Excalibur with both hands.

"The world burned me first," he whispered. She wondered what he meant by that.

Then Mordred slid his blade across Cardoc's throat.

Blood splattered all over Amaya, getting in her eyes and mouth. She thought she was going to be sick. The world was going hazy again.

No, no, no.

She took a deep breath, feeling the grooves of the sword once more. This was real and it was happening. She was going to make it through this. She was born for this. She was a Pendragon.

Mordred smiled as he unsheathed his sword. Amaya embraced this last moment of peace. The calm before the storm. Then, with a loud scream, her blade met his.

ELDORA PEREZ

The remaining guards flooded the courtyard, shooting arrows and loading things into tall, wooden catapults. They all were aiming at Astrea.

Elle was able to dodge the arrows, but it was much more difficult for Astrea. She took up so much space in the sky, it was almost hard to miss her. She cried as dozens of arrows buried themselves in her skin.

Elle reached for the arrows that were on her back, trying to keep her balance. Shooting from the back of a horse seemed like a walk in the park now. She tensed all her muscles, tightening her stomach and squeezing her thighs together.

She nocked the arrow into place and set her eyes on a target. Before Astrea could make any sudden movements, Elle released the arrow. Like a bird swooping in to catch its prey, the arrow dived down in one swift movement and impaled the target. She smiled, exhaling in relief. Not too bad for her first shot.

"Come on, Astrea. Let's get these sons of bitches."

The glow of Astrea's belly lit the ground beneath them. Elle watched the men lower their weapons and begin to cower. They knew what was coming.

Elle secured her bow on her back and held on tight. She squeezed her eyes shut as she felt the rumble growing in Astrea's stomach. It grew louder and deeper. Elle felt the heat spread throughout the scales on her back.

Then with a loud roar, the bright flames escaped her mouth.

Elle opened her eyes and saw the courtyard light up in flames. Much to her surprise, this did not stop the men. They were growing in numbers, bringing out even more weapons, each one more terrifying than the last.

She grabbed her bow and began shooting arrows once more. She aimed for the ground at the men who were loading what seemed like large balls of fire into the catapults. It was hard to see through all the smoke and flames.

The large balls of fire began flying through the air. Astrea turned sharply, making Elle lose her balance. With her bow still in hand, she held onto her back tightly. She couldn't shoot like this.

Astrea zigzagged through the sky in a chaotic manner. This wasn't fair to her. *There's too many of them. She'll never make it.*

"Astrea! Back to the trees!"

Astrea turned too quickly, sending Elle flying off her back.

She shut her eyes, bracing herself for what was to come. She heard the wind whistling in her ears as she fell. But it was strange. It didn't feel like falling. Not like she'd imagined it would. It was more like floating. Like a cloud in the sky.

She didn't dare to look. That would make it worse somehow. When the impact didn't come, she grew suspicious. With an exhale, she opened her eyes.

She was in fact not falling at all. She was hovering just inches above the ground. But how?

She looked up and saw Edmund standing in front of her. Amidst the fiery chaos, he was reaching his arm out to her. He had saved her.

"Edmund."

"I've got you," he said, setting her down gently on the floor.

Overhead, she watched Astrea settle in the trees outside of the city. She was going to be okay.

She grabbed an arrow off her back and nocked it into place.

LUNA ANBRIS

More and more wounded soldiers began filtering into Liana and Luna's tent, desperately needing healing. It was too much for just two of them to handle. Liana had once told her there were dozens of mages before the Great War. The castle was filled with an entire group of them. But the enemy viewed them as creatures of magic. In the end, only one survived. Liana.

Luna felt her stomach all tangled up into knots, wondering if the next person who walked through that door was going to be one of her friends. Or worse…they'd never leave the battlefield.

"Has anyone seen Amaya?" Luna yelled over all the screaming patients. No one answered.

"Luna, my dear, we cannot worry about her right now. I need your help healing these men."

"*Don't get involved*," Luna's mother's voice echoed in her mind.

"No," she whispered under her breath. Something was wrong.

She knew it wasn't fair to leave this all to Liana, but she couldn't shake this feeling. So, she made an irrational, impulsive decision. Making sure her dagger was secured tightly underneath her dress, she fled, hearing Liana's protests fade into the wind.

AMAYA PENDRAGON

Excalibur was heavy, but not impossible to wield. She let the sword take control, just as Merlin had said. Her mind turned to her mother's stories. She let her mother's words guide her movements, like she was there, narrating that very moment.

Maybe she'd be someone's bedtime story one day. Maybe she would be that loose thread that held together a broken relationship.

Although Amaya was quick and agile, Mordred was strong. He was much bigger than her, forcing her back into a corner. It was almost like a dance. The two of them went back and forth, while Mordred took the lead.

She ducked, just barely missing his swing, throwing him off his balance. She took advantage and shoved her blade into his right thigh. Although he cried out in pain, he was not hindered.

She saw something shift in his eyes. Ambition turned to anger. He gripped his sword with both hands and let all hell break loose.

Amaya fought back with everything she had. But it wasn't enough.

With one big swing, Mordred knocked Excalibur right out of her hand.

She felt a sharp pain tear through her stomach as she dove for the sword. She looked down and saw Mordred's blade buried deep in her skin.

She fell to her knees as he ripped the sword from her body.

"Well, isn't this a familiar sight? A Pendragon begging for her life at my feet. You look an awful lot like your daddy," he mocked her, placing his blade under her chin.

"Why didn't you kill me when I first arrived? You knew back then, didn't you?"

"I knew from the moment you set foot in my kingdom. But you were lost. Weak. Stupid. I realized you had no idea who you were. Your own fear was eating you from the inside out. I didn't need to kill you because you were already killing yourself."

"Or maybe you're just as scared as me." She dug her nails into her wound. "Why did you keep those letters? You could've burned them."

"Those letters held much more than you can imagine. You will soon be nothing but ash, just like they are."

Whatever. It didn't matter now. Amaya ran her fingers along the deep grooves of the sword to ground herself. She tried to stay present in the moment, no matter how much she wanted to dissociate and launch her mind elsewhere. She needed to stay conscious and gather any last strength she had.

"I don't think so," Mordred said, stepping on her hand making her lose her grip on Excalibur. She cried out in pain.

I guess this is how it ends, she thought. At least she went out fighting. That's all she ever wanted for herself. To not let her anxiety get the best of her. She closed her eyes, not waiting to see Mordred's face when he claimed his victory. She imagined her friends carrying on their legacy for years to come. She knew they'd thrive no matter where they were. She'd miss them.

Just as she thought it was over, she heard a familiar voice. It almost sounded like Luna. "Lou?"

Luna was running towards them with a small dagger in her hand. She slid across the floor and sliced Mordred's ankle. He collapsed to the floor in pain, allowing Amaya to grab Excalibur once more. She struggled to her feet and quickly shoved the blade into his chest.

His faux appearance melted away with his strength. His aging eyes regained their youth while his muscles thinned. His gray tips grew black and his once sharp jaw rounded. King Kay was gone. This was Mordred.

"You took everything from me. My parents. My home." She glanced back at Luna. "But I should also thank you. If it weren't for you, I would've never gotten this family." She ripped the sword from his body, causing his torso to hit the floor.

It was strange to think about. All that suffering and pain gave Amaya her greatest gift of all. The universe had a funny way of working things out. She thought of a world where Arthur lived. Elle, Iris, and Luna? She would've had to do life without them. If she could go back and stop things from happening the way they did, she wouldn't change a thing.

Amaya stood over him as he choked on his own blood. All the color drained from his face, leaving his eyes empty and lifeless. And that was that. She had killed someone. She had killed Mordred.

The pain started taking control once more as her adrenaline started to wear off. She let Excalibur fall from her hands. The world was getting darker and she was tired. She sat down on the cold stone floor, letting her eyes drift shut.

She heard a muffled voice, "Amaya, just hang on, okay?"

LUNA ANBRIS

Luna's body was vibrating with anger and rage. She was rattling with energy and yet nothing was happening. Why wasn't it working?

She began to sob uncontrollably, trying to force the life back into her friend. Her grip was tight around the wound. Amaya was not going to die. She wasn't.

Wherever Mordred's soul was now, she hoped he was suffering. Part of her wished Amaya hadn't killed him so she could've done it herself.

She dragged Amaya's cold body into the moonlight, soaking in the bright rays that fell gently into the room. This should've given her more than enough power to heal her. But still…nothing.

"WHY ISN'T IT WORKING?"

Then it hit her. Something Liana had told her that very first day. *Mages are pure of heart.*

Luna's mind was poisoned with hurt and anger. Her intentions weren't pure. They were violent and vengeful.

She took a deep breath and tried to clear her mind.

Amaya. This is about healing Amaya.

She looked down at her friend and thought about how warm she made her feel. How losing Amaya would be like extinguishing the flame that lived inside of her and kept her going. Her love for her was stronger than any hate she could ever have for Mordred.

Amaya not dying wasn't enough. Amaya needed to *live*.

She reached out to her, gently this time.

AMAYA PENDRAGON

Amaya felt a cold hand press against her wound, sending warm vibrations throughout her body. It hurt, but in a good way. Like stretching muscles that are sore. She felt life return to her body all the way down to her fingertips. Even with her eyes closed, she could sense a glowing light surrounding her. It felt safe.

"Amaya, please," the voice cried.

She opened her eyes and saw her friend glowing in the moonlight. Her eyes were red with tears. "Lou? What's going on?"

"You're gonna be alright. I healed you."

She saw Mordred sprawled on the floor out of the corner of her eye. She did it. They were going to be okay.

"Come on, let's get you on your feet," Luna said, pulling her off the floor.

She clutched onto Luna, still feeling a bit disoriented. "It's over, Lou. We did it."

Luna smiled. "No, you did it." Suddenly, Luna's knees became shaky. She clutched her stomach and doubled over.

"Lou?" Amaya's voice was small and childlike. She saw the deep red soaking through Luna's dress. Luna's face grew pale as she collapsed into Amaya's arms. The red stain continued to grow. "Luna, what happened?" Amaya cried.

"Mordred. I guess he got me," she whispered.

"I told you to keep yourself safe." Amaya began to panic, searching around the room for a solution, "You're gonna be okay. We're gonna go find Liana and everything will be fine. Just hang on a minute longer. Everything's going to be fine."

Luna placed a trembling hand on Amaya's cheek, forcing her to look at her. Luna's eyes were filled with this look that said, "It's too late."

"Luna, please don't do this. Please."

"I know you've always felt invisible. Like you didn't matter. Just because you have some fancy title and a new sparkly crown now doesn't mean that you are somebody. Because you have always mattered, Amaya. You've always been somebody to me. Don't ever think otherwise."

"I don't know how to do this without you, Lou."

"You don't have to. You'll see me in the stars. In the way the moonlight hits the water. In Elle. Iris. And in yourself. I will be there."

Amaya wrapped her hand around Luna's and squeezed it tight. She bit her tongue, trying to suppress the sobs that were building in her throat. Moments ago, she had just been stabbed through the abdomen with a sharp blade. This hurt more.

The blue light that once danced on Luna's skin lifted into the sky like lanterns. They swayed like kelp beds in the ocean and filled the air with her light. They traveled into the night sky and faded into the stars, leaving Luna dark and gray.

IRIS YUKI

I ris and Elle found Amaya on the floor, clinging to Luna's lifeless body. They knew trying to pull her away would be pointless. So they didn't. The girls fell to their knees and mourned with her.

Iris wasn't sure how long they stayed like this. Now, time moved differently. Or at least it felt that way.

"Let's take her body," Elle said. "She deserves a proper funeral."

Iris peeled her heavy body off the ground and whipped her face dry. Her head was throbbing and her ears rang. She felt sick.

Sick with grief.

She slid her arm under Luna's limp torso and lifted her off the floor. Elle took the bulk of her weight while Amaya hadn't moved a muscle. She was frozen with a blank stare plastered on her face like a mask.

As much as it pained her, Iris had to pull her out of her trance. "Amaya, we need to go. We're not leaving here without you."

She didn't budge.

"Amaya, for once in your life, please don't be so goddamn stubborn." She felt more hot tears burn her cheeks. She was tired. Angry. She just wanted to go home with the family she had left. She reached her hand out to her, desperate.

Amaya accepted.

"This is all my fault." Maeve buried her head in her hands. "Luna should be alive. Not me."

"Maeve, it shouldn't have to be one or the other. You *both* should be here right now," she turned to face her. "Don't ever think this is your fault. Don't act like you're expendable." Iris tried to keep her mouth shut. She was filled with pain and didn't want to say the wrong thing.

"What's going to happen now? Without Castemaga? Without all the other witches?" Maeve's lip began to quiver. "Without my mom?"

"That's not something you need to worry about. We will rebuild it. Even bigger and better than before. I promise I won't let anything happen to you." Her gaze shifted to Amaya. "She's queen now. She's not going to let anything happen to us, okay?"

Maeve broke down and collapsed into her arms. For once, Iris welcomed the embrace and held her tight. "I've got you," she said. "I've got you."

AMAYA PENDRAGON

A very bruised and bloodied Merlin collapsed into an embrace the moment he saw Amaya. "It's over," he said. "You did it."

She wondered if killing Mordred worked, giving Merlin his magic back. She was too tired to ask. Too numb. There was nothing he could say to make her feel better at that moment. Nothing he could say could bring Luna back.

"Why aren't you celebrating? We did it, Amaya!"

She couldn't bring herself to say it.

Iris and Elle shot him a sorrowful glance, telling him everything he needed to know. "Oh," he said softly. "Amaya, I'm so sorry."

She shoved passed him and disappeared into the Elderen Wood.

ELDORA PEREZ

No one knew what to say, or what to do. Part of Elle wanted to run after Amaya. But she knew Amaya wanted to be alone. She just hoped she wouldn't blame herself for this.

"So, uh, did it work?" Elle asked, changing the subject and filling the silence. "Do you have your magic back?"

He smiled, facing the trees. So many of them were nothing but ash and dust now. It broke Elle's heart.

As he closed his eyes, a gust of wind rushed through the leaves and branches. It rippled through the entire forest, extinguishing every last flame with it. Within seconds, the wood was dark and cold.

"It will take time to heal," he said. "But it will heal. And when it does, it will be more beautiful than ever."

"So, what now?" Iris asked.

"We go home," a voice said behind them.

Elle's heart leapt out of her chest. *Evan.*

He limped towards her, his curls matted and full of dirt. She jumped in his arms like a lovesick schoolgirl. Seeing him in front of her made her realize how fearful she was of losing him. Like all her emotions, she had pushed it aside and pretended it wasn't true. But the feeling was so overwhelming she couldn't hide it anymore. "I thought I was never gonna see you again," she admitted.

"You really had that little faith in my fighting skills?" He smiled into her neck.

"I almost took your head off with an arrow the first time we met. I had every right to be worried."

He cupped her face in his sweaty hands and kissed her like he was afraid of losing her too.

The knights stepped forward to carry Luna's body back to Camelot. Elle and Iris trailed closely behind them, their hands interlocked. Even in death, Luna was glowing like the sun. No–like the moon.

They found Amaya, curled up in a ball amongst the ash and rubble. Elle placed a gentle hand on her shoulder. "We need to go. Please."

This time Amaya didn't argue. She quietly rose and joined them.

AMAYA PENDRAGON

The castle maids took Luna's body and put her in a beautiful blue gown. They combed her hair and cleaned her face of the blood that once stained it. Amaya, Iris, and Elle picked flowers of all different kinds and weaved them into her red hair.

Just the three of them traveled to Lake of Avalon where a small boat was waiting for them. They decided to do this at night, so Luna could be under the moon and the stars. The three of them rested Luna's body in the boat and scattered more flowers around her. "She looks beautiful," Iris said.

"It's Luna. Of course she does," Elle said through the tears.

The moon was full that night. Its glow rippled on the small waves that echoed throughout the lake. It was strange to see Luna's skin so dim. Amaya would miss the blue colors that filled the air when she stepped into a room.

"Together?" Elle asked.

Iris and Amaya nodded. The girls placed their hands on the edge of the boat.

"One," Iris said.

"Two," Elle said.

"Three," Amaya said, letting only one tear slip.

The boat made a loud scraping sound as it moved through the sand and into the water. They stepped back, wrapping their arms around each other and watched her fade into the distance.

They stayed like this for a while, leaning on each other for comfort. They told stories and laughed about old times. Amaya could feel that something had shifted between them. Their strong bond had grown even stronger. Luna's death was like a needle that thread them all together tightly. No matter what happened next, they were going to get through it together. Just like they'd always done.

"Let's go home," Amaya finally said. This time, those words held a new meaning.

AMAYA PENDRAGON

About every maid in the castle rushed into Amaya's room with fabric spilling from their arms. They stood her on a small box and extended out her arms. They tugged and pulled at her limbs, wrapping fabrics of all different textures and colors around her.

"How do you feel about this style, your highness?"

Amaya was taken back by the title. "Um, it's great." *Come on, Amaya. You're a queen, you're supposed to talk like one.* It was strange to think that her mother was a queen once. She hadn't really thought about that until now. It was hard to imagine her wearing beautiful gowns, administering councils, and running a kingdom. She wished she could have seen that.

The maids sat her down and examined her face. They lathered her skin with all sorts of strange powders and pigments, making her cough and sneeze. When they reached her hair, they began complaining about its length. They found it to be far too short for a lady and extremely difficult to style.

"Well, I happen to like the length. I cut it myself," Amaya said.

"Yes, your highness. My apologies." The maids began to panic. Amaya was not used to having this kind of authority over people. She wasn't sure what to make of it.

They brushed through her hair, letting the gentle waves rest nicely against her head. Once they were satisfied, they handed her the dress they had selected for her. The top of the dress was a tightly fitted corset with hooks that ran down the front and laces in the back. It cinched in deeply at her waist and burrowed out at her hips. The skirt ran down all the way to the floor, pooling at her feet.

To top it all off the dress was a deep red. "Pendragon red," one of the maids had said. Gold sparkles dusted the red fabric, making it shimmer when she twirled. It was perfect.

"There is the Queen of Camelot," Merlin said, stepping into the room.

"Do I look alright?"

"More than alright. How are you feeling?"

"If I'm being honest, I'm trying really hard not to throw up right now."

"You've got this. I will do all the talking. You do not have to speak. Only if you want to. I will be up there with you the whole time, okay?" Amaya nodded, trying to find comfort in Merlin's words. "I have to go, but good luck," he said, pulling her into a hug. "Arthur would be proud of you," he whispered.

She really hoped so. Being in Camelot had changed her. She was beginning to realize some things were bigger than her fears. That didn't mean she was unafraid, but her desire to make a difference was stronger. She wanted to help these people and make Camelot what it once was. She wanted to protect the Elderen Wood and make sure no harm came to a being of magic ever again.

It ended now.

The Throne Room was flooded with all sorts of people once more. It was hard to believe that this was all for Amaya. She recalled when no one showed up to her thirteenth birthday party. Now hundreds of strangers were dressed in their finest clothes all on account of her.

She hid behind the large, draping curtains trying to catch her breath. She jumped when a voice whispered, "Hey," behind her.

"Edmund," she smiled. It was comforting to see a familiar face. "I feel like I'm gonna be sick."

"Here," he held out the paperclip that she had given to him weeks ago.

"I had almost forgotten," she took it in her hands. "Thanks, Edmund." It was strange how something so small could be so impactful. In her drift into space, it felt like a rope pulling her back to earth. A lifeline.

"You can do this. I always knew you were special. I never doubted it. I will be forever honored to serve you as my queen."

She threw her arms around him and basked in his warmth.

Amaya stepped forward and kneeled before Merlin. He held a beautiful crown made of golden leaves above her head. The crowd held their breath as Merlin uttered the words, "With the power invested in me, I crown you...Amaya, Queen of Camelot." He rested the crown on her head as the crowd cheered. She rose and turned to face them, giving them a gentle smile.

"Long live the queen!" Everyone began to chant. Elle and Iris cheered louder than anyone, absolutely beaming with pride.

She pretended it was just the four of them in the room. That it was just her and her friends. Even Luna was there in her mind. No one else really mattered anyway. She was doing this all for them.

Merlin told her she did not have to speak. But she was sick of fear always getting in the way. She took a deep breath, trying to calm the anxious feeling swirling in her stomach. *It's just Elle, Iris, Luna and you. No one else is here. Just us.* If she could stay present in the moment when fighting Mordred, she could stay present now.

She fidgeted with her paperclip behind her back. "People of Camelot, I am speaking to you today as your queen. I would like to apologize for the misfortune Mordred has brought on you. Not only you, but the entire Elderen Wood has suffered at his hand. In the name of my father, I give you my word that I will bring a new day."

She clenched her fists, attempting to stop her hands from shaking, as her gaze drifted to Elle. "Eldora Perez, will you please join me up here?" It was time to keep Evan's promise. Elle's head turned as she shot Amaya a confused look. Amaya nodded and gestured to her. Although confused, Elle did as she asked.

"Elle, would you please kneel?" Amaya said.

"Uh, okay," Elle complied.

Amaya unsheathed Excalibur, which was resting comfortably against her hip. The crowd leaned in in anticipation. "Eldora Perez. I, Queen Amaya, hereby knight you Sir Elle...Knight of Camelot."

ELDORA PEREZ

E lle slowly rose, feeling the rush of adrenaline surge through her
body. She stared at Amaya in utter disbelief. She was the first
woman knight of Camelot. Amaya had just declared that in front of
the entire kingdom.

She looked out to the crowd, fearing their reaction. To her surprise, everyone's face held a smile as they clapped and cheered. Even
the knights were jumping up and down with joy. It looked like she
had finally won their favor. In the middle of them was Evan, who was
looking at her with that familiar, stupid smile. She wanted nothing
more than to run right into his arms.

"Thank you, Amaya," Elle said.

"Don't thank me. Thank him," Amaya gestured to Evan. Of
course this was his doing. She wasn't the slightest bit surprised. "Elle,
stay up here with me. I'm not finished," Amaya whispered to her. "I
would also like to give Iris Yuki the title of Court Witch, and Edmund
the title of Court Sorcerer." She paused and shifted her tone. "These
titles died with my father, but today I am giving them new life."

Iris and Edmund joined them with the biggest smiles on
their faces.

Amaya continued, "These people are the bravest, most selfless
people I have ever met. They've done everything from the goodness
of their hearts and used their strengths to strengthen others. There
is no one else I would rather have joining me at my side. I will serve

this kingdom alongside my friends." Her voice softened. "And in the name of Luna Anbris. For we owe this victory to her and her alone. She died saving us. All of us. We should all be forever grateful for that."

Everyone in the room placed their hands on each other, taking part in the mourning of Luna. So many people were in tears, especially Liana. Elle hoped she did not blame herself for what had happened. It was strange seeing so many strangers cry for her friend. Amaya was right. They wouldn't be standing there if it weren't for Luna.

After a beat, the crowd cheered once more for the great Queen Amaya and her new Royal Court. Elle felt the warmth of her friends and the comfort of Evan's smile gazing back at her. For the first time in a long time, she felt right at home.

AMAYA PENDRAGON

Amaya spent the following day tucked away in her room. She was tired in more ways than one. The first snow had fallen in Camelot that day. It dusted the trees and brought new beginnings. Amaya opened her window and was hit with the chill of the winter air. The colors of the sunset bounced off the snowy roofs. It was beautiful. Peaceful.

She opened her closet and grabbed the biggest cloak she could find. She wrapped it around herself, tightly like a warm hug. She slipped on some boots and ran out the door.

She wondered if she'd ever get used to passing Luna's empty room. It sat there as a constant reminder that she was gone. Losing Luna was like a crack in their once solid foundation. With time, it could be repaired. But it would never be what it once was.

Edmund had suggested moving into the royal suite, since it was in fact hers now. She declined. Although the empty room at the end of the hall would haunt them like a ghost, the memories that this corridor held were too precious to abandon.

"Fancy a drink?" Amaya asked, peeking her head into Iris's room. She was buried under a mess of blankets.

She sighed. "You know I'm not one to turn down alcohol."

"Did someone say drinks?" Elle said, stepping into the room. Her frizzy hair was dusted in fresh powder.

"Where did you come from?"

"I was just taking Astrea for a ride. Apparently dragons love the snow."

Iris let out a small chuckle. "God, our lives are so freaking weird."

"Okay, come on, weirdo." Amaya pulled her out of bed.

Just like any other day, Gwaine's was filled from wall to wall with loud, friendly folks. However, blending in wasn't so easy this time. Some people bowed; others raised their glasses. At one time, all the attention would have terrified Amaya. Although she still felt that pit in her stomach, it was growing smaller every day. She controlled her breath and relaxed in the comfort of her friends beside her.

They sat at a table in the far corner of the room, away from all the chaos. Wren sat on the edge of the table and winked. "What'll it be, your highness?"

Amaya smiled and rolled her eyes. "Three tankards of your finest mead, please."

"You got it!"

Elle sighed.

"What's wrong?"

"Nothing it's just…Luna isn't here to order for you anymore."

Amaya glanced at the empty seat next to her. The moonlight fell through the open window, touching the seat with its light. Elle wasn't entirely right. Luna might not have been there physically, but she was still there. Just as a part of Merlin had lived in the three of them, a part of Luna lived in her. And it always would.

Until the end of time.

For Amaya, change was like the rain. Although it may come unexpectedly, when the sun breaks through those dark clouds, new life begins to blossom.